PARADOX

PETER M. BROWNE

Paradox/Peter M. Browne – 1st ed.

Printed in the United States of America

PeterMBrowne.com – info@petermbrowne.com

ISBN: 978-1-7360217-6-7

In the vastness of the universe, human life is but a fleeting spark, a paradox of significance in its cosmic insignificance, speaking the humbling truth of our existence.

—The Author

AUTHOR'S NOTES

Welcome to Paradox

This novel delves into the contradictions that define us — how we navigate the space between who we appear to be and who we truly are. At its heart, it is a psychological thriller that explores the darker side of human nature, the conflicts we carry within ourselves, and the forces — seen and unseen — that shape our lives.

The story pulls you into a world of complex, flawed, and profoundly human characters, where secrets and truths cohabitate. *Paradox* offers a raw glimpse into the shadows of humanity and the unseen threads that bind us all.

Peter M. Browne

PROLOGUE

In the grand narrative of human existence, a spectrum of behavior unfolds, as diverse and intricate as the colors of a rainbow. At one end stands the virtuous, their compassion and empathy forming the pillars of society's ideals. At the other lies the void, where empathy is absent, and darkness thrives. Between these poles, most of us walk an uncertain line, balancing between the masks we wear and the truths we dare not share.

Some, however, are different. Their footsteps stray from the line entirely, weaving into the shadows where morality twists and fractures. These are the manipulators, the predators, the ones who navigate life with a calculating gaze and an unsettling calm. They blend in. They charm. And when they strike, they leave us questioning how well we ever understood them — or ourselves.

This story is not merely about them. It is about the spaces in between — the contradictions we all carry and the moments when our fragile constructs of morality begin to crumble.

The old ones knew this truth well. They whispered of powers that tested the boundaries of human will, of those who dared to wield forces beyond understanding. And of the price such power demands.

In the end, we all reach the same destination. But it is the path we walk along the way that define us. As you turn these pages, beware: the labyrinth of the human soul is vast, and few who pass through emerge unscathed.

CHAPTER 1

Long before the United States government forcefully removed thousands of Native Americans from their ancestral lands, the Muscogee people thrived in what is now the Southeastern United States. Known to the English as the Creek Nation, the Muscogee developed a complex and highly organized society, their culture rich with traditions passed down through countless generations.

The Muscogee resided in self-governing villages, each with its own council, often strategically placed near rivers. These rivers were vital for trade, transportation, and sustenance, serving as physical and spiritual lifelines. The Muscogee believed these waterways linked the earthly realm with the spirit world, a belief that permeated their rituals, stories, and way of life.

Their understanding of the universe was rich in meaning and symbolism. They believed that in the beginning, the world was submerged under a vast expanse of water. Out of this primordial sea emerged the land, shaped by the divine forces that governed the universe. Animals, plants, rivers, and stones were not mere objects to the Muscogee. They were beings imbued with spirit and purpose, entities with whom they could communicate and who demanded respect and reverence.

Medicine men and women, individuals believed to possess extraordinary powers, held a central role in Muscogee society. They acted as healers, spiritual guides, and intermediaries between the physical and spiritual worlds. They could interpret dreams, cast out illness, and perform rituals to ensure the prosperity of their people. Some walked the fine line between light and darkness, wielding powers that could heal or harm, bless or curse.

The Muscogee also placed great emphasis on the balance between opposites — light and dark, male and female, order and chaos. Life was a delicate dance between these forces, and maintaining harmony was key to their survival. This belief extended into their social structure, where the roles of men and women, young and old, were clearly defined yet complementary.

However, with the arrival of European settlers, this balance was disrupted. The Muscogee, skilled traders and warriors, initially sought coexistence through alliances and trade agreements. But as the demand for land grew, tensions escalated. The Muscogee found themselves caught in the crossfire of colonial expansion, their lands increasingly coveted for their rich soil and strategic rivers.

The early 19th century brought a series of devastating blows. The Creek War (1813-1814), a civil war within the Muscogee (Creek) Nation, was fueled by the involvement of the United States. The conflict primarily arose between the Red Sticks, a faction opposing American expansion and seeking to preserve their traditional way of life, and the White Sticks, who were more accommodating to American influence.

The Battle of Horseshoe Bend, fought on March 27, 1814, became a pivotal conflict during this war. General Andrew Jackson, a man whose fiery temperament and unrelenting determination would later catapult him to the presidency, stood at the center of the action. Jackson, clad in a weathered blue coat with brass buttons dulled by months of campaigning, was a commanding figure even on the chaotic battlefield. His sharp, hawkish eyes seemed to pierce through the smoke and chaos as he surveyed the Red Stick fortifications across the river. His face, etched with lines of both experience and exhaustion, was framed by a shock of unruly auburn hair that defied the authority he so zealously demanded from others.

Despite the tension, there was an air of resolve in Jackson's movements. He gripped the hilt of his sword tightly, its polished surface catching the sun, and pointed it toward the Red Stick stronghold.

"We strike now!" Jackson bellowed, his voice cutting through the clamor of men and horses. "The barricade will fall, but not without courage. I expect every man here to fight as if the fate of this nation rests on his shoulders—because it does!" He turned to a nearby officer. "Signal Coffee's men to cross and encircle them from the rear. No mercy until this is done."

Drummers began to beat a rhythm of advance, and Jackson strode among his troops, his voice booming over the cacophony. "These warriors will fight like cornered wolves. Do not falter! The barricade may stand strong, but the will of these men will break. We'll show them what it means to face an American army!"

The command to attack was given.

Across the river, the Red Sticks, led by Chief Menawa, stood on the ramparts of the fort, their faces grim but resolute as they watched the massing U.S. troops. Menawa himself was a vision of defiance, a living embodiment of Muscogee pride and power. His bare chest glistened in the sun, streaked with bold red and black paint in striking, angular patterns that seemed to radiate both menace and sacred protection.

Feathers of raven and hawk adorned his long, dark hair, which flowed in the wind like a banner of war. Around his neck, he wore a necklace of bear claws and carved bone talismans, each piece representing the strength of his ancestors and the spirits that guided him. A crimson sash encircled his waist, and his fringed deerskin leggings were stained with the earth of his homeland. He carried a war club in one hand, its head carved from stone and inlaid with intricate designs, and in the other, a flint-tipped spear that gleamed with deadly purpose.

His dark eyes swept over his warriors; their faces painted in preparation for the battle that awaited them. He raised his voice so all could hear, the words carrying the weight of their shared history and the grim determination of their fight.

"Today is a good day to die," Menawa declared, his tone steady and unyielding. His war paint, accentuating the fierce lines of his face, seemed to make his eyes burn brighter as he looked into the souls of his men. His words, like an unspoken oath, rippled through his ranks, stiffening the spines of his warriors as they prepared to defend their home and honor to the last breath.

Jackson's strategy involved a two-pronged assault. While part of his force, including Cherokee and White Stick Creek allies, crossed the river to surround the Red Sticks from the rear, Jackson launched a frontal assault on the fortified encampment with his main force.

Under heavy fire, Jackson's troops breached the Red Stick barricade and engaged in brutal hand-to-hand combat. The Red Sticks fought fiercely but were eventually overwhelmed.

When the tide of the battle turned against the Red Sticks, and the barricade was breached, Menawa refused to surrender. Though shot multiple times, he was carried from the battlefield by the few surviving warriors who refused to abandon their leader. As they retreated into the woods, his blood left a trail, a grim reminder of the cost of resistance.

Though Menawa survived that day, the battle marked the end of the Red Stick resistance. His wounds would heal, but the scars of that day, both physical and spiritual, would never fade. For the rest of his life, he would carry the burden of their loss—a testament to his people's fight for freedom and survival against impossible odds.

It had been a devastating loss for the Red Sticks, with over 800 of their warriors killed.

Following the battle, on August 9, 1814, the remaining Creek leadership was forced to sign the Treaty of Fort Jackson. Despite the fact that many of the signatories had been allies of the United States, the treaty required the Creek Nation to cede over 21 million acres of land—about half of their remaining territory in what is now Alabama and Georgia—to the United States.

By the 1830s, under the shadow of the Indian Removal Act, the Muscogee, along with other tribes in the Southeast, faced the grim reality of displacement. The U.S. government, driven by the hunger for land and resources, initiated a campaign to remove all Native Americans from their ancestral homes. Thousands of Muscogee were forced to leave, their journey westward marked by hardship, suffering, and death — a "Trail of Tears."

CHAPTER 2

The humid air clung to the dense foliage of the Florida wetlands, where the cries of herons echoed through the cypress trees. When most Native Americans in Florida were forced to march westward to the barren lands of Oklahoma, a small band of Red Stick Muscogee evaded the soldiers. They vanished into the swamps, their knowledge of the land guiding them to a desolate, marshy area upstream from the Blackwater River where it met the Gulf of Mexico. There, they established Cusseta, a hidden sanctuary in a world that had little use for such inhospitable land. But to the Muscogee, this place was sacred.

Because the Muscogee believed, the world was once submerged underwater, and from the waters, life emerged. This proximity to the river wasn't just practical; it was spiritual. The land itself was alive, vibrating with the energy of ancestors, spirits, and forces beyond human understanding.

The Muscogee were a superstitious people, guided by rituals and rites that connected them to the earth and the heavens. They believed in the power of dreams, visions, and omens. Certain individuals were believed to be touched by the divine or the dark forces lurking just out of sight.

By the late 1880s, among the descendants of those first Muscogee settlers, one man emerged—a figure spoken of in equal parts awe and trepidation. He was known only as *He Whose Name Is Never Spoken*, for to utter his name was to tempt the spirits, to summon the unknown. He was a healer, a man who mended the sick with whispers and poultices no one else could explain, a man who called to the spirits when no one else dared.

His presence was unforgettable, though few could agree on what they'd seen. Some claimed his eyes were black as pitch, endless and unblinking, while others swore they held a strange light, a flicker of something otherworldly. His hands—calloused, strong, and always steady—worked miracles, though their touch lingered like a memory, as though his power left a mark. He was a tall man, broad in the shoulder, his voice a low rumble that carried more weight than thunder. Yet others who saw him in passing would later swear he seemed smaller, slighter—a shadow barely there at all.

No one could quite pin down the truth of him, and perhaps that was the point. The more you looked, the less you saw.

It was said his touch could draw fever from a dying man's body or soothe the cries of a colicky infant. Those who sought him in desperation often found their prayers answered, though the price of such miracles was something no one fully understood.

The same hands that could heal were rumored to hold darker gifts—powers not meant for casual use. If he ever turned that power upon his enemies, it was not without cause, but the results were no less chilling.

A man who wronged his neighbor might find his cattle dead in the morning. A bitter woman who spread lies could awaken screaming, swearing she'd seen a shadow at her window, calling her name.

One night, a desperate farmer came to *The Man's* dwelling, his face pale and drawn. His wife had fallen ill, her body wracked with fever for days, and no medicine had helped. The farmer with weathered hands and a voice heavy with worry, approached the shadowed figure seated by a fire, embers glowing like distant stars.

He didn't turn as the farmer stammered out his plea. "Please… I've come for your help. They say you can do what no other can."

The Man finally looked up, his gaze unsettling in its intensity. The firelight flickered across his face, making his features seem to shift and blur. "What you ask is not simple," he said, his voice like the murmur of wind through ancient trees. "To call upon the spirits is to make a trade. Are you prepared to pay the cost?"

The farmer hesitated, his fingers twisting the brim of his hat. "I'll do anything. Just… save her."

Without another word, *The Man* rose and gestured for the farmer to lead the way. As they walked, the farmer's mind flickered with an image of his wife as she had been last summer—laughing as she hung the wash on the line, her hair catching the light of the sun. He clenched his fists, forcing himself to focus. Whatever it took, he would save her.

The air inside the farmer's cabin was thick, heavy with the scent of death hanging from the rafters.

He Whose Name Is Never Spoken knelt beside the woman, her body fevered and trembling. He placed one calloused hand on her forehead, the other over her heart and closed his eyes. A silence fell, so deep it seemed even the forest outside was holding its breath.

Then, in a voice barely above a whisper, he began to speak — not to the farmer, but to something unseen. The words were ancient, their meaning lost to time, but they resonated in the air, vibrating with a power that felt both sacred and dangerous.

As *The Man's* whispers filled the air, the fire seemed to dim, its flames dancing to a rhythm no one else could hear. A sudden chill swept through the room, and the shadows along the walls seemed to ripple and shift, as though alive.

The farmer stood frozen, his heart pounding as he watched *The Man's* hands hovering over his wife's body. The room seemed to darken, the shadows stretching and twisting as though alive. The faint hum in the air grew louder, a droning that pressed against the man's ears, making him feel as though he were standing on the edge of a great chasm.

Suddenly, the woman gasped, her eyes fluttering open. Her fevered trembling stopped, and her breathing slowed, becoming deep and even. The room seemed to exhale with her, the oppressive weight lifting as quickly as it had come.

Slowly, her eyes fluttered open, their dark depths unusually sharp, reflecting the faint glow of the firelight. She blinked, her gaze snapping to her husband with a clarity that made him take a half-step back.

"It is done," *The Man* said, rising to his feet. He turned to the farmer; his face unreadable. "She will live."

Tears filled the farmer's eyes as he stumbled forward, reaching for *The Man's* hands. "Thank you—thank you! How can I repay you? Name your price."

The Man's dark eyes bored into the farmer, and for a moment, the farmer felt as though he were being weighed, measured, judged. "The spirits have already taken what they require," *The Man* said, his voice low and distant. "Be grateful it was not more."

The farmer swallowed hard; his relief mingled with unease. "I don't understand…"

"You do not need to," *The Man* replied, his tone final. "Care for your wife. And remember: life given is a gift, not a guarantee."

The farmer nodded, following *The Man* to the door of the cabin with a mix of gratitude and fear. As *The Man* crossed the threshold into the cool night air, he glanced back. Silhouetted by the moon light behind him *The Man* seemed larger than life, a figure beyond this world.

Stories circled about *The Man's* eyes—dark and knowing, as though they could see beyond the veil, where spirits tread. He spoke little, but when he did, the words seemed to hum with a weight of their own. Some called him saint, a man chosen by the spirits to protect his people. Others called him sorcerer, for what power could move the earth and sky without explanation? And yet, no matter what they believed, they came to him. They always came to him.

He Whose Name Is Never Spoken was neither saint, nor sorcerer. He was something in between, as complex and powerful as the forces he commanded. Those who remembered him did so with reverence and fear, knowing that his power had been used to combat evil — but also that power, no matter how well-intentioned, could shift when the line between light and darkness blurred.

His legend did not end with his death. It sank into the bloodline, passed down like an inheritance both sacred and dangerous. As the Muscogee intermarried with European settlers, his legacy did not vanish — it simply hid. A quiet hum in the family's bones, waiting for the right moment. Waiting for the right soul to carry it forward.

One such descendant, born to Ramon Blackstone, a great-grandson of *He Whose Name is Never Spoken*, grew up in a world far removed from the shadowed swamps of her ancestors. Ramon Blackstone was a man who commanded attention without effort. He was not loud, nor did he wield overt displays of power; instead, he possessed a quiet, gravitational pull — like the eye of a storm. When he entered a room, conversations would falter mid-sentence, as if people instinctively sensed the weight of something ancient trailing in his wake.

His features were carved with an angular precision that time seemed reluctant to soften. High cheekbones, a strong jaw, and dark, thoughtful eyes that seemed to hold secrets just beyond reach. A streak of silver sliced through his otherwise black hair, like a blade marking a lineage both noble and cursed. Ramon carried himself with the ease of a man who could bend reality to suit his will, a power that others obeyed before they could reason why.

Ramon never spoke of his heritage or the powers whispered to run through their blood. To his daughter, he was simply "Dad" — the man who could make anything happen. He was the giver of Christmas mornings that sparkled with impossible gifts and the steady voice that quieted her nightmares. Yet there was always something unspoken, primal, in the silences between them. When his gaze lingered too long, it felt as though he could see the invisible threads of the world and knew just how to pull them.

The swamps of their forebears were distant, but Ramon carried them with him — an echo of damp earth, secrets buried in moss, and the faintest chill that lingered in his presence. Whether by blood, magic, or something older still, he was a man who walked between worlds, leaving his mark wherever he stepped, even if no one could see it.

Ramon's sister, Milagro — known to everyone as Aunt Millie — was a woman who could command a kitchen like a battlefield and meddle in lives with the precision of a master strategist. She was a plump, matronly figure, with rounded shoulders and hands always busy — kneading dough, folding laundry, or pointing accusingly at someone. Her face, while soft and lined with age, carried a sharpness around the eyes, as though she missed nothing. Millie's graying hair was perpetually pinned back in a tight bun, secured by what seemed like a hundred bobby pins that rattled softly when she shook her head in disapproval. An apron — usually stained from some task she'd just finished — clung to her frame like a second skin, the pockets full of tissues, candies, or tools she'd stuffed there earlier and forgotten.

Millie had lived her life as both witness and sentinel to the family history, carrying her grandmother's stories like sacred scripture. She remembered the whispered warnings about *He Whose Name Is Never Spoken*—how his bloodline carried a dark power, as unpredictable as a storm. Where her brother Ramon wielded his presence with quiet subtlety, Millie felt the power—like an itch under her skin—and never pretended otherwise.

From the moment Carla was born, Millie had kept an eye on her niece with a mixture of affection and unease. At first, she told herself the girl was just willful, stubborn, full of the fire that burned in all the women of their family. But as Carla grew, flashes of something deeper, something sinister, began to surface. Millie watched for it—small moments others might dismiss—but she saw.

Like that day in the kitchen.

Millie had just finished scolding Carla about the way she treated her boyfriend, Tom. "Don't think you can keep walking all over people, Carla," she'd said, her voice sharp, wooden spoon tapping rhythmically against her palm like a warning drumbeat.

Carla, sitting at the table, looked up slowly. It wasn't her usual sulky glare. This look—the one Millie would never forget—sent a cold ripple down her spine. Carla's eyes narrowed, dark and unblinking, the way a predator might stare before it pounced. For a split second, Millie could've sworn her niece's shadow lengthened unnaturally on the wall behind her.

It's just the light, Millie thought, but her fingers twitched nervously at her apron strings.

"Why don't you mind your own business, Auntie!" Carla said, her voice steady, but the way she spat the words carried an edge that was almost unnatural. She stood abruptly, her movement animated, deliberate. Millie's breath caught as Carla stalked out of the room, shoulders rigid — her entire body coiled like something was barely being restrained.

The room fell silent, unnervingly so.

Millie turned to the young man Carla had left behind, a sheepish boy whose confidence seemed to shrink by the seconds. He was slouched in his seat, picking at the hem of his jeans like he wished he could disappear. Millie narrowed her eyes, her voice low and firm.

"Watch out for this one," she said, her next words carefully chosen. "She's a manipulator. Mark my words, boy — one day she'll be filled with regrets. She will live long and die alone."

He snorted a laugh, waving her off. Millie took a step closer, her presence looming despite her small frame. Her hands balled in her apron, wrinkling the fabric as though to steady herself. "I'm serious. You don't know what you've gotten yourself into."

Before he could respond, the kitchen lights flickered — one pulse, then another — before snapping back to life. He glanced upward; brow furrowed. "Huh. That's weird."

But Millie's breath hitched. Her fingers instinctively brushed the small cross hanging from her neck, tracing it as her lips moved in silent prayer. An unnatural coldness seemed to settle into the room, as though something unseen had brushed past them both. She shivered, forcing a smile when the young man noticed her pallor.

"You alright?" he asked, eyebrows raised.

"Oh, I'm fine," she said quickly, though her voice trembled just enough to betray her. She turned her back to him, busying herself with a dish in the sink, hands scrubbing too hard.

Peter M. Browne

But deep down, Millie knew. Carla's actions weren't just the tantrums of a defiant teenager. No, there was something darker in her niece—something that reminded her too much of the stories her grandmother had whispered long ago.

And for the first time, Millie found herself afraid of her niece.

CHAPTER 3

Buck Dyson had been a long-haul trucker for over 30 years, a seasoned road warrior with countless miles etched into his rugged appearance. Now in his mid-50s, Buck's appearance was a testament to the grueling life he led on the open road. Standing at a solid six feet tall, his frame was broad-shouldered and sturdy, a physique maintained by years of manual labor.

His face, weathered and tanned from the sun's relentless glare, was adorned with a thick, salt-and-pepper beard that reached down to his chest. The beard, meticulously groomed, gave him an air of rugged wisdom and authority. His hair, matching the beard's color, was often tucked under a well-worn baseball cap, but when revealed, it showed signs of thinning, the inevitable passage of time.

Buck's eyes, a piercing blue, held a depth that spoke of endless highways and the solitude of the long haul. They were sharp, always scanning the horizon, alert to the subtle changes in weather or the movements of other vehicles. Crow's feet at the corners of his eyes hinted at a life filled with squinting into the sun and many hours of laughter with fellow truckers.

His attire was practical and comfortable, favoring flannel shirts layered over plain T-shirts, sturdy denim jeans, and well-worn leather boots. A heavy, silver belt buckle, a memento from a trucking competition years ago, was his only concession to adornment. Around his neck hung a small, gold cross, a quiet acknowledgement of his faith and the comfort it brought him on lonely nights.

Buck's hands were calloused and strong, with a grip that could reassure or command respect. His fingers bore the signs of a life spent maintaining his rig, with dirt often embedded under the nails despite his best efforts. On his left hand, he wore a simple gold wedding band, a constant reminder of his wife Esther and the family waiting for him back home.

Despite his gruff exterior, Buck had a warm, hearty laugh that could fill a room and a deep, resonant voice that carried stories of the road. He was a man of few words, but when he spoke, it was with a sincerity and straightforwardness that drew people in. His bearing was calm and steady, qualities that made him a respected figure among his peers.

Buck Dyson was more than just a trucker; he was a living embodiment of the freedom and challenges of life on the road. His life was a testament to the hard work and dedication required to navigate the vast, open highways of America.

Buck's current rig was a 1975, "arrest me" red, Kenworth, his pride and companion on the endless roadways crisscrossing the United States. It was a second home for a seasoned traveler of the interstate.

With its signature long nose, the truck's design married aerodynamics with the ruggedness required to face the varying moods of the country's weather and the challenges of the varied terrain.

Under the hood, the truck boasted a powerful PACCAR MX-13 engine, revered for its reliability and efficiency. With horsepower that peaked around 485, it commanded the force needed to haul heavy loads, like steel girders, oil rigging, pipeline pipe, or ship containers, up mountains and across the plains with unwavering steadiness. The engine's design focused on maximizing fuel economy without sacrificing performance, a critical feature for long-haul trips that stretched from the sunny coasts of Florida to the bustling harbors of Maine or the highways to the west.

The transmission, an Eaton Fuller 18-speed, provided smooth shifting and control, allowing Buck to navigate the nuances of speed and torque with the finesse of a seasoned maestro. The versatility of an 18-speed gearbox was crucial for adapting to the varied demands of his routes, from the steep inclines of overpasses to the stop-and-go congestion of city traffic.

Inside, the cab of the Kenworth was more than a mere driver's compartment, it was a mobile living space, designed with the long-haul trucker's comfort and convenience in mind. The sleeper unit was spacious, featuring a compact yet cozy sleeping area that offered a semblance of home comfort on the road. With a high-quality mattress, ample storage for personal items, and even space for a small refrigerator and microwave, the sleeping quarters was a sanctuary for rest and rejuvenation.

The driver's area, a cockpit of efficiency, with ergonomically designed seats that provided support during long hours behind the wheel. The dashboard housed an array of controls and displays, all within easy reach, designed to keep essential information at Buck's fingertips. From fuel efficiency stats to engine diagnostics, every piece of data helped ensure a smooth operation and swift response to any issue that might arise on the road.

The flatbed trailer hitched to the back of Buck's Kenworth was an impressive sight, stretching nearly fifty-five feet in length, its surface a vast expanse of reinforced steel and weather-resistant decking. Built to accommodate the massive bulk and weight of whatever cargo, was consigned. The trailer's design balanced strength with the agility needed to navigate the twists and turns of the "last mile" roadways of the inner city.

For Buck, his rig was more than just a vehicle; it was his livelihood, a bearer of burdens both physical and emotional, and a constant in a life spent in transit. The road had been a solitary companion for the better part of his life. The endless highways and the rhythmic hum of the engine were constants in a world that changed too quickly.

During the years when his children were navigating the tumultuous days from adolescence to adulthood, Buck found himself alone, on the road, more often than not. The cab of his truck was his refuge, a place where time seemed to stand still even as he moved from state to state.

To fill the silence and break the monotony of long hauls, Buck often picked up hitchhikers. Each new face was a story, a temporary reprieve from the quiet. These passengers, with their varied backgrounds and destinations, brought with them fleeting connections that Buck cherished. They were mirrors reflecting the myriad paths life could take, and Buck, in his own personal style, openly shared his views of the world.

In the universe of long-haul trucking, where the cab of a truck served as both office and sanctuary, the amenities provided catered to nearly every necessity of life on the move. Buck's Kenworth was fully equipped, however, the one aspect of daily life not accommodated within the confines of his mobile domain was personal hygiene. For that, truck stops became indispensable oases, vital pit stops that offered not just fuel for the truck but also rejuvenation for the driver.

The Flying J, Love's, and TA truck stops dotted Buck's routes like beacons, their familiar signs promised a chance to refresh and recharge. These stops were more than just places to refuel; they were communal hubs where truckers from all walks of life converged. The showers, always clean and well-maintained, provided a much-needed respite from the confines of the cab. They offered the luxury of hot water and plenty of it.

But the true heart of these truck stops was the dining areas, where truckers gathered around Formica tables with mugs of coffee that seemed to never run cold. Here, amidst the hum of vending machines and the clatter of utensils, a unique culture thrived. Truckers, a breed known for their independence, found community over shared meals and stories. These spaces became forums for exchange — tales from the road, tips on navigating tricky routes, and the latest news on road construction and weather conditions that might affect their journeys.

Buck found a sense of belonging in these brief gatherings. The camaraderie amongst truckers was a given, a bond forged with the understanding of what it meant to spend life in motion. Conversations flowed easily, from lighthearted jokes about the quirks of their rigs to more serious discussions about fuel costs—a constant concern that impacted their livelihoods. And while complaints about traffic snarls or the challenges of time-sensitive deliveries were common, so too were stories of breathtaking sunrises witnessed from behind the wheel or the unexpected beauty found in the most remote corners of the country, not something you'd expect macho truckers to share openly, but this was their sanctuary where they could speak freely.

In these moments, shared over cups of coffee or quick meals, a collective narrative unfolded—one of resilience, adventure, and the unspoken respect for the road and those who traveled it. For Buck, these interactions were a reminder that, though the job demanded solitude, he was part of a larger community, a network of individuals who shared his experiences, his challenges, and his love for the open road.

As the years passed and his children grew, setting off to build their own lives, the empty spaces in Buck's home seemed to echo the emptiness of his truck's cab. It was during this chapter of his life that Esther, Buck's wife, began to join him on the road, adding a vibrant and dynamic presence to his solitary journeys. With her imposing stature and an aura that was both comforting and commanding, Esther brought a new dimension to Buck's travels. She was a big woman, not heavy or overweight, but rather large in stature, standing nearly as tall as Buck with a frame that exuded strength and resilience.

Esther's presence was as undeniable as it was warm. Her broad shoulders and sturdy build spoke of a life lived with purpose and determination. She carried herself with a confidence that was immediately apparent, whether she was helping Buck secure a load or engaging in friendly banter with fellow truckers at a roadside diner. Her hands, though strong and capable, were also gentle, revealing her nurturing side as she tended to the needs of their makeshift home on wheels.

Her face, framed by thick, curly hair that had streaks of silver running through it, was expressive and open. Deep-set eyes of a rich, earthy brown were windows to her soul, reflecting both kindness and an unyielding strength. They sparkled with a mixture of curiosity and wisdom, always attentive and empathetic to those around her. Her laughter, a hearty and infectious sound, could lighten the mood of even the most stressful situations.

Esther's attire was practical yet stylish, often consisting of comfortable jeans, sturdy boots, and colorful blouses that added a touch of femininity to her robust appearance. She had a penchant for wearing scarves, which she skillfully tied in various ways, adding a splash of color and flair to her outfits. Around her neck, she wore a locket containing photos of their children, a constant reminder of the family that rooted her to her sense of purpose and love.

Despite the rough-and-tumble life on the road, Esther maintained an air of grace and dignity. She had a talent for creating a cozy atmosphere in their truck, transforming the small space into a welcoming retreat after long hours of driving.

Esther's commanding presence extended beyond her physicality; she had a natural ability to lead and organize, often taking charge of logistical details and ensuring that everything ran smoothly. Her voice, warm and steady, could both soothe and command attention, making her a respected figure among her peers, at home or on the road. She had a knack for diffusing tense situations with a calm presence and wise counsel, earning the admiration and respect of those who crossed her path.

In Buck's eyes, Esther was not just a companion but a partner in every sense of the word. Her unwavering support and shared sense of adventure made the long hauls more bearable. She shared Buck's love for the open road, but it was her passion for crime novels that truly transformed their trips together. She would read aloud to Buck as he drove, her voice a soothing counterpoint to the drone of the highway. Together, they delved into mysteries and thrillers, solving fictional crimes as the landscapes blurred past. These shared stories became their collective adventures, moments of connection that deepened their bond.

Yet, this upcoming trip to Pensacola was different. It was a relatively short run, a straightforward job transporting a luxury yacht from the manufacturer to its new owner. He would be dead-heading back, so it would be a quick turn-around. Esther, working on a church project, decided to stay behind, leaving Buck to face the road as he had in the years before his children had grown.

The decision was practical, but as Buck prepared to depart, he couldn't help but feel the absence of her usual presence beside him. The truck felt emptier without Esther's commentary on the latest plot twist or her laughter at the more absurd moments in the book she was reading. Buck enjoyed the way she could weave theories and predictions, her imagination painting vivid pictures that danced between the reality of their journey and the fiction of the tales. The silence in the cab would be a reminder of the days when hitchhikers were his only company, a reminder of a quiet that he hadn't felt for some time.

Buck arrived at the Sarasota Marine around 7 AM, to pick up his cargo. It would take a little over an hour to load and secure the boat onto the trailer. His delivery, a brand-new Fathom 500 luxury sports yacht headed for the Pensacola Marina. As he was checking all the tie downs he couldn't help but admire the vessel. Buck was familiar with this model having transported more than a few of these up and down the coast.

The yacht was cradled in a custom-fabricated harness, designed to distribute its weight evenly across the flatbed's frame, preventing any undue stress during transport. These supports were padded with high-density foam and wrapped in durable, non-abrasive materials to protect the yacht's pristine finish from scratches or damage from the vibrations of the road.

This sleek 50' sports yacht, boasted an elegance that matched its innovative design. With a streamlined hull that cut through the water like a knife through silk, it was a marvel of modern engineering. The yacht's most distinctive feature was its reversed radar arch, an avant-garde twist that not only enhanced its futuristic silhouette but also improved its aerodynamics and performance at sea.

Below deck, the Fathom 500 offered an oasis of comfort and style. Designed to accommodate six guests in lavish comfort, the interior was a statement of contemporary comfort, with plush seating, state-of-the-art entertainment systems, and oval windows that offered breathtaking views of the endless sea.

The yacht's crowning jewel, however, was the cockpit with its dual captain's seat, making for cozy cruising, the elaborate dashboard with gauges and switches too numerous to mention, a wood grained steering wheel, and dual chrome throttles.

There was one other striking feature, its bathroom facility, which housed a revolutionary revolving shower door. Inspired by the iconic beaming station of Star Trek, this shower was a marvel of technology and design. With a simple touch, the semi-circular door would rotate, enveloping its occupant in a cascade of water from every angle. The walls of the shower were lined with lights that could mimic the starry night sky or the deep blue of the ocean, adding a layer of sensory experience to the already exceptional shower.

As Buck came around the stern the two giant propellers, protruding from the hull spoke to the twin 450 HP marine engines that allowed this vessel to cruise at 45 MPH.

Above the propellers, painted on the transom, in sea green, was the vessel's name, "My Lovely". Buck couldn't help but wonder who the lucky lady was.

CHAPTER 4

It was around 11 AM as Buck approached the entrance ramp to Interstate 10 West. The sun was climbing higher in the sky casting a bright golden glow over the asphalt. The morning had unfolded uneventfully, a testament to the predictability that Buck strived for in his trip planning.

He had made a quick stop for fuel at the Flying J and a cup of coffee, the only diversions from the rhythm of the road, the steady hum of the engine and the passing scenery.

It was the sight of a hitchhiker, a solitary figure standing on the side of the road, with a worn backpack slung over one shoulder, that caught Buck's attention.

He was holding a sign with, "Pearson's Point," scrawled in bold, black letters, unmistakable even from a distance. He was dressed in faded jeans and a weathered jacket, his face partially obscured by a baseball cap pulled low over his eyes.

Buck's eyes narrowed as he read the homemade sign, a flicker of recognition crossing his face. Pearson's Point wasn't just another name on a map; it was a place he had passed many times, its proximity to the Gulf of Mexico and the Florida state-line making it a familiar landmark on his routes. It was only a few miles from Buck's destination—Pensacola. Yet, despite its familiarity, Buck had never had cause to stop there, the town remaining a peripheral note in the chronical of his travels.

Aware of the logistical challenges posed by the approaching clover-leaf exit ramp and the precious cargo he was transporting, Buck began to calculate several moves ahead. Any truck driver who was worth his pay knew that you always watched the road at least ten car-lengths in front, to avoid any surprises. He had seen his share of accidents from drivers looking no further down the road then the tip of their hood ornament.

The 50' yacht affixed to his flatbed demanded careful handling and forethought for every turn and stop. Deciding to assist the hitchhiker required a safe and practical approach, not stopping too quickly or too close to the exit ramp.

With a practiced eye, Buck scanned the road ahead, looking for a suitable spot to pull over safely before reaching his exit. Finding a stretch of shoulder sufficiently wide and stable, Buck signaled and eased his rig to a stop, well beyond the hitchhiker.

As the rig came to a gentle halt, Buck watched through the rearview mirror as the hitchhiker, reading the trucker's intentions, began to run towards the now stationary vehicle. The young man's relief was evident, even from a distance, as he approached the Kenworth, his hurried steps kicking up small clouds of dust along the roadside. Buck watched the hitchhiker close the distance, his strides long and determined.

The hitchhiker was young, perhaps in his mid-twenties, with a backpack flapping on his shoulder, as he ran and a look of relief crossing his features as he approached the truck. Buck observed him carefully, noting the way the young man's eyes scanned the rig and its unusual load, a mix of curiosity and interest in his gaze.

As the hitchhiker reached the passenger side, Buck rolled down the window, the morning air carrying the scent of pine and asphalt. "Headed to Pearson's Point?" he asked rhetorically, his voice carrying a hint of warmth.

The young man nodded, a grateful smile breaking through his cautious exterior. "Yes, sir. If you're going that far, I'd really appreciate a ride."

Buck considered him for a moment longer, then nodded toward the passenger door. "Climb on in. It's a long ride to Pearson's Point."

As the hitchhiker hoisted himself into the cab, Buck felt the familiar stir of curiosity and anticipation that accompanied new acquaintances on the road. This young man, with his sign for Pearson's Point knew where he was going. Buck liked that. He hated those travelers only going a few miles up the road, wasting his time. He was looking for someone to keep him company, talk and break up the monotony.

"Buck Dyson," he offered as the hitchhiker closed the door.

"Brad Williams, I appreciate the lift." Brad was a young man in his mid-20s, with an appearance that spoke of both youth and hardship. His tall, lean frame suggested he was once athletic, but the rigors of life had worn him down. Dressed in faded jeans that had seen better days and a weathered jacket that hung loosely on his shoulders, he looked like someone who has been struggling with life's challenges.

His face was gaunt, with sharp cheekbones that hinted at missed meals and restless nights. A layer of scruff covered his jawline, giving him a rugged, unkempt appearance. His eyes, a striking green, were perhaps his most notable feature—vivid and expressive, they held a mix of exhaustion, determination, and a glimmer of hope. Dark circles under his eyes betrayed sleepless nights, and a few stray locks of sandy brown hair escaped from under the brim of his well-worn baseball cap, which he wore pulled low to shield his eyes from the sun and the gaze of strangers.

Brad's hands, visible as he clutched his backpack, were calloused and rough, the result of various odd jobs and the physical toil of surviving without a permanent home. His backpack, once probably a vibrant color, was now dulled and frayed, filled with the sparse belongings he had managed to hold onto—necessities for life on the road and reminders of a more stable past.

Despite his disheveled appearance, there was a quiet dignity about Brad. He carried himself with a sense of resilience, his posture straight even when fatigue seemed to weigh heavily on him. His voice, when he spoke, was soft but steady, carrying a slight rasp that hinted at countless conversations with the wind and the elements.

Brad's story, though unspoken, seemed to radiate from him—a tale of lost opportunities, fleeting dreams, and a relentless quest for a place to belong. There was a hint of vulnerability about him, yet his eyes revealed an underlying strength, a determination to keep moving forward despite the odds.

As he settled into the passenger seat of Buck's truck, Brad's presence brought a new energy to the cab. Though clearly down on his luck, there was an unspoken understanding between the two men — both travelers on the same endless road, each carrying their own burdens and stories, finding a brief moment of solace in the company of a friendly face.

With a quick check of the mirrors, Buck eased the 18-wheeler back onto the highway, the rig and its cargo moving forward once more. Buck took the I-10 exit ramp with caution as they headed westbound.

They shared some introductory information and then the cab grew silent. As the miles stretch out before them, the tree covered landscape unchanged, the interior of Buck's truck became a confined space where conversations typically unfolded over the hum of the engine, now felt heavy with quiet. Buck who loved to listen, felt the need to break the silence, yearning to hear the sound of voices, even if initially his own.

Clearing his throat, Buck decided to share a story he attributed to one of his wife Esther's crime novels. Maybe it was the mention of Pearson's Point that brought it to mind, or maybe it was just the long stretch of road ahead. Either way, he found himself speaking before he could question his choice of topic.

"You know, this stretch of I-10 always reminds me of one of Esther's novels," he said, glancing over at Brad. "It's a story that chilled me to the bone — about a serial killer. The media in the book called him 'The Highway Killer.'"

Buck continued with a vivid description of the killer's modus operandi, detailing how this phantom of the highways targeted homes just off the beaten path, homes that stood isolated, their occupants unaware of the danger lurking so close. He spoke of the killer's cunning, how he would feign pulling over to take a break, setting up triangular reflectors to alert approaching drivers and ward off suspicion, using the cover of night to his advantage.

Buck proceeded, "Under the veil of darkness, the killer moved like a phantom through the woods, reaching his chosen house with a kind of eerie precision. In the book, the break-ins were so silent and calculated it was as if he belonged there. The killer's weapon of choice was a knife, its blade described as glinting in the moonlight, and what followed..." Buck paused, his voice steady but low, "...well, it wasn't the kind of scene you'd want to imagine."

He went on, describing how the killer, after committing his crimes, stayed in the house. "He'd cook a meal for himself, like something out of a twisted routine, then sit down to eat in the very house he'd turned into a nightmare. When he was finished, he'd clean up after himself, erasing any trace of who he was—at least, anything personal—and vanish back into the night. Esther always said it was that detail, that cold normalcy, that made the book so disturbing."

Buck cast a quick glance at Brad before continuing. "In the story, the authorities couldn't make heads or tails of it. No signs of forced entry. No fingerprints. No weapon left behind. Nothing but... what was done.

"They couldn't even connect the dots at first. It wasn't until years later they pieced together that these scattered crimes across the South were all tied to one person—or at least, that's what Esther's book suggested."

As Buck narrated, his tone remained steady, but Brad felt a creeping unease settling over him.

Something about the methodical nature of the crimes, the killer's calm, unhurried routine—it stirred a vague memory in the back of Brad's mind. The details felt too familiar, not like something from a book, but like something real.

Brad's discomfort grew, the air thick with his burgeoning suspicion. "This...sounds a lot like a true crime story, not just something from a novel," Brad ventured, his voice marked with a cautious unease.

Buck paused, a slight shift in his manner. "You know," he began, a reflective tone coloring his words, "Esther's read me so many of those stories over the years, it's hard to keep straight which were true crime and which were fiction. You may be right." His admission carried a nonchalance intended to downplay Brad's observation.

However, Brad's mind raced, connecting dots from childhood memories, whispers of an unsolved crime that had once terrorized Pearson's Point. "I remember hearing about a series of killings like that when I was a kid. They never caught the guy, as I recall." His words hung between them, conjuring memories long forgotten.

The moment passed, but the seed of curiosity had taken root. Buck's story, intended as a way to pass the time, had inadvertently opened a door to the past, hinting at truths hidden beneath the surface. Brad felt something, indescribable, that would remain with him long after he and Buck parted ways.

Seeking to steer the conversation away from the dark narrative that had settled between them, Brad posed a question that he knew the answer to, but inquired anyway. "How much further is it to Pearson's

Point?" he asked, his voice casual, betraying none of the turmoil Buck's story had stirred within him.

Buck glanced at the road ahead before answering, "We're still a couple hours out. What's drawing you to Pearson's Point? My recollection is, it's a nowhere town in the middle of nowhere." His tone was one of genuine curiosity, a shift from the storyteller back to the trucker sharing his cab.

Brad sensed an opening, a chance to reclaim some sense of normalcy in their exchange. "I'm looking for a new start," he began, his words carrying the weight of his recent reflections. "I've been to a few different places, tried my hand at various jobs, but nothing's really panned out. A friend told me about the easy life in Pearson's Point, so I figured I'd give it a shot."

Buck nodded; his expression thoughtful as he considered Brad's words. "You seem awfully young to have faced any significant setbacks. But you know what they say, 'nothing beats a try but a failure.' Just keep at it. You've got time on your side." There was an encouraging note in Buck's voice, a hint of solidarity that seemed to bridge the gap between their experiences, if only for a moment.

Brad appreciated the shift in conversation, grateful for the chance to get a stranger's opinion of his experiences. He would more than likely never see Buck again, so he could speak freely, though he hadn't initially, when asked his reasons for heading to Pearson's Point.

Brad's story unfolded like a map of missed turns and dead ends, his words spilling out as he stared at the road ahead. "I got married young," he began, his voice tinged with a mix of nostalgia and regret.

"Thought it was the kind of love that could last forever. Turns out, forever was about a year."

Buck glanced at him, one hand resting lightly on the wheel. "That young, huh? Guess you didn't know yourself yet, let alone someone else."

Brad nodded. "Yeah, hindsight's a hell of a thing. After the divorce, I was… lost. Didn't know what the hell to do with myself. So, I joined the service."

"The Army?" Buck asked, curiosity flickering in his tone.

"Yeah," Brad confirmed. "Infantry. Figured the structure, the discipline… it'd give me some purpose. And it did, for a while. But when I got out, I realized all the skills I'd learned didn't really mean much in the civilian world. Turns out, there's not a huge demand for guys who know how to clear buildings or handle a rifle."

Buck grunted. "It's a tough adjustment. A lot of guys go through it. You try the whole college thing after that?"

"Yeah," Brad said, letting out a dry chuckle. "Junior college. Thought I'd give it a shot. But man, it felt like trying to learn a foreign language. I just didn't fit there. Dropped out after a couple of semesters."

Buck shook his head. "That's rough. So what, you went straight to work after that?"

"Construction," Brad replied. "Hard work, long days. Felt good to be doing something real, you know? Something with my hands. But it wasn't enough. I didn't want to be one of those guys swinging a hammer till they're sixty. So, I tried starting my own thing—a lawn care business. I was actually doing okay for a bit."

"Yeah?" Buck asked, his tone lightening slightly. "That's good, man. What happened?"

Brad sighed, his hands tightening on his knees. "Trailer got broken into. They took everything—mower, trimmer, blower, you name it. No insurance, no savings. That was the end of that."

"Damn," Buck muttered. "That's a tough break."

"Yeah," Brad agreed. "After that… it felt like every time I tried to pull myself up, life had a way of knocking me back down. The more I tried, the more it felt like I was chasing something I couldn't catch."

Buck was silent for a moment, letting Brad's words settle in the air. The hum of the engine filled the space between them.

"You ever think," Buck began, his voice thoughtful, "that maybe the problem isn't the path you're on, but the way you're walking it?"

Brad glanced over, frowning. "What do you mean?"

"Just that sometimes, it ain't about starting over, or finding some new path," Buck said. "It's about figuring out why the hell you're walking in the first place. What's driving you. Otherwise, you'll just keep hitting the same damn walls, no matter what road you're on."

Brad was quiet, his gaze fixed on the horizon. "Maybe," he said finally. "Maybe I just haven't figured that out yet."

Buck nodded. "Well, it's never too late to start looking. Hell, you've already got the bruises to show you've been in the fight. That's something."

Brad allowed himself a small smile. "I guess that's one way to look at it. How did you know you wanted to be a truck driver?" Brad asked, his gaze fixed on the road ahead, but his mind searching the horizon for answers.

Buck considered the question, his hands steady on the wheel. "I'm a simple man with simple needs," he began, his voice a reflection of the calm certainty that seemed to guide him. "Driving, the road—it's straightforward. You start at one point, and you get to another. And at the end of the trip is a paycheck."

"And how has it worked out for you?" Brad pressed on; his curiosity piqued.

"It's been good for me," Buck replied with a nod. "It's a way to earn a good living. Been doing it for years, and it's provided for me and mine just fine."

Brad's questions penetrated deeper, seeking the foundation of Buck's life choices. "What did you do before this?" he inquired; the question loaded with the weight of his own crossroads.

"Before this?" Buck echoed, a hint of nostalgia in his tone. "This has been my life for so long, it's hard to remember a before." He paused, checked his rearview mirror and signaled a lane change.

He shook his head, "Some of these old folks don't know how to do the speed limit."

"Where were we? Oh yeah, I was a shop mechanic for a short while. I worked on these big rigs. But I didn't like the confinement. I've always liked the freedom of the open road."

"And any regrets?" Brad's question hung in the air, a delicate probe into the fabric of Buck's experiences.

Regrets were tricky, Buck knew. They had a way of coloring the past in shades of what could have been. Yet, as he pondered the question, he found his answer with ease.

"My wife and I, we're happy. Raised three kids, put them through college so they can do better than I did. No, I can't say I have any real regrets. Life, with all its turns, has been good to Buck Dyson," he smiled a contented smile.

Brad absorbed Buck's responses, each word, perhaps, a clue laid on the path of his own search for meaning. Here was a man who had found contentment in the simplicity of his choices, a life measured not by the breadth of its adventures but by the depth of its commitments. Was there more to Buck's story — A private side he was not sharing with Brad?

The truck moved along, a silent companion to the two men lost in their own thoughts. The landscape outside blurred into glimpses of shadows and light as they each pondered the revelations of their conversation. After a stretch of silence, filled only by the sound of the road, Buck spoke up, his voice cutting through the quiet with a contemplative tone.

"You mention your misfortunes, and the sense that perhaps you're an unlucky person," Buck mused, glancing briefly at Brad. "Let me tell you, son, I believe we make our own luck. Think lucky, and you'll be lucky. I myself have been very lucky."

Brad turned towards Buck, sensing the depth behind his words. "It feels like there's another story behind that comment," he ventured, a hint of cautious curiosity coloring his voice.

The cab was engulfed in a protracted silence, the kind that speaks volumes, as Buck seemed to retreat into his own reservoir of memories. Outside, the landscape began to shift, signaling their approach to Pearson's Point. It was Buck who finally broke the silence, his voice steady and clear.

"Pearson's Point starts at the bridge coming up. You'll want to get out at the next exit."

CHAPTER 5

Carla Peterson sat stiffly on the edge of the cream-colored couch in Dr. Elizabeth Mercer's office, her manicured nails tracing invisible lines along the fabric's seam. The room smelled faintly of lavender, the kind of soft, artificial calm that irritated her more than soothed. Light filtered gently through the gauzy curtains, painting everything in shades of serenity. Yet, for Carla, it was an unwelcome reminder of how out of place she felt. Her world was anything but serene.

Across from her, Dr. Mercer sat with her legs crossed, a leather-bound notebook resting lightly in her lap. The therapist's pen hovered, poised to capture Carla's words, but she hadn't spoken yet—not really. Dr. Mercer's calm gaze seemed to strip away her defenses, like sunlight melting a carefully constructed frost. Carla glanced at the clock on the wall, though she knew she had plenty of time left in the session. Her lips pressed together tightly, and her fingers stilled.

"I don't even know why I'm here," Carla blurted finally, her voice sharp, cutting through the tranquil silence. "I don't need therapy. I just…things aren't how they should be. That's all."

Dr. Mercer didn't react immediately. She tilted her head slightly, letting the words linger in the air like a challenge. "Sometimes acknowledging that things aren't how they should be is where the work begins," she said evenly, her tone light but unwavering.

Carla scoffed, leaning back and crossing her arms over her chest. "Right," she muttered. But her gaze drifted again to the curtains, to the diffused sunlight that felt mocking.

The decision to seek therapy had come after many months of denial. She wasn't the type of woman who spilled her problems to strangers, especially not one with degrees hanging neatly on the wall, perfectly framed like trophies. Carla prided herself on control, on knowing exactly how to navigate people and situations to her advantage. A beguiling smile here, a carefully chosen word there—that was her game. But for some time now, these tactics had provided no satisfaction.

Her mind flickered to Richard, her third husband—a strategic choice.

"Richard's...fine," she began, as if responding to an unspoken question. Her tone was clipped, dismissive. "He's everything you're supposed to want in a husband—stable, reliable, decent. But decent doesn't exactly make your pulse race, does it?" The words slipped out before she could catch them. She grimaced, but Dr. Mercer said nothing, simply writing something down.

Carla's gaze darted toward the notebook, then back to the therapist's face. "He's like puddy in my hands," she continued, her voice harder now. "I thought that would be enough. That I could mold him into the perfect husband. But you can't mold someone into things they are not, can you?"

Her laugh was brittle, and it broke off abruptly. She turned her face away, her eyes landing on the muted painting hanging on the wall. For a moment, she studied its soft, abstract swirls, trying to ignore the pit in her stomach that rose every time she thought of her ex-husbands — or her sons.

The therapist's silence pressed on her, inviting her to continue, but she bristled against it. "And my son..." she said reluctantly, her voice faltering. Her fingers tightened on the edge of the couch. "he's grown, and doesn't call. When he does, it's always tense. Like he can't wait to hang up. He blames me for everything, you know? As if I didn't do my best."

Her laugh came again, hollow and bitter. "Of course, what do they know about what it takes to survive?"

Dr. Mercer leaned in slightly. "Do you blame them?"

The question hit Carla like a quiet blow. Her lips parted, but no words came. Instead, she stared down at her perfectly polished nails, as if the answer might be etched in the fine gloss of crimson red.

Carla had called Dr. Mercer on a whim, late one afternoon, after her latest disagreement with Richard that was followed by days of the silent treatment. Her son had phoned earlier the same day — a strained, obligatory conversation that left her gut churning. The magazine ad had been there on the coffee table, taunting her with its promise of solutions. And though she'd hated herself for it, she'd dialed the number, her voice trembling when she asked for an appointment.

Now, sitting here, under Dr. Mercer's patient gaze, she wasn't sure whether she felt relief or resentment for that fleeting lapse of control.

For a moment, her mind wandered back in time.

In her younger years, Carla had been pleasant to look at, though not conventionally beautiful. Her attractiveness lay in her beguiling ways and her knack for making men feel valued, though she could really have cared less about them. It was a means to an end, a way to manipulate men to obtain what she needed from them. Now, in her fifties, Carla's appearance had matured, but the sharpness in her eyes and the subtle charm in her manner remained unchanged, honed by years of perfecting the art of persuasion. Her clothes, makeup, and nail polish were always an overstatement, a compensation for her insecurity and her need to be seen. The vibrant colors and bold patterns of her attire clashed with the understated elegance of Dr. Mercer's office, making her presence even more pronounced. The thick layers of makeup, meticulously applied to mask the passage of time, and the glossy, brightly painted nails spoke volumes about her desperate desire to maintain appearances and command attention. Her hair, dyed to an unnatural shade of black, added to the contrast, a stark, almost defiant statement against the inevitability of aging. The lines on her face hinted at a life lived with calculated intent, every interaction a chess move in her intricate game of survival.

Dr. Mercer's voice brought her out of her reverie.

"Let's backtrack a little. Tell me about your first marriage, " Dr. Mercer prompted, notepad in hand, the click of her pen punctuating the silence like a metronome.

Carla sighed, her manicured nails tracing the paisley pattern on the armrest.

"Thomas Clark was his name. Tom was... comfortable, like an old shoe. But who wants to dance in old shoes?" Carla's lips curled into a wry smile, her gaze losing focus as she revisited those early years.

The therapist nodded, encouraging her to continue.

"I was young, vibrant. I needed excitement, the pulse of the crowd, the thrill of the music. Tom just wanted to stay in, watch another documentary," she scoffed, the disdain in her voice painting a clear picture of her impatience for the mundane domesticity Tom had offered.

Dr. Mercer asked, "Why then, did you marry Tom?" Carla drew back. A subconscious gesture, distancing herself from the old Carla.

"He was one of several guys I was dating at the time. When I got pregnant, Tom was the only one who stepped up. He never questioned if the baby was his. I wasn't going to be a single parent, and Tom was good-looking, a hard worker, and knew his way around the bedroom. Things were good in the beginning. He was a family man and a good provider, but that wasn't enough for me. I yearned for the attention other men wanted to give me. I had a wandering eye."

"And when you decided to leave Tom?"

"I needed more, Dr. Mercer. I was suffocating." Her hand fluttered to her chest, as if she could still feel the constriction of those days.

The conversation drifted to her second marriage — her so-called "fun" years with Reggie, though they had been anything but. Carla painted a vivid picture of those reckless adventures: the endless parties, the thrill of life in the fast lane, and the gnawing anxiety of overdue bills and empty cupboards.

For a moment, her face lit up as she thought of Reggie. A smile tugged at her lips, but it quickly faded. She slowly shook her head, her tone shifting.

"Reggie Williams," she began, a wistful edge to her voice. "He was a handsome man, a real head-turner. All the ladies wanted a piece of Reggie — and plenty of them got it." She let out a bitter chuckle. "I thought the excitement would be enough. That fun could fix everything. But it didn't."

Her polished exterior cracked, just slightly, revealing a rare glimpse of vulnerability. "Reggie was a child," she admitted with a sigh. "In the end, I had three kids to look after, not two."

Dr. Mercer's office was a sanctuary of sorts, a place where Carla's words could carve out the truth she so deftly avoided outside its walls.

"And your decision to leave Reggie?"

Carla's eyes hardened. "Survival," she stated flatly. "I wasn't going to drown with him."

The conversation shifted back to her current husband, Richard. Secure. Stable. Successful. The words were a checklist, and he had met them all. But Carla's heart was an account that no amount of security alone could balance.

"He worships me," she said, not without a trace of pride. "But it's all so… tepid."

"Apparently, that wasn't enough for you, Carla?" Dr. Mercer leaned forward slightly, her tone probing but measured.

"It should have been," she countered quickly, the words sharp, defensive. "He's a good man. We have a good life."

"But?"

Carla's facade began to crack, the fissures revealing something raw beneath. She glanced toward the window, the afternoon light cutting through the blinds, tracing faint lines on the floor. "But I feel trapped once again." Her voice softened, faltering. "Tom had offered me a kind of stability I now realize I wasn't ready for. Back then, I craved freedom—freedom to be myself, like an untamed bird flying far from a cage I hadn't realized I'd built myself. I told Tom flatly, 'I'm never going to marry again,' and I believed it with every fiber of my being."

Her lips pressed together as she exhaled a bitter laugh. "And now? Now I'm in a golden cage, Doctor. The bars are polished, and the view is beautiful—but the door is still locked."

Dr. Mercer remained quiet, letting her words hang in the room, as Carla leaned back into the chair. For a fleeting moment, she closed her eyes, the memories of Tom's steady presence flickering like an old reel of film. He had been everything Richard was now, but she had run from it then. And now, she had run right back to it—only this time, the stakes felt higher, the walls closer.

"Tom had given me the kind of stability I didn't want," she continued, her voice tinged with something that felt like regret. "And now Richard has given me the kind of stability I can't escape."

She looked up, meeting Dr. Mercer's gaze. "Is it me?" she asked, the words heavy with exhaustion. "Am I the one building the cage every time?"

Dr. Mercer tilted her head, considering her question. But before she could respond, Carla let out another breath, her eyes dropping to her lap. "I thought I wanted freedom. I thought I wanted love. And now, I don't even know what I want anymore."

"Happiness comes from within," Dr. Mercer instructed. "From finding contentment with who we are, not just what we have."

Carla's laughter was sharp, a shard of glass from the mirror she refused to look into. "Contentment," she mused. "A quaint idea."

The hour waned, and with it, Carla's willingness to peer further into the depths of her own narrative. Dr. Mercer closed her notebook, a silent signal that their time was up.

As Carla stood to leave, smoothing the creases from her designer skirt, Dr. Mercer offered a final thought. "Remember, Carla, paradoxes exist within us all. It's in reconciling those conflicting parts that we find our true selves."

Carla paused, a shadow of contemplation flickering across her features before she masked it with a practiced smile. "I'll see you next week, Doctor."

The exterior door clicked shut behind Carla as she left Dr. Mercer's office, the soft sound reverberating in her chest like the closing of a vault. For a moment, she lingered on the stoop, her hand gripping the metal rail as though it could steady the unspoken weight pressing down on her. The brightness of the day made her squint. She slipped on her sunglasses, a shield not just against the glare of the sun but against the glaring truths she wasn't ready to face.

The air was warm but carried a faint chill, a deceptive kind of weather that reminded her of her own life—appearing inviting on the surface but with an undercurrent that could leave you cold. Her heels struck the pavement with a sharp, purposeful rhythm, an attempt to impose order on the chaos swirling in her head.

Dr. Mercer's words echoed faintly, their soft cadence replaying like a song she couldn't skip. Therapy was supposed to help, wasn't it? To provide clarity? But the truths unearthed in that serene room felt less like revelations and more like accusations. Carla huffed, adjusting her handbag on her shoulder, the leather strap digging into her skin like a rebuke.

Her life was built on facades—layers of charm, control, and artifice stacked so high she sometimes forgot what lay beneath. She had perfected the well-rehearsed smile, the polished laugh, the strategic compliment. It had worked for years, fooling everyone, even herself. But in moments like this, when her defenses slipped, the truth rose like an unwanted guest. She walked the remaining distance home, her head in a fog.

As she stepped through the front door, the phone rang, Richard's voice chimed through before she could greet him.

"Don't forget about the dinner party tonight. And don't forget to smile."

She hung up and stared out the window, her reflection blurred in the golden light of sunset. She had everything she'd ever wanted, hadn't she? And yet, the emptiness pressed in, suffocating.

Peter M. Browne

CHAPTER 6

The dinner party was a blur of clinking glasses and hollow laughter. Carla moved through the room like a seasoned performer, her smile perfectly practiced, her gestures poised. The guests basked in her charm, oblivious to the gnawing emptiness beneath her polished exterior. She watched them closely, each wearing their own mask, and wondered if any of them felt the same dissonance she did—the growing gap between the life they presented and the life they lived.

Late into the night, after the last guest had left and Richard had retreated to bed, Carla sat alone in the dimly lit living room. A half-empty glass of wine rested in her hand, the silence of the house pressing in like an unwelcome guest. She stared at the polished floors, the neatly arranged furniture, the curated artwork—all of it part of the stage she had built. But tonight, even the stage felt fragile, its foundation shifting under the weight of her thoughts.

Her gaze drifted to her reflection in the darkened window. For a moment, she didn't recognize the woman staring back. The contours of her face were sharp, but the eyes lacked clarity, as if clouded by years of denial and discontent. Who was Carla Peterson without the masks? Without a man? Without the gilded cage that had become her life?

The glass slipped from her fingers, landing softly on the carpet. She leaned back, her head resting against the sofa, and let her eyes close.

Carla found herself standing in a swamp, the air thick with humidity and the pungent scent of decaying earth. Shadows danced across the water's surface, and the distant hoot of an owl echoed through the oppressive silence. A figure stood on the opposite bank, cloaked in shadows that seemed alive, shifting and writhing around him.

He Whose Name Was Never Spoken.

Carla froze as his glowing eyes locked onto hers. Though his features were obscured, his gaze pierced hers, stripping away the layers she had so carefully constructed.

"You are one of us," his voice whispered, the sound coming from everywhere and nowhere. His words carried the weight of an accusation. "You cannot escape what you are. And you cannot escape the consequences."

"What consequences?" Carla's voice was barely a whisper, her throat tightening.

"The one you've already begun to feel," he said, his tone heavy with finality. "You have squandered what was given to you, bending it to serve only yourself. Change your path, Carla, before it is too late."

The swamp seemed to close in, the air suffocating, the shadows reaching out toward her. She tried to move, to speak, but her body was frozen in place.

And then she saw it — a faint reflection in the water. It wasn't her own face staring back, but something darker, something unrecognizable. The figure began to fade, his voice lingering in the humid air.

"Make the right choice."

Carla woke with a start, her heart pounding. Her sheets were damp with sweat, twisted around her body like vines. The dream clung to her, vivid and oppressive, as though it had been more than just a creation of her subconscious. She sat up, glancing at the mirror across the room, half-expecting to see something — or someone — besides herself staring back.

The grandfather clock in the hall chimed softly, ushering in the early hours of dawn. Carla swung her legs over the side of the bed, her movements slow and deliberate, as if the weight of the dream still lingered. She padded to the window and drew back the curtain, the cool light of morning spilling into the room.

Stepping out onto the terrace, she inhaled deeply, the crisp air a welcome contrast to the suffocating heat of her dream. The sky was a wash of soft blues and pinks, a fleeting promise of renewal. But even the beauty of the morning couldn't quiet the unease curling in her chest.

The house behind her felt cavernous, its silence a reminder of the distance between her and Richard, Brad, and even herself. She thought about her son — distant and polite, his calls tinged with obligation rather than affection. She thought about Richard, sleeping soundly in the next room, unaware of the growing chasm between them.

Her life had become a series of performances — roles she played so well that even she sometimes forgot they weren't real. But the dream had shaken her. Its message was clear, even if she didn't want to acknowledge it: something had to change.

As the sun rose higher, Carla leaned against the railing, her eyes fixed on the horizon. She wasn't sure what lay ahead, but one thing was certain—she couldn't keep living like this. The path she had taken, paved with manipulation and self-interest, had led her to this empty, lonely place. The dream's warning echoed in her mind, a challenge she couldn't ignore.

"Make the right choice," she whispered, her breath forming a cloud in the crisp morning air.

And as the sun climbed higher, casting its golden light across the terrace, Carla turned and walked back inside, her shadow stretching long and thin behind her.

Carla's home was a testament to her need for control, each room carefully curated down to the smallest detail. The living room was pristine: the sleek, white leather sofa perfectly aligned with the edge of the beige rug, a glass coffee table holding a single, immaculate orchid in a crystal vase. The abstract art on the walls hung level, chosen not for personal meaning but for how its muted tones complemented the space.

She stopped in the center of the room, her gaze darting from one perfect element to another. Her chest tightened. The order mocked her. The stillness pressed in like a weight. She stared at the orchid; its delicate petals unwavering, serene.

"Perfect," she muttered, the word sharp and bitter as broken glass. Her hand shot out, sweeping the vase off the table. It smashed against the floor, water pooling around shards of crystal. "Not anymore."

Her steps quickened as she moved through the house. She grabbed the edge of a photo frame in the hallway — one of the many staged family portraits, their smiles all teeth and no warmth — and ripped it from the wall. She studied it for a moment, her lip curling.

"Do any of you even know who I am?" she asked, her voice rising. "I don't." Without waiting for an answer, she threw the frame to the ground. The glass shattered in a satisfying burst, and she stepped over the pieces as she stalked toward the dining room.

The long, elegant table stood like a monument to a life she no longer wanted. Fine china, crystal glasses, silver cutlery — it was all set, perfect, unused. Her fingers brushed the edge of a glass. For a moment, she hesitated, then flicked it with the tips of her fingers. It tipped, rolled, and fell, shattering against the polished wood floor.

Her laughter was sharp and bitter. "I made my choices," she said, her voice rising with each word. "Married the man who could give me what I needed. Built this perfect, hollow life. Controlled every detail. And for what?" She grabbed one of the chairs and shoved it to the ground, the crash reverberating through the room. "To end up married but being alone."

Her breathing grew heavier as she stormed into the kitchen. The pristine countertops gleamed under the recessed lights, the stainless-steel appliances standing at attention like soldiers in a parade. Without pausing, Carla opened a cabinet and yanked a stack of neatly arranged plates out, sending them clattering to the floor in a cacophony of breaking porcelain.

She turned back toward the hallway, her eyes wild, her steps heavy. "I'm done with this," she muttered under her breath. "Done playing this game. Done pretending everything's fine while I'm suffocating in here."

Upstairs, the bedroom was a sanctuary of muted luxury. The bed was immaculate, its crisp, white linens stretched tight, the throw blanket folded with precision at the foot. Carla yanked the blanket off and threw it across the room. The bedside lamp followed, tumbling to the carpet with a dull thud.

In the closet, rows of clothes hung neatly by color and type, shoes lined up in perfect symmetry. She grabbed at the hangers, yanking dresses off the rods and tossing them onto the floor. Shoes went flying, one hitting the mirrored closet door with a sharp crack.

"This is it, huh?" she said, her voice trembling. "All the things I thought would make me happy. And here I am, drowning in them." She kicked a pile of clothes, sending them scattering across the floor.

Finally, Carla stopped in front of the mirror, her reflection fractured by the chaos behind her. Her hair was wild, her face flushed, her chest heaving with exertion. She stared at herself, a bitter smile twisting her lips.

"There's going to have to be some changes made" she said, her voice carrying a strange finality. "I'm done faking it. It's over!"

When Richard finally woke, the first thing he noticed was the noise. The sharp clatter of pots, the slam of a cupboard door—sounds that didn't belong to his usual morning routine. He squinted at the clock and frowned. Carla was never up this early, and she certainly wasn't making noise.

The second thing he noticed was the smell of coffee, rich and dark, wafting into the bedroom. Pushing off the covers, Richard shuffled toward the kitchen, rubbing sleep from his eyes.

Carla stood at the counter, a mug in hand, her back to him. The mess around her was startling: cabinet doors left ajar, a trail of coffee grounds on the countertop, the vase of lilies that usually adorned the kitchen table conspicuously absent. He glanced down and saw it lying shattered in the trash bin, white petals wilting among shards of glass.

"Carla?" he ventured cautiously.

She turned slowly, her face calm but her eyes blazing with something Richard couldn't quite name. She set her mug down with a decisive clink.

"Sit down," she said.

"What the hell's going on?" he asked, hesitating by the doorway.

"Just sit."

Her voice carried an edge he wasn't used to, sharp and unyielding. He moved to the table and eased into a chair, his eyes darting nervously around the kitchen, taking in the chaos.

Carla poured him a cup of coffee, sliding it across the table without a word. She leaned against the counter, arms folded, watching him as if deciding how much to say — or how to say it.

"What's going on?" he asked again, his voice quieter now, uneasy.

Carla tilted her head, studying him for a moment before answering. "I'm done playing this game, Richard."

His brow furrowed. "What game?"

"This—" she gestured around the kitchen, the house, the life they'd built together. "The pretending. The smiling. The dinner parties and polite conversations. I've been choking on this life for years, and I can't do it anymore."

He stared at her, stunned into silence. Carla had never spoken to him like this. She reserved that voice— the sharp, cutting one—for others. He'd witnessed her use it many times, dismantling waiters, family members, even her own friends, with a precision that made him uneasy. Each time, he'd thought quietly to himself, I hope she never gets pissed at me. Yet here she was now, turning that edge on him, and it was sharper than he imagined.

"Did something happen?" he asked carefully, trying to piece together what might have set her off.

"Yes," she said, her voice tight. "I happened. I've been twisting myself into knots trying to live up to some picture-perfect version of life, and I'm done. Done pretending I'm happy. Done pretending this—" she gestured vaguely at him, the table, her own mug, "—is enough."

Richard blinked, her words hitting him like cold water. He opened his mouth, then closed it, struggling to process the shift in her tone.

"This isn't like you, Carla," he said finally, his voice laced with confusion. What is really the problem?"

Her laugh was bitter, a short, sharp sound that made him flinch. "Of course, you'd think that. You've spent so much time ignoring the cracks in this marriage, why wouldn't you assume I'm the problem?"

"I didn't say that," he replied quickly, defensively.

"You didn't have to," she shot back. "You're perfectly content with the status quo, Richard. You get your stability, your quiet little life. Meanwhile, I'm drowning in it."

Richard shifted uncomfortably in his chair, his hands gripping the edge of the table. "What exactly are you saying, Carla?"

"I'm saying I need more," she said, her voice breaking just slightly before she steadied it. "And I don't know how to get it."

The words hung in the air like a storm cloud, heavy and foreboding. Richard looked at her, his expression a mixture of disbelief and hurt.

"You're serious," he said after a long pause.

"Dead serious."

He looked down at the coffee she'd made for him, the steam curling up in quiet, mocking tendrils. For the first time, he couldn't read her. This was a side of Carla he didn't recognize, and it terrified him.

After a moment, he pushed back his chair and stood. "I'm going to get ready for work," he said stiffly, his voice void of emotion. "We can finish this conversation later."

Carla watched him go without a word.

When she heard the bathroom door close upstairs, she picked up her mug and took a long sip, her thoughts churning. The scene from earlier echoed faintly in her mind — the sound of dishes and glasses hitting the floor — and she realized that it had felt... good — to assert her freedom.

Peter M. Browne

CHAPTER 7

Back in the day, Buck Dyson was known in his Sarasota community not just as a long-haul trucker but as a pillar of steadfastness and reliability. He and his wife, Esther, lived in a modest yet well-kept home that reflected the values they held dear: hard work, integrity, and a sense of community. Their house, a single-story ranch-style home, sat comfortably in a working-class neighborhood where everyone knew each other's names.

The front yard was evidence of Buck's dedication and pride in his home. A neatly trimmed lawn stretched out before the house, bordered by vibrant flower beds that Esther lovingly tended. A sturdy oak tree provided ample shade, its branches often the gathering spot for neighborhood kids playing games. The back yard, with its inviting swing and potted plants, served as a welcoming space for friends and family to gather and cook out.

The house itself was painted a warm, earthy tone, with white trim that highlighted its clean lines and simple architecture. Large windows allowed plenty of natural light to filter through, creating a cozy and bright interior. Inside, the décor was practical and unpretentious, with comfortable furniture that showed signs of good use. Family photos adorned the walls, capturing moments of joy and milestones over the years.

The kitchen, often filled with the aroma of Esther's cooking, was the heart of the home. It was here that Buck and Esther spent many evenings, when he was home, sharing meals and discussing the events of the day. The kitchen table, a sturdy wooden piece that had seen countless family dinners, was the center of many lively conversations and heartfelt moments.

The neighborhood itself was a tight-knit community where people looked out for one another. Neighbors exchanged greetings as they tended to their gardens or washed their cars. Children played in the streets, their laughter echoing through the neighborhood. Block parties and barbecues were common occurrences, fostering a sense of unity and camaraderie among the residents.

Buck's garage was a reflection of his meticulous nature. It was well-organized, with tools neatly arranged on pegboards and shelves. His truck, when not on the road, was parked in the driveway, a symbol of his livelihood and dedication. The garage also housed his collection of memorabilia from years on the road — maps, trinkets, and souvenirs that told the story of his travels across the country.

Despite the long hours and demanding nature of his job, Buck always made time for his community. He volunteered at local events, offered a helping hand to neighbors in need, and was a familiar face at community meetings. His reputation as a dependable and hardworking man was well-earned, and his presence brought a sense of stability and trust to those around him.

When home, he was the devoted family man, his world orbiting around his wife and three children. His love for them was a quiet, steady flame, illuminating their lives with warmth and security. On the rare occasions when he was home, dinner was a very special time filled with discussions, laughter, and the occasional story of the road.

On each return he was met with the same excitement. As Buck's truck rumbled to a stop in the driveway, the sound was like a beacon to those inside. The truck door barely had a chance to close behind him before the excited shouts of his children filled the air.

"Daddy!" The youngest, Lily, sprinted into his arms, her enthusiasm infectious.

Buck scooped her up, spinning her around as she giggled uncontrollably. "Well, if it isn't my little ray of sunshine," he beamed, setting her down gently. "What've you been up to, huh?"

Lily launched into a detailed account of her day, her words tumbling out in a rush. Buck listened intently, nodding and chuckling at the right moments, his heart swelling with love.

Through the kitchen window, Esther watched the scene unfold with a soft smile. "You know, the dining room's missed your laughter, Buck," she yelled out, her tone light but laden with unspoken emotion.

Buck looked up toward the window, meeting her gaze. "And I've missed being the cause of it," he replied, entering the kitchen through the side door, he wrapped his arms around her. They shared a look, a moment, that spoke volumes of their shared history, love, and resilience.

As they gathered around the dinner table, Buck took his place at the head, his presence anchoring the room. "I heard you aced your math test, Jake," he said, turning to his eldest with a proud nod.

Jake, tried to maintain a cool demeanor, but couldn't hide his smile. "Yeah, wasn't too bad. Studied a lot for it."

"And Sarah, your mom told me, Mrs. Henderson said you're leading the science project team. That's quite the achievement," Buck continued, his attention shifting to his middle child, who blushed at the mention of her success.

Sarah shrugged, her modesty front and center. "Just doing what I love, Dad."

As they ate, the conversation flowed freely, ranging from school projects to neighborhood happenings and the occasional gentle discussion on a variety of topics. Buck's contributions were thoughtful, often laced with humor, drawing laughter and thoughtful nods from around the table.

When talk turned to a recent challenge Sarah faced, Buck's tone softened, his advice woven with the wisdom of experience. Sarah, had been struggling with a group project at school, where she was being teased. She sat, her eyes downcast as she fiddled with her fork, "The kids were making fun of my suggestions for the project."

Buck listened, his gaze never leaving her face, seeing beyond the school project to the heart of the matter. "Sarah, just like on a sports team, every player's contribution is vital. You've got to stand strong, know your worth," he said, reaching across the table to squeeze her hand. "And remember, teasing's like a flat tire on my truck—it won't get them far. Talk to your teammates. See if you can solve this problem yourself. Okay? If not, we're here to help you."

The weight on Sarah's shoulders seemed to lift, a small smile breaking through. Buck provided not just a strategy for resolution but a lesson in resilience and courage.

Esther reached across the table, squeezing Sarah's hand. "We're a team, remember that. Together, there's nothing we can't handle."

To his neighbors, Buck was the embodiment of the good Samaritan. When not on the road he could often be found beneath the hood of a neighbor's car or atop a ladder, fixing a loose shingle on an elderly resident's roof. His knowledge of mechanics wasn't just limited to his rig; he was the go-to for anyone in need of a fix, his hands as skilled with a wrench as they were steady on the steering wheel.

On this particular day Buck was where he often was when not on the road—under the open hood of someone's car. Mrs. Thompson's old Chevrolet, parked in her driveway. The elderly widow stood by, watching Buck work, her hands clasped together, her eyes alight with gratitude.

"You're sure you don't mind doing this, Buck? I hate to take you away from your family on your Saturday at home," Mrs. Thompson said, her voice concerned. She knew Buck's time at home was limited and precious.

Buck looked up from his work, wiping his brow with the back of his hand. "Not at all, Mrs. Thompson. You know I enjoy helping out where I can. What kind of neighbor would I be if I let you miss your granddaughter's birthday because of a stubborn car?" he replied, his tone light and reassuring.

"Oh, I don't know what we'd do without you, Buck. You're a blessing to this neighborhood," she said, her eyes shining with unshed tears of appreciation.

"Just keeping things running, Ma'am. Besides, it's nice to be able to put my hands to good use off the road," Buck said, his attention returning to the engine before him. His hands moved with practiced ease, the wrench turning with precision under his skilled grip.

As he worked, a young boy from next door, Tommy, came running over, a toy truck clutched in his small hands. "Mr. Buck, Mr. Buck!" he called out, breathless with excitement. "Can you fix my truck too? The wheels are stuck."

Buck straightened up, a smile breaking across his face as he turned to the young boy. "Let's have a look then, Tommy," he said, gesturing for the boy to come closer. Kneeling down to be at eye level with Tommy, Buck took the toy truck in his hands, giving it the same careful attention, he afforded the real vehicles he worked on.

After a moment of inspection, Buck made a slight adjustment to the truck's axle, a twist here and a turn there. Handing it back to Tommy, he said, "Try it now."

Tommy's face lit up with delight as his toy truck came to life, its wheels spinning without the previous hindrance. "Wow! Thanks, Mr. Buck! You can fix anything!" he exclaimed, his admiration for Buck evident in his wide eyes.

Buck chuckled, ruffling Tommy's hair gently. "Just doing my part, buddy. Now, go on and play. And be careful with that truck," he advised, standing up to return to Mrs. Thompson's car.

As the morning turned into afternoon, Buck finally closed the hood of the Chevrolet with a satisfied nod. "All set, Mrs. Thompson. She should run smoothly now. Just remember to take her in for regular check-ups."

Mrs. Thompson beamed at him; her gratitude visible. "Thank you, Buck. I don't know how to repay you for all your help."

Buck waved off her thanks with a smile. "Seeing that car get you where you need to go is thanks enough for me. Take care, Mrs. Thompson."

In the community, Buck's faith was well known. Not a regular at the local church, due to his travels, but he was as comfortable discussing scripture as he was talking about football or the best route to take from Jacksonville to Boston. His faith was a compass, guiding his actions and decisions, imbued in the respectful way he treated everyone he met. His belief in doing unto others as you would have them do unto you wasn't just a scripture passage; it was a way of life.

On another week-end at home, Buck Dyson found himself perched atop a ladder, addressing the loose shingles on Julia Henderson's roof. The single mom watched from below, her hand shielding her eyes from the sun.

"You really don't have to do this, Buck. I can call the roofing company," Julia called up, her voice carrying a note of worry.

Buck paused, hammer in hand, and looked down at her with a reassuring smile. "Nonsense, Julia. It's no trouble at all. Besides, the professionals will over charge you for this simple fix. Consider this my Sunday service to you."

"But you're missing the actual service at church," she pointed out, her brow furrowed.

Buck chuckled, resuming his work. "My faith doesn't require a pew, Julia. I believe in putting it into action, in helping out where I can. Like the Good Book says, 'faith by itself, if it does not have works, is dead.'"

Julia smiled, shaking her head in admiration. "You always have a scripture ready for every occasion, Buck. Your faith is truly lived."

Just then, a young man from the neighborhood, Billy, approached. "Hey, Mr. Dyson, I heard you were back in town. I've got this issue with my car, and I was hoping you could take a look?"

Buck nodded, securing the last shingle before descending the ladder. "Of course, Billy. Let's see if we can't get you fixed up."

As they walked towards Billy's car, Buck listened intently to the young man's troubles, not just with the car but with life's larger challenges. Buck offered advice, blending practical tips with nuggets of wisdom, his faith subtly guiding his words.

"You know, Billy, sometimes the routes we're on take unexpected turns. But there's always a way through if you keep the faith and a clear head," Buck advised as he tinkered under the hood.

Billy watched, absorbing more than just mechanical knowledge. "Thanks, Mr. Dyson. Not just for this, but for the advice too. You're not just good with cars, you know?"

Buck stood, wiping his hands on a rag, a gentle smile on his face. "Life's a bit like an engine, Billy. Sometimes it needs a bit of tweaking to run smoothly. Just remember, whatever path you're on, make sure it's one that you can look back on and be proud of."

As the car roared to life, Billy's gratitude was evident.

"It was backfiring because the timing was off. Not a big deal," Buck remarked as he closed the hood. He turned to Billy, "Stay out of trouble now."

"I will, Mr. Dyson. Thank you."

Buck was more than just the sum of his good deeds. He was known for his congenial nature, a friendliness that seemed to come as naturally to him as breathing. His laughter was infectious, his bearing approachable, making him well-liked and respected both within his circle and out in the broader community. On the road, his reputation as a Good Samaritan extended to fellow truckers and strangers alike, always ready to lend a hand or an ear.

Yet, like any man, Buck was not without his flaws. His mood could shift like the weather, occasional clouds darkening his usually sunny disposition. These moments were fleeting, like summer storms, quick to pass but leaving a kind of tension in their wake. It was in these times that his high expectations for himself and those around him were most evident, a perfectionist streak that could both motivate and intimidate.

Buck took great pride in his rig, maintaining it with an almost religious zeal. To him, the truck was more than just a vehicle; it was an extension of who he was. His knowledge of its mechanics was extensive, each adjustment and repair carried out with a meticulousness that spoke of a deep respect for the machine that was his livelihood.

Buck, always a pillar of strength in his family's eyes, a man who navigated the world with an unshakeable calm and an iron will. His rare presence at home was like the sun emerging from behind the clouds, bringing warmth but also casting long shadows that hinted at the mysteries of his life on the road.

At the local park, the sun dipped low, casting long shadows over the baseball diamond. Buck stood along the sidelines, cheering as his son, Jake, rounded second base. The game was a nail-biter, and for once, Buck was there in the flesh, his usually demanding schedule fortuitously open.

The crack of a bat against a ball, a cheer from the crowd, then a sudden shift. Jake slid into third, but not without cost. As he stood, a trickle of blood ran down his leg, a stark red against his white uniform. The game paused; coaches and players huddled around him.

From the stands, Buck's presence loomed large, yet as he caught sight of the blood, his usual stoicism faltered. His face paled, and for a moment, he looked as if he might pass out. Esther, ever observant, noticed the change immediately. She wrapped her arm around him, guiding him to sit down.

Later that evening, after assurances that Jake was fine and the wound was superficial, Buck and Esther sat on their back deck, enveloped in the calm after the storm. The day's scare with Jake's injury had unsettled something deep within Buck, and the silence between them was thick with unvoiced thoughts.

"Buck, I know you're squeamish at the sight of blood," Esther ventured, breaking the stillness. Her voice was gentle, probing the layers of a man she knew so well and yet was always discovering anew.

"Yeah, I don't know what it is..." Buck said softly, in his voice evidence of his discomfort with the subject. He looked out into the darkness, searching for answers in the night. "I've been in combat, seen my buddies get shot, seen too much death and pain. It never phased me then, but now when it's my kid, it goes right through me..."

Esther, sensing there was more beneath his words, nudged gently, "It's different with family, isn't it? The fear, the worry..."

Buck shook his head, a rueful smile touching his lips as he corrected her, "No, it's not just the family. In the service, those guys were my family too. It's more like I've used up all my tolerance for bloodshed and pain, I guess." He sighed, struggling to articulate a feeling that eluded even him. "Somewhere along the line, something inside me changed. I just... I can't stand to see it. One drop just flashes me back to all that needless bloodshed and loss of life." The air went silent as they sat in the warmth of the Florida evening.

Time marched on, Buck logging thousands of miles each trip. The children once so small they'd danced on his boots as he walked were all grown up. Jake went off to Florida State on a baseball scholarship and then on to Stetson Law School in Tampa, Florida.

Sarah, always the geek, ended up in Silicon Valley working for a small startup company working on medical robotics. Back in high school Sarah had proposed that her "Odyssey of the Minds" team create an autonomous robot to enter into the competition. Her teammates made fun of her for her outlandish idea but Buck had told her to stick to her guns. On her own she produced a prototype that convinced her teammates it could be done. They went on to win second place in that year's competition.

Little Lily was all grown up too, but she remained in Sarasota as an elementary school teacher.

Now that Buck and Esther were empty-nesters. Esther started riding along with Buck keeping him company on his long hauls and entertaining him with her true crime stories.

She did not accompany him, though, on his short trip to Pensacola, to deliver that yacht. She had committed her time to the local church, that week, to work on the upcoming banquet.

The next week, they were back on the road again. Buck was filling Esther in on his trip to Pensacola.

"I picked up a young hitchhiker just outside of Lake City, on his way to Pearson's Point. It reminded me of the crime story that had taken place there, that you read to me."

Being a crime aficionado, she instantly recalled. "You mean the highway murders they never solved."

"Yeah, when he mentioned Pearson's Point it just reminded me of that story. I thought it was fiction," he suggested.

"No that was a true crime story. They never caught the guy," she added.

"What makes you think it was a guy?" He remarked in jest.

Esther just waved him off.

"I'm going to pull in here for some fuel for us and the truck," referencing the sign for the upcoming truck stop. Buck took on one hundred gallons of diesel for the truck and coffee and donuts for them.

As they exited the Love's Truck Stop just south of Savannah Georgia, Buck glanced over at Esther who was fanning the pages of her latest crime novel looking for where she left off.

"Ah, here we go," she said, as she began to read aloud.

Peter M. Browne

CHAPTER 8

Carla found herself once again in Dr. Mercer's office. The familiar surroundings, once a battleground for her deflections, now seemed to hold her accountable. Dr. Mercer, diminutive in physical appearance but maintaining a large presence, waited, patient as ever, for Carla to break the silence that had settled between them. Despite her small stature, Dr. Mercer's persona commanded respect and attention. As usual, she was conservatively dressed, her attire always professional and understated, yet impeccably neat. Her glasses, perched atop her head and tucked into her hair, added to her scholarly appearance. The frames, simple yet elegant, hinted at her practical nature. Dr. Mercer's hair, graying but still thick, was pulled back in a no-nonsense style that matched her straightforward approach to therapy. Her eyes, sharp and observant, missed nothing, and her expression was one of calm assurance. In her presence, Carla felt the weight of her own thoughts and emotions, knowing that Dr. Mercer would patiently and persistently guide her towards confronting them.

"I've been thinking about what you said," Carla began, her voice less certain than it had been before she arrived. "About how happiness comes from within."

"And what have you concluded from your reflection?" Dr. Mercer inquired, her gaze both gentle and probing.

Carla hesitated, the words like pebbles in her mouth. "I've realized that everyone around me is responsible for my unhappiness. If Tom had been more adventurous, if Reggie had been more responsible, if my children..." Her voice trailed off, her instinct to lay blame as reflexive as breathing.

Dr. Mercer leaned forward slightly. "And where do you see yourself in all of this, Carla?"

The question hung in the air, a challenge she wasn't sure she wanted to accept. For a fleeting moment, Carla's defenses wavered, and she found herself teetering on the edge of self-awareness. She glimpsed her reflection in the window, the fading light casting shadows that seemed to reveal more than they concealed.

But the moment passed, the walls she had built so meticulously over the years proving too formidable to tear down in an instant. "I... I did everything I could," she said finally, retreating to the safety of her familiar narrative.

Dr. Mercer nodded; her expression unreadable. "Let's try a different approach next time," she suggested, her tone hinting at a deeper strategy. "I want you to think about the roles you've played, not just with your husbands or your children, but with yourself. "Who is Carla when she's not performing for someone else?"

Dr. Mercer's question hung in the air, deceptively simple, yet charged. Carla's breath caught, a faint tremor fluttering in her chest. She masked it quickly, letting out a laugh that sounded too hollow, even to her own ears. "You do love your theatrics, Doctor," she quipped, her voice smooth and practiced, deflecting as always.

But the words lingered, digging at her. Carla leaned back into the couch, her gaze drifting to the ceiling as if searching for something distant, just out of reach. "I don't know," she admitted finally, her voice oddly calm, detached. "People... just give me what I want. Sometimes, I don't even have to ask. It's like they... know."

Dr. Mercer's pen scratched softly against her notepad. "And how does that make you feel?"

Carla turned her head slowly, deliberately, locking eyes with the doctor. Her gaze was sharp, unblinking, like a scalpel poised to slice through layers of pretense. For a moment, Dr. Mercer felt as if the air had shifted, the room closing in just slightly. Carla's lips parted, but she hesitated, her faint smile hovering like a secret too heavy to reveal.

"I feel..." Carla began, her voice calm and measured. Then her smile grew, sharp at the edges. "POWERFUL."

The single word seemed to echo in the small office, resonating not just in the air but somewhere deeper, somewhere primal. It carried an unnatural weight, low and sonorous, as though it had been plucked from the depths of the earth itself.

Dr. Mercer froze, her pen pausing mid-stroke. The room fell utterly silent. The ambient hum of the world beyond the walls — the traffic, the muffled voices, even the faint buzz of electricity — vanished, leaving behind a void so profound it pressed against her chest.

A chill slithered across Dr. Mercer's arms, sharp as icy fingers. She rubbed her hands over her sleeves, her rational mind immediately reaching for explanations: faulty ventilation, a draft from somewhere unseen. Yet, the temperature had undeniably dropped. The stillness was uncanny, as though the air itself was watching, waiting.

"Powerful?" Dr. Mercer echoed; her voice softer, almost unwilling to disturb the fragile silence. She cleared her throat, steadying herself. "In what way?"

Carla's smile widened, a flicker of amusement glinting in her dark eyes as she registered the subtle shift in Dr. Mercer's manner. She noticed the doctor's tightening grip on the pen, the faint crease forming between her brows, the telltale stillness of someone trying too hard to appear composed. It pleased Carla in a way she couldn't quite articulate, a quiet affirmation of the effect she could have on people. She did not answer the doctor's question. She simply held her gaze, unblinking, unyielding, watching as discomfort flickered across the other woman's face like the shadow of a passing cloud.

The silence stretched again, and this time, Dr. Mercer felt an almost primal urge to look away, though she forced herself not to.

The chill deepened, like the breath of something ancient brushing the back of her neck. A bead of sweat trickled down her spine, despite the cold. Reflexively, her eyes darted to the air vent. Her throat tightened; her pulse quickened.

And then, as suddenly as it had come, the heaviness lifted. The hum of the world returned, faint but unmistakable. The room warmed, the chill dissipating like a passing shadow.

Dr. Mercer straightened in her seat, masking the unease that lingered in her chest. "Until next time, Carla," she said, her tone crisp and professional.

Carla rose gracefully, smoothing the hem of her skirt as if nothing had transpired. She turned to leave; her movements unhurried. As the door clicked shut behind her, Dr. Mercer let out a breath she hadn't realized she was holding, her hand trembling slightly as she set down her pen. She flexed her fingers, as though testing to see if they still belonged to her, and leaned back in her chair, her heart pounding faintly in her ears.

For a long moment, she simply sat there, her gaze fixed on the door, her mind struggling to assemble the scattered pieces of her composure. *What was that?* she thought, her clinical detachment faltering. She had been a therapist for years, had seen countless patients, some more intense than others, but never had she felt... that.

The chill still lingered in the corners of her awareness, despite the warmth returning to the room. It wasn't just the temperature — it had been something else, something harder to name, like an unseen presence pressing against her skin, brushing her thoughts.

She reached for her pen again, tapping it nervously against the edge of her notebook. Her notes from the session were sparse, disjointed — "powerful," "unsettling," "unnatural aura" — phrases jotted in a hurried scrawl. The word "unworldly" stood out, underlined twice.

Dr. Mercer frowned, shaking her head as if to dislodge the feeling. It's just another patient, she told herself. And yet, she couldn't ignore the way Carla had looked at her — like she could see through her, past her, down to something raw and vulnerable.

She stood and moved to the window, pushing it open slightly to let in fresh air. The evening breeze carried the faint scent of rain, grounding her in the tangible, the real. But the unease remained, a whisper in the back of her mind, insisting that what had just happened was far from ordinary.

"Powerful". The way Carla had said it, her voice resonating like a note struck too low, sent another shiver coursing through Dr. Mercer. She closed her eyes, rubbing her temples. The rational part of her wanted to chalk it up to an over-reaction, but in a place she didn't like to examine too closely, she felt it — something unnatural had happened.

And as she returned to her desk, she found herself wondering: *Who is Carla Peterson, really?*

CHAPTER 9

Brad had always heard the saying in Pearson's Point: "No one moves here; they only move away." Growing up, he witnessed the cycle firsthand — the way people seemed destined to replay the lives of the generations before them. It was a cycle he desperately wanted to break, which led him to leave in search of something more, something better. But now, years later, Brad had come back, not as the success story he had hoped to become, but with a sense of defeat he couldn't shake off.

Pearson's Point hadn't changed much. It still had that small-town feel that made secrets hard to keep and personal victories or failures the talk of the town. Returning meant facing people who would remember him as Carla's son, the bright kid with big plans, now a man whose aspirations had dimmed.

The sun was setting as Brad walked up to the house, the familiar sight bringing a mix of emotions. Carla stood on the porch, her figure silhouetted against the fading light, curiosity playing across her face, as she saw the person approaching — then recognition struck.

"Bradley, you didn't tell us you were coming," Carla said, her voice a tone of surprise as she descended the steps to greet him. Her use of his full name, reserved for moments of significance, wasn't lost on him. But at the same time, it wasn't the warm greeting from a mother excited by her son's return.

"Yeah, I didn't know when I'd get here," Brad replied, his voice carrying a weariness that wasn't just from the road. He managed a small smile, but it didn't quite reach his eyes.

They stood there for a moment, the years and distance between them hanging in the air. Finally, Carla stepped forward, wrapping him in a hug that felt both familiar and foreign. Brad stiffened initially, then relaxed, allowing himself this small comfort.

As they separated, Carla looked up at him, her eyes searching his. "I'm glad you're home, Brad. I know you've had some tough breaks," she offered without emotion.

Brad shifted uncomfortably, the weight of his return pressing down on him. "Yeah, well, not much here says 'successful return,' does it?" he said, trying to keep his tone light.

Carla sighed, a hint of impatience in her voice as she led the way inside. "Success isn't just about running off to who knows where, thinking you'll find something better, Brad, it's about facing reality, making do with what you have. Maybe that's something you'll finally understand now that you're back."

Brad bristled at her words; the familiar sting of her judgment sharp as ever. "I'm not back because I've given up, Mom. I just... need to figure things out," he said, his voice tight with frustration.

Carla turned to him, her gaze scrutinizing, as if assessing whether he believed his own words. "Figure things out," she echoed, her tone laced with skepticism. "Well, don't think that just because you've come crawling back, everything will be handed to you. You're going to have to work, prove you're not the same person who left."

They settled into an uneasy silence, the kitchen between them feeling both too small and too vast. Brad looked down at his hands, the sense of defeat creeping in despite his best efforts to keep it at bay.

"I'm not asking for handouts," Brad finally said, his voice low. "I just thought... maybe, living here could be different, this time."

Carla's expression softened slightly, but the edge in her voice remained. "Starting over means taking responsibility, Brad. It means not making the same foolish mistakes. I hope, for your sake, you're ready to do that."

Her words hung in the air, a challenge and a reminder of the gulf between them. Brad nodded, more to himself than to her. "I am. I have to be."

The conversation shifted then, to practical matters — job prospects in Pearson's Point, the condition of the house, the comings and goings of familiar faces. Yet, beneath the surface, Brad's resolve hardened. Carla's skepticism, her judgments, they were obstacles to overcome, but they wouldn't define him. Not anymore. He was determined to prove, to his mother and to himself, that coming back wasn't a retreat. It was the first step toward a new beginning, however uncertain the path ahead.

The sound of a car pulling into the driveway signaled Richard's return from work, a moment both had been unconsciously dreading.

Richard entered the house with a weary sigh, the lines of his day etched deeply into his face. His eyes landed on Brad, and for a fleeting second, a complex mix of emotions flitted across his expression—surprise, resignation, and a trace of displeasure. "Brad," he said, his greeting terse, a nod more out of obligation than warmth.

Brad stood, the chair scraping on the tiled floor. "Richard," he replied, the name carrying years of distance and disconnection.

Carla watched the exchange, a knot of anxiety tightening in her stomach. She knew Richard's thoughts almost as well as her own; Brad's presence was a disruption, a catalyst for the kind of domestic strife Richard abhorred.

"I didn't realize you were visiting," Richard said, carefully hanging his coat, his words measured. The word 'visiting' hung between them, a pointed reminder of Brad's outsider status.

Brad's jaw clenched at the implication. "Not visiting, I'm back," he corrected, the defiance in his voice more for his own benefit than Richard's.

Richard's sigh was heavy, laden with the foresight of conflicts to come. "Well, that's going to be quite an adjustment for everyone," he said, glancing at Carla, who remained silent, her earlier resolve wilting under Richard's practical, unemotional gaze.

Dinner was a quiet affair, the conversation skirting around the elephant in the room. Richard, ever the appeaser, attempted small talk, but his efforts were stymied by the undercurrent of tension. Brad contributed where he could, but the responses were short, the atmosphere stifling. Carla, caught between her husband's disapproval and her son's defiance, felt an old, familiar pressure building—a pressure that would inevitably force her to choose sides.

After the meal, Richard retreated to his den, a silent signal that he had no intention of delving into the complexities of Brad's return that evening. Carla busied herself with the dishes, her movements sharp, her silence a barrier. Brad, feeling the weight of his presence as an imposition, offered to help but was met with a curt refusal.

Brad stepped outside, seeking refuge from the stifling atmosphere of the kitchen. Inside, Carla lingered at the sink, her hands mechanically scrubbing at dishes already clean, her mind racing with thoughts of amends and resolutions.

Richard, observing her from the doorway, broke the silence with his characteristic pragmatism. "You're thinking about Brad," he stated, more an acknowledgment of fact than a question.

Carla paused, her back still turned to him, the weight of years of unresolved conflicts heavy on her shoulders. "I've never really been there for him, not in the ways that mattered," she admitted, her voice barely above a whisper, laden with a regret that was new to her. "It's time I tried to make it right. This might be my last chance."

Richard crossed the room to stand beside her, but there was no comfort in his proximity. "Carla, he's an adult," he reminded her, his voice carrying the usual note of disapproval. "This isn't about us 'not helping.' He's got to make it work for himself. We've never picked up the pieces for him because, let's be honest, you never wanted to and I supported you, to keep the peace. Are you saying you want to start now?"

Carla's hands stilled in the dishwater, and she turned to look at Richard, her expression one of defiance mixed with a trace of guilt. "Yes I do," she said, the words coming out almost as a challenge to herself as much as to Richard. "Maybe it's time I tried to be more of a mother to him. God knows, he's deserved better than he has gotten," looking towards Richard with accusing eyes.

Richard's brow furrowed, and he leaned back against the counter, skeptical. "And what about the next time he stumbles? What then, Carla?"

"It's not like we can't afford to help. We've just been selfish." She corrected herself, "I've been selfish."

Richard, did not respond.

She dried her hands on the towel, tossing it down with a snap of fabric. "I'm not blind to who I've been, Richard, nor to the part I've played in pushing him away. But he's here now, and I won't turn my back on him. Not anymore. I have to try to make this right. He's my son." She brought her hands to her face an unconscious acknowledgement of the shame of her treatment of Brad and her other son Gregory with whom she can never make amends. He was killed while on active-duty in the Korea.

Richard watched her, the hard lines of his face softening slightly. "Alright," he conceded, warily. "But remember, Carla, Brad is who he is. He's always been a dreamer, reaching for something just beyond his grasp. If you're going to do this, be prepared for the possibility that it might not change a thing."

Paradox

Carla stood firm, her resolve unshaken even as Richard's words echoed the bitter truths of the past. "He was no more a dreamer than any other young man," she retorted, her voice rising with defiance. "It's just that, somehow, misfortune seems to cling to him like a shadow. I can't help but feel that a little love and support might dispel that darkness."

Richard's gaze lingered on her, a silent acknowledgement of the shift in her stance. "Alright," he said, his voice marked with reluctant acceptance.

Carla wasn't done. "Were we just too selfish or just didn't care enough?"

"They are your kids, not mine. I was simply following your lead. If you have a change of heart I'll support you as I always have. Just don't make me out to be the bad guy, " Richard's meek attempt at defiance.

Carla glanced out the window at Brad's silhouette against the twilight sky. She felt a stirring of something long dormant—a desire to connect with her son, to offer him the support she had withheld for so long, which she now realized had been her attempt to control him and his brother.

"How has that worked for you?" she asked herself.

As the night wore on, the house settled into a quiet that was more reflective than uneasy. Brad, lost in his thoughts under the vast, indifferent sky, and Carla and Richard, within the walls of their home, were each grappling with the complexities of familial relationships and the arduous path towards understanding and acceptance.

Peter M. Browne

CHAPTER 10

When Carla returned to Dr. Mercer's office, she thought she might be ready to make some changes in her approach to life. She understood what Dr. Mercer had been telling her about her choices and could look back and see her contribution to the disappointments in her life. It was a bitter pill to swallow, but there was no changing the past.

As she took her usual seat on the couch, Dr. Mercer noticed something different in Carla's countenance. Her usual confident posture seemed subdued; her gaze downcast.

"Something troubling you?" Dr. Mercer asked gently.

Carla stared at her hands, her perfectly manicured nails glinting under the light as she began to spin her wedding band. A long moment passed as Dr. Mercer waited patiently for a response. Carla's eyes finally met Dr. Mercer's, but she quickly looked away, inspecting the ceiling, the floor — looking anywhere but at her therapist. She had come to a painful realization about herself, one that she felt compelled to share with Dr. Mercer, but the words seemed caught in her throat. Finally, she just blurted it out.

"I'm a very jealous person," she whispered, her voice low and tentative. "I've always been. As a child, if a friend had something I didn't, I'd find a way to take it or break it. Ever since our divorce, Tom has been the main object of my jealousy. Every success of his feels like a failure of mine. It eats away at me, consumes my thoughts." She sunk down into the couch. "Is there something wrong with me, doctor? I don't know."
Dr. Mercer's approach was usually to listen without judgment, but today she sensed Carla's deeper struggle, a raw vulnerability that needed a different approach. She would take on the role of counselor.

"Jealousy is a very human emotion, Carla," she began, her tone compassionate. "It's not unusual to feel envious when you see others — especially someone you once had a close relationship with — achieving success. It's part of the complex web of emotions that come with comparing ourselves to others."

She paused, letting her words sink in. "But it's important to understand that these feelings often have less to do with the person you're jealous of and more to do with what's happening inside you. Jealousy can be a sign of something unresolved — perhaps a sense of loss, regret, or a fear that their success somehow diminishes your own self-worth."

Carla's expression softened slightly, though her hands remained tense.

"The key," Dr. Mercer continued, "is not to suppress these feelings but to explore them. Ask yourself why Tom's success triggers this reaction. Is it a reflection of something you feel you're lacking? Or is it a reminder of a path not taken? By understanding the root of your jealousy, you can start to address the underlying issues — and perhaps find a way to transform that energy into something more positive for yourself."

Carla's response came quickly, her voice sharp with unfiltered emotion. "I hate him for his success. I wanted to see him living in a van, down by the Blackwater river, while I'm living high on the hog, so that he would regret ever losing me. But now it's the opposite. Each of his successes cuts deep. I wish him sickness, death, and eternal damnation." She looked to Dr. Mercer for an answer. "Am I obsessing?"

Dr. Mercer stayed quiet, her expression calm but attentive. Carla shifted uncomfortably, as though she expected a reproach, but the silence urged her to continue.

Her hands twisted together in her lap as she spoke, her voice growing lower, edged with something darker. "I tried to make him fail," she admitted. "Not just fail — but fail miserably. I wanted him ruined."

Dr. Mercer gave no response, simply letting the confession unfold.

"I don't even know how to explain it," Carla went on, her words spilling out faster now. "But I have this... way of influencing things. Bending people to my will. I thought I could use it to destroy him. I wanted him humiliated, broken. I wanted his world to collapse all around him. So, I focused on him — on his downfall. I tried everything I knew." Her voice cracked, and she pressed a trembling hand to her forehead. "But nothing worked. Somehow, everything I did, every effort to make him stumble, seemed to backfire. Instead of falling, he rose higher. A car dealership. A new house. A younger wife who's prettier than I ever was. It was like…" Her voice dropped to a whisper, her tone unsteady. "It was like the power was mocking me."

Dr. Mercer leaned forward slightly; her tone cautious but probing. "When you say you tried to influence things, Carla, what do you mean by that?"

Carla's gaze darted up, searching the doctor's face as though gauging how much she could safely reveal. She let out a bitter laugh, shaking her head. "You wouldn't believe me if I told you."

"Try me," Dr. Mercer replied softly.

Carla hesitated before answering. "It's not like I cast spells or anything," she said, her voice tense. "It's just… when I focus on something—really focus— people or situations bend in my favor. It's been that way my whole life. I didn't even have to think about it most of the time; things just went my way. But with Tom…" She shook her head, her voice trembling. "It was like trying to shove someone off a ledge and falling off myself instead."

Dr. Mercer studied her carefully, her expression neutral but attentive. "You've spoken before about feeling like things align in your favor when you want them to," she said slowly. "That sense of control can be… powerful. But when it doesn't work the way you expect—like with Tom—it must feel unsettling."

Carla's lips twisted into a faint, bitter smile.

Dr. Mercer nodded slightly, allowing the silence to stretch between them for a moment before speaking again. "When things don't go your way—like you said, when it 'turns on you'—how does that make you feel?

Carla tilted her head, her dark eyes narrowing as if gauging Dr. Mercer's capacity to understand. "I don't know," she said slowly, her tone thoughtful but guarded. "All I know is, when I want something — when I focus on it hard enough — things usually happen. But no…" She trailed off, her voice growing softer. "With Tom, it turned on me."

Dr. Mercer set her pen down deliberately, her voice calm but measured. "You described feeling powerful, like things often go your way. When they don't — what's your first instinct?"

Carla's jaw tightened. "To find a way to get even." Dr. Mercer raised an eyebrow, silently prompting her to continue.

Carla exhaled sharply. "It's not just Tom. I've always been vindictive. Someone takes my parking spot? Their car gets keyed. A neighbor lets their dog poop on my lawn? Trash shows up in their yard by morning." She laughed bitterly. "Petty? Maybe. But I don't just get mad — I get even."

Dr. Mercer leaned in, her gaze steady. "And if you can't get even? What then?"

Without hesitation, Carla replied, "I keep trying."

Dr. Mercer's expression softened; her voice measured. "It sounds like this experience with Tom is forcing you to look at that approach differently. Whether or not the 'power' you describe is real, it's clear the outcome mattered deeply to you. Maybe the pain you're feeling isn't about power, but about control — or even fear."

Carla's gaze snapped up, her eyes narrowing. "You think I'm afraid?"

"No," Dr. Mercer replied firmly. "I don't think it's about power in the way you're describing it. What you're calling 'power' might actually be about your ability to focus intensely on what you want — your determination, your persistence. But when those feelings are driven by jealousy or the need to get even, they can start to feel out of control. Those emotions have a way of clouding judgment, making things spiral in ways we don't expect."

Carla sat back; her expression unreadable. For a moment, neither of them spoke; the weight of the conversation filled the room.

Finally, Carla broke the silence. "So, what now? You want me to just stop feeling this way? To let him get away with everything?"

Dr. Mercer leaned forward, her tone firm but compassionate. "Carla, these feelings you're experiencing—this need to have your way, this jealousy—they're intense, and they're very real. But clinging to them, feeding them, won't undo what's already happened. All they do is keep you stuck, unable to move forward."

Carla's shoulders sagged, her bitterness giving way to a heavy sense of despair. "Then what am I supposed to do with all of this?"

"It's not about pretending those feelings don't exist," Dr. Mercer said gently. "It's about understanding them—where they're coming from, why they feel so consuming. Maybe even what purpose they serve for you. Only then can you start letting go, little by little."

Carla looked away; her voice quiet. "Letting go doesn't seem fair. He doesn't deserve it."

"Letting go isn't about him," Dr. Mercer replied. "It's about freeing yourself. Carrying this anger, this need for revenge—it's like holding fire in your hands. The only one who gets burned is you."

We need to explore what Tom represents to you— not who he is, but what he symbolizes. His success triggers something personal, something unresolved. By working through that, you can begin to reclaim your focus and let go of this fixation."

Carla's eyes glinted with skepticism, but her voice softened. "And if I can't?"

Dr. Mercer's expression didn't waver. "You can. But it will take time, patience, and effort. The first step is acknowledging that your worth isn't tied to his failures — or his successes. Let's figure out how you can start focusing on your own life, your own goals, and finding fulfillment outside of this dynamic."

Carla said nothing, blotting at the corners of her eyes.

"It's not an overnight process, but with time and effort, you can learn to let go of this anger and move toward a life where Tom's success — or anyone else's — no longer has the power to disturb your peace."

Carla responded, "I'm not sitting around stewing about Tom on a daily basis, but in the quiet moments I'm aware that leaving him was my choice. He is just living his life not throwing his success in my face but it feels like he is without having to do anything."

"Perhaps it's a reflection of a sense of competition, or unresolved emotions from your past relationship."

"That's the thing," Carla interjected. "I have always viewed it as a competition. I wanted to be better than he, to be richer than he, more accomplished than he and I am none of those things and it cuts me to the quick."

Carla paused, "I'm a spiteful person. I feel that Tom ruined my life and he has been able to walk away without any recourse and created a great life for himself."

"Recognizing that you feel spiteful is a significant step, Carla, but it's also important to challenge that narrative. You see Tom's success as a sign that he walked away unscathed, but the truth is, his life and choices don't diminish your own worth or potential. Holding on to spite only gives him more power over your emotions, and it keeps you trapped in the past.

"It's natural to feel resentment when you perceive that someone else has moved on easily while you're left struggling. But the idea that Tom ruined your life suggests that you're attributing all the control over your happiness to him." Dr. Mercer paused. "You said that you have the power to shape outcomes. Use it then, in a positive way.

"Let's explore what it looks like to direct that power. If we can shift the focus from what Tom has done to what you can do now, we might find a path forward that isn't defined by jealousy, anger or resentment, but by your own choices and growth."

Carla bowed her head and slowly shook it from side to side, "That's just the point. I can do nothing. I have no skills other than to be able to attract men to care for me. I'm defined through the men I marry. My successes are vicarious. I strived to be independent but have been unable to manage on my own."

"Carla, it's understandable to feel trapped when your sense of self has been so closely tied to others for so long. But recognizing this pattern is the first step toward breaking free from it. You've relied on others to define your worth, but that doesn't mean you're incapable of finding your own path.

"It's true that stepping away from what's familiar—using your charm and relationships as a means of security—can feel daunting. But the fact that you're here, questioning these patterns, shows a desire for something more. Independence doesn't have to mean doing everything alone; it can start with small steps toward discovering what you're passionate about, what makes you feel fulfilled beyond your relationships.

"We can work together to explore what those steps might look like. It might be uncomfortable at first, but every step you take toward self-reliance, no matter how small, is a step toward redefining yourself on your own terms."

Carla looked up to meet Dr. Mercer's gaze, "I hear you doctor, when you say, we can work together. But what does that look like? How do we begin? How do we progress? What is the end goal? I am not going to magically transform into some person with broad skills that is in high demand. I'm not going to become an artist, a musician or author at 56 years old."

"Carla, I appreciate your honesty, and you're right — there's no magic wand that will suddenly turn you into someone else. But transformation doesn't have to be about becoming someone entirely new; it's about uncovering and strengthening parts of yourself that have been overshadowed or ignored.

"There are ways we can approach this:

"Understanding Your Core: We'll start by exploring what you genuinely enjoy or what has interested you in the past, even if those things seem trivial now. This could be hobbies, interests, or skills you might not have fully pursued. Discovering these can give us a foundation.

"Setting Small, Achievable Goals: We'll break down your journey into small, manageable steps. It could be as simple as exploring a new interest, taking a class, or volunteering in an area that interests you. These aren't about immediate success but about building confidence and discovering more about yourself.

"Developing Emotional Resilience: Together, we'll work on your emotional resilience—learning how to handle setbacks, disappointments, and the feelings of inadequacy that might arise. This might involve mindfulness techniques, cognitive restructuring, or just regular reflection.

"Redefining Success: We'll also redefine what success means to you; beyond the roles you've been playing. Success doesn't have to be about high demand skills or public achievements. It can be about finding peace, satisfaction, and a sense of purpose in whatever you choose to do.

"Celebrating Progress: Finally, we'll make sure to recognize and celebrate the progress you make, no matter how small. Each step forward is a victory, and over time, these steps can lead to significant change.

"The end goal isn't to become someone else but to become more fully yourself, someone who can find fulfillment and value beyond the confines of your past relationships. It's about finding a sense of independence that works for you, even if it looks different from what you might imagine."

Carla left Dr. Mercer's office with a heavy heart, the weight of the doctor's words pressing down on her. In her mid-50s, the thought of embarking on a long, introspective journey to uncover some hidden version of herself felt exhausting, even absurd. This was who she was—who she had always been.

Dr. Mercer had asked, "Why didn't you go to college?" Carla had answered quickly, dismissively,

"Grew up too fast. Married too young. The rest is history." But as she walked to her car, the question lingered. She thought about her childhood—how she had always been given more than her siblings, how her parents had bent over backward to make her life easier. She had been the baby, the favorite, the one who could get away with anything.

Her parents had meant well, she supposed, but all they had done was teach her to take. To expect the world to cater to her whims. Her brothers and sisters had gone on to college, built their own careers, and struggled to make their way in the world. But not Carla. She had relied on charm and manipulation, on bending people to her will. She had always taken the easy route because it was there for her, paved and waiting. And now, here she was, twice divorced, bitter, and empty.

Dr. Mercer's promise that things could be different if Carla wanted them to be rang hollow. "What if this is who I am? What if there's nothing else?"

The idea of change, of peeling back layers to reveal some truer, better self, seemed like a fool's errand. Carla didn't want to transform; she wanted to survive. She realized that she wasn't interested in healing old wounds or forging a new path. She was comfortable in her discomfort, content with the sharp edges that defined her life.

Why pretend to be anything other than what she was? She would continue to hate Tom, to tolerate Richard, and criticize whoever she pleased. If that made her spiteful, so be it. She would embrace it. No more sessions, no more introspection—just Carla, unapologetically herself, living life on her terms, even if those terms were filled with bitterness and discontent.

She knew how to project a happy façade. She had been doing it her whole life.

CHAPTER 11

Brad had always felt like an outsider, even more so upon his return to Pearson's Point. His parents' home, under the pseudo-dominion of his stepfather Richard, was a constant reminder of his uneasy place by the awkward tension between them.

"Keep your stuff out of the living room," Richard's voice barked from the kitchen, as Brad stepped in from the hallway. Brad had inadvertently left some papers on the coffee table the previous night.

Brad stiffened, his jaw locking. It wasn't the words that stung, but the tone—territorial, dismissive, like he was an intruder instead of family. He bit back a retort, knowing it wouldn't make a difference. Richard was just the latest in a long line of Carla's shields, the person she positioned front and center so she could play the part of the long-suffering mediator. He'd seen it before, and yet, standing there in the house that wasn't his, it still burned. This was temporary, he reminded himself. Just a pitstop on the way to something better.

Later that morning, Brad rolled up his sleeves at the Tire Barn, a cold breeze slicing through the open garage doors. The air smelled like burnt rubber and motor oil, while the rhythmic hiss of the air compressor filled the space. He worked in silence, wrench in hand, his mind half-focused on the stubborn lug nut in front of him. A beat-up sedan sat on the lift, its wheels caked with grime, but Brad didn't care about the car. It was just another in a long line of vehicles that kept his hands busy and his wallet just full enough.

"Yo, Williams, you gonna take all day with that thing?" Rick, one of the other mechanics, called over, his voice dripping with impatience.

Brad tightened the wrench with a sharp twist, forcing himself to stay calm. "Almost done," he muttered, though Rick wasn't listening.

Every car he fixed, every oil pan he drained, was a step closer to getting out of that house, out from under Richard's shadow and Carla's badgering. But as he wiped his hands on a grease-streaked rag, he couldn't shake the nagging thought that no matter how far he went, the weight of Pearson's Point—and all the baggage it carried—would follow him.

After a long day, hands stained with grease and spirit buoyed by ambition, Brad found himself sharing beers with Reed, a fellow mechanic whose laid-back nature belied a keen intellect.

"You know," Brad started, the clink of bottles punctuating his revelation, "we see all these trucks and cars, moving stuff from point A to B. What if we jumped into that? Like, helping people move with the right kind of vehicle?"

Reed, taking a slow sip, raised an eyebrow. "You're talking rental trucks instead of cars?

"Exactly, but more local, more personal. I'm thinking of calling it 'Your Move,'" Brad said, excitement in his voice.

Reed leaned back, considering. "It's not a bad idea, Brad. But it's a big leap from fixing cars to running a rental business."

"I know, I know. But I've been saving up, and I've done some research on how often people move around. We could start small—one or two trucks, maybe a trailer."

The conversation flowed into the night, dreams blending with the harsh realities of startup costs, business plans, and potential roadblocks.

Reed was a few years older than Brad, probably edging into his early thirties, but his quiet, steady nature gave him a presence that felt seasoned beyond his years. He stood a bit taller than Brad, his frame broad and sturdy, built through years of lifting heavy tools and crawling under trucks. Reed's hands were scarred, marked with faint, white lines of old cuts and burns, the kind that spoke of years in the mechanic's trade—a silent reminder to his profession and hard-won experience.

His face, framed by thick, dark hair that he often kept swept back, carried the look of someone who'd seen enough of life to know when to keep his mouth shut and when to let his opinions roll out slow and measured. He had a perpetual five o'clock shadow, making him look slightly rugged, but his dark eyes held an unexpected warmth—a hint of something softer beneath the tough exterior.

Reed didn't talk much, but when he did, people listened. It wasn't just what he said, but how he said it, words coming out in a low, gravelly tone that made everything sound deliberate and thought-through. He had the kind of patience that's rare in young men, which worked as a counterbalance to Brad's eagerness. Reed listened to Brad's ambitious, idea absorbing it in silence before offering his own view.

Where Brad was all fire and energy, Reed was like stone, grounding them both. And though he might not admit it openly, Reed respected Brad's ambition, seeing something of his younger self in the kid's hustle. He might even have felt a twinge of envy for Brad's unjaded hope in what they could build together.

Underneath Reed's easygoing manner, there was an edge — a keen intellect that only surfaced when he found something worthy of his attention. He was quick with numbers, able to calculate expenses on the fly, and had a talent for thinking through problems in a way that Brad would come to rely on. Reed had spent years fixing cars and trucks, doing honest work for people who didn't have much. He understood how to keep a business steady, to focus on the bottom line, and to not let dreams run wild without a plan.

As Brad went on about "Your Move," Reed leaned back, his expression thoughtful. "It's not a bad idea, Brad," he said, a hint of a smile tugging at the corners of his mouth. "But it's a big leap from fixing cars to running a rental business." That was Reed all over — cautious, calculated, his mind always working a few steps ahead.

And yet, there was something in Reed's eyes as he listened — a glint of curiosity, maybe even a touch of ambition he'd thought he'd buried. After a few sips of his beer, he finally set down his bottle and nodded. "Alright, let's talk numbers."

In the dim light of the bar, Brad and Reed began to settle into a more serious tone. They worked the idea of "Your Move" with enthusiasm, but now it was time to face the gritty details head-on.

Brad leaned in; his voice steady but marked with a hint of concern. "Okay, let's talk numbers, Reed. That's your thing", Brad continued. "Startup costs aren't going to be small. We're looking at buying trucks, maybe a trailer, not to mention insurance, licensing, and a storefront office."

Reed nodded, pulling a napkin towards him and grabbing a pen from his shirt pocket. "Let's break it down then. Start with what we've got and what we'll need."

They scribbled figures and estimates, calculating the cost of used vehicles, repairs, and the essentials to get "Your Move" road-ready. The numbers weren't daunting, but they were substantial. "I'll start saving more aggressively. I'll cut back on anything non-essential. Every penny's going to count," Brad offered.

They began to toss around options. "What about just a single truck and one box trailer to start with?" Reed suggested. "Sort of a proof of concept. If it works we can always expand."

"Not a bad approach," Brad agreed. "What's a used truck go for these days?"

"Around four or five-grand. We don't want something too cheap. If it's in good condition I can spruce it up. Make it look like new," Reed smiled confidently.

"What about a trailer? Any thoughts?"

"Yeah, I think Rob McPherson Construction has one for sale. It has a broken hitch tongue that can easily be welded."

"You sure? Why's he selling it then?"

"He bought a brand-new bigger rig for his business."

Over the following weeks, Brad and Reed met tirelessly after work, drafting and redrafting their business plan. They outlined their vision for "Your Move," target demographics, marketing strategies, and financial projections.

Under the dim light of a hanging bulb in Reed's garage, surrounded by tools and the faint smell of motor oil, the two friends leaned over a sprawl of papers scattered across a makeshift table. Each sheet detailed a fragment of their dream: "Your Move," a business that was starting to feel more real with every late-night session.

"Okay, so who are we really targeting with this?" Reed asked, tapping a pen against the table, eyes scanning the demographics research they had compiled.

Brad, always the visionary, didn't hesitate. "It's the people right here in Pearson's Point. Small businesses, maybe, and definitely folks moving in or out of apartments. They can't all afford the big moving companies, right? So, they end up borrowing someone's truck or pack up their car for multiple trips back and forth."

Reed nodded, scribbling notes. "Right, right. Local and personal, got it. How do we get the word out?"

"That's the fun part," Brad said with a smirk, pulling up a chair. "We'll get some flyers made and post them about town in places where people congregate; grocery stores, strip-malls, the community center, the library, gas stations and yeah, the Tire Barn."

Reed's eyes lit up. "That sounds good and that won't cost a lot."

Brad leaned back, his mind racing ahead. "And our cash? We've got to make sure we can keep the lights on. I did some crunching of the numbers, and—"

"Show me," Reed interjected, his tone apprehensive.

Spreading out the financial projections, Brad pointed to the figures. "Here's where we start. It's tight, but we really have little operating expenses, a phone and some office space. We can rent a couple of parking spaces from Tire Barn's lot to start."

"But, what about day-to-day operations? We can't afford to quit our jobs until…" Reed didn't finish the thought. But, Brad fully understood.

Brad met his gaze, determination etched in his features. "We know it won't be easy. But we've got a plan, and we've got each other to figure it out. Every problem's just a solution in disguise, right?"

Reed couldn't help but smile at Brad's optimism. "Right. But about the additional investment…?"

"That's where my mom comes in. She offered to give me a loan. I'm going to approach her tomorrow. See if she was just talking. She does that sometimes," his eyes lacked confidence in her words.

The mention of Brad's mom brought a brief silence between them, both aware of the weight of asking for such a favor.

"You sure she'll go for it?" Reed asked, concern flickering in his eyes.

Brad shrugged, "It's a jump ball. We'll see."

The night wore on, their conversation weaving through plans, potential setbacks, and dreams of what "Your Move" could become. Each word, each laugh, and each moment of doubt shared between them only solidified their resolve.

As they packed up for the night, the garage seemed less like a cluttered workspace and more like the birthplace of their future.

As Brad and Reed stepped out into the cool night air, energized by their planning session, they faced the logistical realities of running "Your Move" while still holding down their jobs at Tire Barn. They knew they couldn't just dive in without a solid plan for managing the day-to-day operations of their new venture. Walking slowly, they continued their conversation, now focused on the practicalities of making their business work.

"You know," Reed began, breaking the silence, "we can't quit our jobs, not until this thing really takes off. But that means we need a plan for handling customers during the day."

Brad nodded, his mind racing through possibilities. "Right. We need someone reliable, someone who can man the fort while we're at the Tire Barn. What about part-time help? A college student, maybe, looking for a few hours of work?"

Reed considered the idea, the possibility taking root. "Not bad. They could handle inquiries, do the paperwork, hand out the keys. We could set up a small office space...rent something cheap but functional."

"Yeah, and we can use pagers to stay in touch while we're at work. That way, we're always just a call away if there's a problem," Brad added.

"But what about the initial cost?" Reed questioned, ever the voice of caution. "Hiring someone, even part-time, means added expenses. Plus, the office rental."

Brad's optimism didn't wane. "We factored it into our startup costs. Look, we'll keep operations lean. The person we hire can work peak hours only — say, late afternoon to early evening during the week and then Saturdays. We'll cover Sundays and mornings before heading to Tire Barn."

"And marketing?" Reed asked, shifting the topic slightly. "We need to get the word out without breaking the bank."

"Grassroots, my friend," Brad said with a confident smile. "We use our personal networks. Flyers, local events, community boards. Let's make 'Your Move' feel like a part of the community."

Reed was silent for a moment, then nodded. "It could work. It's going to take some juggling, but it could work."

Brad clapped him on the shoulder. "We'll make it work. We're in this together, remember? 'Your Move' isn't just a business — it's our shot at something bigger."

As they reached their cars, the challenges ahead seemed less daunting. Yes, there were hurdles — finding the right part-time help, balancing their day jobs with their entrepreneurial aspirations, marketing on a shoestring budget. But Brad and Reed were committed. "Your Move" was more than a business venture; it was a dream they were determined to realize, step by careful step.

Over the next few months, Brad and Reed threw themselves into the venture with the fervor of converts. Brad meticulously re-researched the market, updated the business plan, and began saving every penny he could spare. Reed, ever the pragmatist, tempered Brad's enthusiasm with caution, ensuring their plans remained grounded in reality.

The real test came when Brad approached his mother for a loan. Sitting at the kitchen table, the business plan laid out before them like a treasure map, Brad made his case.

"Mom, I know it's a lot to ask, but you said you wanted to help. We've done the homework. 'Your Move' can really work," Brad explained, his hands gesturing towards the documents that spelled out his vision.

Carla, a woman of practical sensibilities, took her time, reading through the projections and considerations laid out on paper. Finally, she looked up, her eyes soft but serious.

"Brad, I want to support you, I do. But this is a big risk. What if it doesn't work out?"

Brad met her gaze, his determination unwavering. "Then I'll find another way. But I have to try this, Mom. I can't spend my life wondering 'what if.'"

"What do you say we have Richard take a look at this?" She enquired, knowing full well that this was her standard operating procedure—make Richard the villain.

"No, Mother!" Brad protested, his posture becoming rigid. His eyes narrowing with distrust. "This is between you and me. I don't want Richard involved in any way."

Carla was reluctant. She was not crazy about the idea. She felt too many things could go wrong when dealing with the public.

"Okay, Bradley! But I want you to agree to purchase double indemnity insurance, in case something goes wrong."

The next few weeks were a blur of activity — buying and refurbishing an old truck and trailer, advertising their services, and navigating the unforeseen challenges of entrepreneurship.

Reed's cousin Meredith, was an artist. They commissioned her, for a nominal fee, to paint their logo on the side of their truck and trailer. It would be part of their advertising budget. The logo "Your Move" depicted a chessboard with the knight in position to capture the queen.

When they finally got their first rental, it was for the trailer. It felt like a victory, tangible proof of their vision, hard work, and dedication.

Paul and Sara Whitcombe were the picture of youthful ambition. In their mid-twenties, they carried themselves with the buoyant energy of a couple ready to take on the world. They looked so alike — both with sandy hair, sparkling blue eyes, and broad, easy smiles — that people often joked they looked more like siblings than husband and wife. But the way Sara's hand naturally sought Paul's arm when she laughed, or the way his gaze softened whenever she spoke, left no doubt about the love between them.

The Whitcombes were on the cusp of a fresh start, moving from sleepy Pearson's Point to bustling Pensacola. Paul had recently landed a job as a proofreader with The Pensacola News Journal — a long-anticipated step up from his years of toiling at the local weekly paper, which offered little in the way of opportunity. Sara, a skilled beautician with a cheerful demeanor that put her clients at ease, knew her trade would make it easy to find work in their new city.

Like many young couples, they were operating on a tight budget. When Paul spotted a flyer for "Your Move" at the grocery store, he pulled it from the bulletin board and waved it excitedly toward Sara. "This looks like a good deal," he said, holding it up. "We can pack everything ourselves, haul it all in one go, and not have to worry about waiting on movers."

Sara raised an eyebrow, her expression skeptical but playful. "What about the sofa? And the mattresses? They're kind of heavy for us to deal with, don't you think?"

Paul grinned and flexed his arm casually, curling it at the elbow to show off a defined bicep that rippled with quiet confidence. "You doubt this?" he asked with mock indignation.

Sara laughed, shaking her head. "You're strong, sure. But are you strong enough to handle a trailer packed with all our worldly possessions? And you've towed a trailer before, right?"

Paul gave her a roguish smile. "How hard can it be? I'll sign us up for the mover's insurance, just in case. Deal?"

Sara nodded, conceding the point. "That sounds wise. And I'll call my brother Henry to help us load the big stuff. Deal?"

"Deal," Paul said, slipping his arm around her waist.

Sara took the flyer, folded it carefully, and tucked it into her purse. The Whitcombes were ready for the next chapter of their lives, and with their boundless optimism, there was little doubt they'd make it work—

even if it meant navigating a bumpy road or two along the way.

A few days later, after sorting through the paperwork at "Your Move," Brad guided Paul and Sara to their rented trailer, an empty but sturdy unit that gleamed in the afternoon sun. The "Your Move" logo proudly on display

"All set," Brad said, helping Paul hitch the trailer to the back of their car and giving the hitch a firm tug to make sure it was secure. "You two got any questions about towing?"

Paul looked at the trailer, the responsibility of maneuvering it dawning on him now that he was actually standing beside it. His excitement was tempered by a touch of anxiety. "Just the basics—any tips on handling turns and stops?"

"Take it slow," Brad advised with an encouraging nod. "Once it's loaded, it'll add a lot of weight, so braking will feel different, and you'll want to take turns a bit wider. But right now, with it empty, you've got a good chance to practice. Once you get it home and start loading, make sure to keep the weight balanced and secure things tight so they don't shift while you're driving."

Paul nodded, absorbing the advice, while Sara shot him a reassuring smile. He felt a bit of the thrill return, imagining the trailer packed with all of their belongings as they headed to their new life. Brad must have noticed his mixture of excitement and nerves, because he gave Paul a reassuring pat on the shoulder.

"You'll get the hang of it," Brad said with a grin. "By the time you get home, you'll be a pro."

Paul returned the smile, his confidence bolstered. "Thanks, Brad. Really appreciate it."

As Paul and Sara climbed back into their car, Paul took a deep breath, his hands steady on the wheel. Sara reached over, giving his hand a reassuring squeeze. "Just think," she murmured, her voice full of warmth, "this is the start of everything we've been dreaming about."

With the trailer in tow, they pulled out of the lot, ready to start the careful process of packing up their lives — and ready, too, for all the opportunities that lay ahead.

The next morning dawned bright and clear as Paul and Sara began the task of packing the trailer. Their small apartment was in chaos, with boxes stacked along the walls and furniture arranged strategically near the door, ready to be loaded.

Henry arrived with his usual easy grin and a beat-up baseball cap that looked like it hadn't left his head in years. He took one look at the stacks of boxes and raised an eyebrow. "So, where's all this going? Are we stacking floor to ceiling and just praying we can shut the door when we're done?"

Paul chuckled nervously. "A little of both, I think. Just have to make it about twenty-five miles to Pensacola, right?"

Henry clapped him on the back. "No worries, man. We'll make it fit. I was born with the Tetris gene." He crouched by the trailer and started examining the space, his fingers tapping against the side of it as if he were already planning the puzzle.

They started with the heaviest items — the old wooden dresser that had belonged to Sara's grandmother, a coffee table, and a narrow bookshelf. Paul and Henry hefted the dresser into the trailer, grunting as they pushed it toward the front for stability.

"This thing weighs a ton," Paul groaned, wiping sweat from his forehead.

"It's all that 'solid craftsmanship,'" Henry teased, settling it against the wall. "They don't make 'em like this anymore because most people don't want to feel like they're lifting a piano."

Sara, standing by with a box labeled "Kitchen Essentials," chimed in. "Just don't scratch it, okay? Grandma might not be around, but she'd find a way to haunt me if something happened to that dresser."

Next came the awkward items—the mattress and box spring. They struggled to angle it through the trailer door, Paul holding one end while Henry maneuvered the other. At one point, Paul nearly lost his grip, and the mattress tilted dangerously to the side.

"Watch it!" Sara yelped, dashing forward. "We don't need any accidents before we even get on the road."

Henry just laughed, his voice light. "Relax, I've got it." He adjusted his grip, wedging the mattress against the side wall. "A little persuasion is all it needed."

"'Persuasion,' huh?" Sara shook her head, amused. "I think you mean brute force."

"Potato, po-tah-to," Henry shot back with a wink.

Finally, they filled in the gaps with boxes, stacking them carefully around the larger pieces. Henry had a knack for spotting every inch of space, tucking in smaller boxes and bags in places Paul would have never thought to try.

When they'd nearly finished, Sara stood back, hands on her hips, surveying their work. "Not bad. I think we might actually get it all in."

"Course we will," Henry said, sounding proud. "Now, let's just hope it doesn't all come crashing down when you hit the brakes."

Paul shot him a look of mock horror, but Henry just grinned and clapped him on the shoulder. "Relax, man. Just take it slow, and you'll be fine."

Sara gave her brother a grateful smile. "Thanks, Henry. Couldn't have done this without you."

Henry shrugged, pulling off his hat and running a hand through his tousled hair. "Hey, that's what brothers are for. Besides, I'm not gonna miss out on watching you two start this big adventure. Just make sure you don't forget to send postcards from that big city of yours."

They laughed, the mood lighter now that the trailer was packed and ready to go. Henry gave them a quick hug goodbye and a reassuring wink. "I'll see you on the other end to help unload. I've got to make a stop, but I'll be there in an hour or so."

Sara scribbled the address of their new place on a piece of paper and handed it to him. Henry barely glanced at it, stuffing it casually into his shirt pocket before climbing into his pickup, which was stacked with the few items that hadn't fit into the trailer. He gave them a wave and rumbled off, leaving them alone in the parking lot.

With the trailer loaded to the brim, Paul and Sara were itching to get on the road. Paul locked up the apartment for the last time, handed the keys to the building superintendent, and joined Sara, who was already buckled in and tapping her fingers on the dashboard with nervous excitement.

Paul started the car, his hands gripping the wheel as he pulled out of the lot, maneuvering slowly and cautiously. They both glanced back at the trailer, watching it sway lightly with each turn. "All right, we're off," he said, giving her a quick, exhilarated smile.

As they navigated through the complex and approached the main road, Paul waited at the entrance, watching cars stream by, a bit of tension in his shoulders. He let a few more cars pass, then finally eased out into the flow of traffic, careful with the weight of the trailer behind them. His route was planned: they'd take Wilson Avenue through town, turn right on Center Street, and eventually pick up South Main Street, which would lead them to the highway.

"I don't know about you, but I'm starving," Paul said, glancing at Sara, a bit of his excitement tinged with nerves.

She brightened at the thought of a break. "There's a Burger King coming up. A burger and fries sound perfect."

Paul spotted the familiar sign a block ahead and began slowing down, preparing for a wide turn into the parking lot. Rather than attempt the drive-thru, he parked across several spaces in the corner, angling the trailer for an easy exit.

They sat inside and enjoyed their meal, talking about their new life and the excitement of living in a bigger city. Paul felt himself relax, some of the nerves easing as he took comfort in Sara's presence and her easy laughter.

After lunch, they climbed back into the car and headed toward the highway. South Main Street was a four-lane road, wide and straight, giving Paul a bit of confidence as he picked up speed, settling into a comfortable rhythm with the trailer swaying steadily behind.

But as they cruised down the street, Paul's gaze shifted to the side, when something caught his eye. For a split second, he thought he was seeing things—his own trailer, passing him in the left lane.

He did a double take, his heart pounding as he realized with horror that it was their trailer, speeding down the road alongside them. Somehow, it had broken loose, and now it rolled freely, its momentum carrying it forward. Time seemed to slow as Paul watched in disbelief. Then, it veered slightly, wobbling on its path, until it swerved back towards their car.

"Paul!" Sara screamed, clutching the door handle as the trailer crashed into the side of their vehicle with a deafening crunch. The impact jolted them sideways, forcing Paul to fight for control as their car skidded off the road. The trailer, flipped onto its side, bursting open and spilling their belongings—a haphazard tumble of clothes, books, dishes, and furniture—across the roadway and down the embankment.

Behind them, cars screeched and swerved, some driving over or around the debris that littered the southbound lanes. Drivers honked, braked, and shouted as they maneuvered around the broken remains of Paul and Sara's belongings.

Paul managed to bring the car to a stop, breathing hard, his hands trembling on the wheel. He turned to Sara, who sat stunned, a thin trickle of blood tracing down from her forehead where she'd struck the windshield. She had forgotten to buckle her seatbelt when they left Burger King. She touched the gash with a shaky hand, her eyes wide with shock.

"Oh my god, Sara—are you okay?" he gasped, reaching for her.

She nodded slowly, though the pain was clear in her eyes. "I... I think I'm okay. Just a cut. It could've been a lot worse," she murmured, her voice wavering.

The two of them climbed out, surveying the damage. Their car was dented, the front quarter-panel pushed in where the trailer had collided with it. Their belongings lay scattered down the street, pieces of their life strewn across the asphalt. Clothes fluttered in the breeze, dishes lay shattered, and the treasured dresser from Sara's grandmother was cracked and splintered.

Nearby, other drivers had stopped, some offering help, others giving wary glances as they picked their way through the debris.

Paul's initial shock gave way to a sinking feeling of dread. All their belongings were ruined. Everything they'd worked to save and carefully packed for this new beginning lay destroyed on the road.

"Good thing we purchased the mover's insurance", Sara whispered.

Back at "Your Move," Brad got the news via a frantic phone call from Paul. "The trailer just... it just came loose," Paul stammered, his voice hoarse and filled with disbelief. "It smashed into us, and everything's... gone."

Brad's blood ran cold. He stood frozen, the phone pressed to his ear, scarcely able to believe what he was hearing. His mind raced, searching for someone to blame. Instinctively, he thought of Reed and the welding job. "It must have been a faulty weld," he muttered, more to himself than to Paul.

But as Brad inspected the trailer later, he saw the break had happened at a different point altogether. It wasn't Reed's fault. The trailer was simply defective — a flaw they'd had no way of knowing existed. "This was just his luck!", he thought.

In the following days, the reality of the disaster set in. Though Paul and Sara's injuries were thankfully minor, they'd lost nearly everything they owned, and Paul's car was damaged. Brad soon found himself at the center of a growing storm of liability, lawsuits and insurance claims. His dream of "Your Move" had turned into a nightmare almost overnight.

Reed sat across from him one evening, a grim look on his face as they reviewed the costs. "This isn't something we're going to bounce back from, is it?" he asked quietly.

Brad shook his head, the weight of failure heavy on his shoulders. "No, Reed… I don't think it is."

"Your Move" was officially out of business, a painful end to Brad's dream, leaving only the hard lessons and the lingering thought of what might have been.

Brad found himself without a company and without a job. He had quit the Tire Barn, prematurely. The dream he'd built from the ground up, lay in ruins. Richard's "I told you so" was a bitter pill to swallow, adding insult to injury.

Carla couldn't resist showing her disappointment, and she had to mention it — if only in the faint sneer that tugged at the corner of her mouth as she regarded her son across the table. The silence between them grew heavy, pressing down on Brad as he sensed the judgment simmering just beneath her measured, deliberate gaze.

Finally, she spoke, her voice quiet but filled with disdain. "I just don't understand, Brad. How does someone keep ending up back at square one?" She took a slow sip of wine, her eyes never leaving his, as if daring him to find a defense.

Brad looked down, his fingers tracing idle patterns on the edge of his plate. He'd heard these words before, in so many forms. To Carla, he was a disappointment by default, a natural consequence of the choices he'd made—and the choices she believed he'd failed to make.

"Mom," he began, trying to keep his tone calm, to keep the resentment from creeping in. "It's not like I haven't tried. Things just... they don't work out for everyone the way they did for you. It's not that simple."

"Oh, please, Brad," she replied, her voice dropping into a soft, mocking laugh. "Life is as complicated as you make it. You—you seem to make everything complicated." She leaned forward, her gaze narrowing. "I've never understood that about you. Some people just... can't get their act together, I suppose."

Brad felt the sting of her words, as sharp and cold as a knife's edge. He took a steadying breath. It was useless to explain that he'd worked hard, that he'd taken risks, only to see them crumble while Carla seemed to coast from one stroke of good fortune to another. She wouldn't believe it, or worse, she'd find a way to turn it into another failure of his own making.

"Maybe," he said quietly, "you just never wanted to understand." He held her gaze, refusing to look away this time. "It's not about 'getting it together.' Some things are out of your control. You of all people should know that."

She tilted her head, her lips pressing into a thin line. "That's the difference between us, Brad. I don't leave things up to chance. I get what I want because I have the ability to do what it takes."

There it was—that hint of triumph, that unspoken reminder that her life was an acknowledgement to her superiority, while his seemed to be a sequence of bad choices and bad luck, all confirming what she'd always suspected: that he was, at heart, a disappointment.

"Not everyone's got a horseshoe up their butt, Mom," Brad muttered under his breath, just loud enough that the words slipped into the air without fully reaching her. It was barely more than a whisper, a quiet release of the frustration simmering inside him—the years of watching her glide through life untouched by struggle, while he stumbled over every obstacle.

Carla's expression hardened; any softness replaced by the brittle edge of judgment. "Luck has nothing to do with it, Brad. That's just another excuse. But I suppose that's all you've ever really had."

The silence stretched between them, thick with all the things they would never say. She sat back, giving him one last dismissive glance before lifting her wine glass as if the conversation had already ended. To her, the matter was settled, his failures neatly confirmed in her mind—just as they always had been.

But as she set her glass back down, her mouth curved into a smirk, and she looked at him with that calculated glint he knew too well. "Oh, and don't think I've forgotten about the loan. I expect you to pay me back, Brad," she said, drawing out each word. "In full."

The words dropped like stones, each one adding to the weight pressing down on his shoulders. Carla didn't need the money — she'd only agreed to loan him the money out of guilt. She'd already written him off as somehow lacking, but she wanted to make amends for her lack of support in the past. But she was not about to subsidize his failure.

Brad swallowed hard, the familiar frustration swelling inside him, but he forced himself to nod. "Of course," he murmured, forcing the words out through clenched teeth. There was no point arguing. No point trying to explain. This was just another power she held over him, and he knew, as he always had, that she wouldn't let him forget it.

Carla's smirk deepened, satisfied, as if she'd finally delivered the final blow. And maybe she had.

Brad's spirit felt shattered, his dream crushed beneath the weight of his mother's disdain. He would pay her back — it would take time, but he would make it happen, piece by painful piece.

He took a job as a furniture delivery man, a humbling role he never thought he'd end up in. Day after day, as he maneuvered the truck through busy streets, the quiet clatter of furniture in the back was a relentless reminder of his place, a silent testament to how far he'd fallen. But somewhere within that humbling work, amid the sweat and heavy lifting, a tiny spark of resilience began to flicker. He clung to it, fanning it each time he remembered Buck Dyson's words: "Nothing beats a try but a failure."

With every mile traveled, every piece of furniture unloaded, he was gathering something—call it grit, or maybe just the pure, stubborn resolve to prove himself, if not to Carla, then to himself. He didn't know what his next move would be, but he knew one thing: he would get back up. For now, each step was small, each hour in the truck hard, but Brad had learned one thing in his short life—sometimes survival was its own kind of victory.

CHAPTER 12

Reed's cousin Meredith, who had painted the logo on the "Your Move" trailer, worked as the secretary for the Pearson's Point Police Department. She had a warmth about her, a soft kindness that made people feel at ease, and her striking appearance — raven-black hair cascading past her shoulders, vivid green eyes that seemed to hold every shade of spring, and a natural prettiness that needed no embellishment — often turned heads in the small town. Meredith was in her mid-twenties, with a caring nature that had earned her the trust and affection of nearly everyone she met.

When she posted a job listing for a police officer position on the department's bulletin board, Brad unexpectedly came to mind. He was the right age, had the physical build, and, as far as she knew, was looking for something more permanent in his life. The next time she ran into him, she decided to bring it up.

"How's everything going?" she asked, her voice carrying an effortless warmth that made Brad look up from his thoughts. "Sorry about what happened to your business venture. I thought it was a great idea."

Brad shrugged, not really wanting to talk about it, but Meredith's empathetic gaze softened the edge of his discomfort. Sensing his hesitance, she pressed on gently. "I don't know if you'd be interested, but the Pearson's Point PD is looking to hire a new officer. If you're looking for a career opportunity..."

Brad raised his eyes to meet hers, his curiosity piqued despite himself. She caught the flicker of interest and smiled, her enthusiasm genuine and infectious. "They're offering a five K signing bonus, a 16-week training program, and you get a patrol car to take home."

"Why are you telling me all this?"

"Because, I think you're a great guy who got a bad break and this could be a good opportunity for you." She paused. "Didn't mean to pry."

"No, no, it's not you it's me. Look can I buy you a cup of coffee and you can tell me all about it."

"Sure."

It didn't take long for Brad to decide to apply for the position. The signing bonus would help him pay his mother's loan back. She said he didn't have to but he wasn't going to give Richard the satisfaction.

Brad passed the physical, went through the training program, and passed the Criminal Justice Basic Abilities Test (CJBAT). He was now an officer of the Pearson's Point Police Department, with his own patrol car.

After that coffee date, Brad and Meredith's relationship took off. At first, it was casual—a movie here, a walk in the park there—but the connection between them deepened with every shared laugh and quiet conversation. By the time Brad returned from the police academy, they were inseparable, their easy companionship evolving into something far more serious.

Brad threw himself into his new role on the Pearson's Point Police Department with unbridled enthusiasm. He loved the rhythm of patrolling the sleepy streets, the small-town familiarity of waving at shopkeepers and chatting with residents. He thrived on community policing, finding purpose in being a reassuring presence at neighborhood events or helping the occasional lost tourist. On the rare occasions when a burglary or domestic dispute arose, he was eager to put his training to use, though such incidents were few and far between. Major crimes were unheard of in Pearson's Point. His courtroom experiences were limited to the occasional traffic ticket dispute, where the drama rarely escalated beyond an annoyed driver's complaint about speed limits.

As time passed, Brad and Meredith's relationship deepened, their bond built on shared values and quiet understanding. They moved in together without pomp or spectacle, merging their lives seamlessly, and soon after, they planned a modest wedding—a small, intimate gathering that reflected their shared practicality.

Carla, however, was anything but pleased. From the moment she heard the word "modest," a storm of indignation brewed within her. This was her only son's wedding, and in her mind, it deserved to be nothing short of a grand affair—a sprawling guest list, a towering cake, and a reception that would cement her social standing. She imagined herself in a dazzling dress, mingling among a glittering crowd as whispers of her impeccable taste filled the air.

But Brad and Meredith wanted none of that. Their vision was clear: a simple ceremony surrounded by only their closest friends and family.

For Carla, this was an affront, a rejection of everything she had always valued. "A wedding is supposed to be a celebration," she huffed one afternoon while Brad and Meredith reviewed seating arrangements at the kitchen table. "Not...whatever this is." Her voice was sharp, her displeasure visible as she glanced pointedly at the modest guest list.

"Mom, it is a celebration," Brad replied evenly, refusing to meet her rising tone. "It's just not a spectacle."

Carla opened her mouth to retort, but Meredith, calm and composed as ever, interjected. "We want something that feels true to us," she said, her green eyes meeting Carla's without wavering. There was no edge to her voice, only an unshakable certainty that left little room for argument.

In years past, Carla would have turned this into an all-out battle, wielding guilt and manipulation to bend Brad to her will. But her sessions with Dr. Mercer had begun to take root, forcing her to confront the patterns of control and selfishness that had strained so many of her relationships. The temptation to press harder gnawed at her, but she bit it back, though not without a few sharp remarks about "lost opportunities" and conspicuous sighs at every mention of the "scaled-down" plans.

On the day of the wedding, Carla arrived in her best attire, still bristling inwardly at the quaint simplicity of it all. The ceremony took place under a canopy of oak trees, their leaves whispering softly in the breeze, with just a few rows of chairs for their closest loved ones. As

Brad and Meredith exchanged vows, their faces lit with joy, Carla found herself unexpectedly moved. For a moment, she wondered if she had been wrong — if perhaps love didn't need grand gestures or extravagant displays to feel profound.

Still, as she smiled politely during the understated reception, a part of her mourned the glittering spectacle that would never be. But for once, she let it pass without protest. This was their day, not hers, and though it went against every instinct in her nature, she chose to let it be.

Brad's career was gaining momentum, each step a testament to his quiet determination. After five steady years with the Pearson's Point PD, he caught the attention of the Pensacola Police Department. The offer came unexpectedly, like a gust of fresh air: better pay, greater challenges, and the tantalizing prospect of making detective. Pensacola, just fifteen miles west on I-10, wasn't far — but for Brad, it was a world away from the sleepy confines of Pearson's Point.

There wasn't much tethering him to his hometown. Meredith, always supportive and eager for a change, agreed that it was time to move forward — literally. Instead of a daily grind of commuting, they packed up their modest life and relocated to the bustling, sun-soaked streets of Pensacola.

The transition wasn't just geographical; it was personal. Over the next five years, Brad rose through the ranks with quiet tenacity, earning a promotion to detective. His unrelenting focus and knack for piecing together fragments of the past eventually landed him a coveted spot on the cold case team.

Here, Brad found his stride. The challenge of resurrecting long-forgotten cases, of sifting through faded evidence and memories to uncover hidden truths, lit a fire in him. His analytical nature thrived in the work, each case an intricate puzzle waiting to be solved. The cold cases, with their echoes of unfinished stories, gave him purpose. For the first time in his life, Brad wasn't just earning a paycheck—he was doing a job he loved.

His first assignment began with the reopening of the Ralph Hammond murder case. His body had been found in Willow's End, a serene park, close to Pensacola Bay, over ten years earlier. Hammond was a pillar of the community, known for his philanthropy and leadership in local charities. His death sent shockwaves through the city, not only because of the loss, but because it threatened to unravel the perfect image the community had curated. The initial investigation went nowhere, the case stalled when people in "high places" applied pressure upon the then police chief, Roger Greer, to steer clear of certain avenues of investigation. As a result, the case went cold.

As the cold case unit cycled through the files Hammond's case was selected as a possible candidate for review. By now, there was a new police chief in charge and he had green lighted the case.

It was assigned to Brad, who approached the cold case with his usual thoroughness. He noticed right away that something about Hammond's death didn't feel right. The crime scene was too clean, too deliberate, and there was an air of theatricality to the murder that hinted at a deeper message.

The first clue came from the autopsy report. Among the findings, the coroner noted an unusual item: a small, barely noticeable tattoo on his right foot—a snake with its tail in its mouth. Brad had no idea what the symbol was or what it meant. But it seemed incongruous with Hammond's public persona to have a tattoo and one discreetly hidden from public view. Brad pondered its significance, aware that tattoos often held personal meanings for their bearers. His first course of action was to find out what this tattoo signified.

He headed for the tattoo parlor, on the corner of West and Wilmington, a place called "Art Rebels." The owner, Art Rebello, was known to the Pensacola PD for doing more than providing body art. They suspected the proprietor also dealt in other questionable activities, like fencing stolen goods, trafficking in narcotics and a bit of loan sharking. It also seemed to be the headquarters for the local motor cycle group known as the "Rhinestone Rebels."

Brad parked his vehicle a block away and proceeded to the tattoo parlor on foot. He did not want Art to see his police vehicle. This part of town was a bit seedy, buildings were rundown, junk cars littered the streets, and the people meandering about were clothed in garments that had seen better days. As Brad walked past those gathered outside they gave him a questioning look. He appeared out of place. He could only be a cop, was the consensus. When Brad reached the dilapidated building that housed "Art Rebels" he paused, out of instinct, checking his surroundings.

As he pushed open the creaking door, the scent of antiseptic solution mixed with the earthy aroma of incense enveloped him. Before stepping past the entrance Brad stopped absorbing the lay of the land.

The dim lighting cast a mysterious ambiance, revealing a myriad of tattoo designs adorning the walls. The floor, made of weathered hardwood, echoed with the buzz of tattoo machines and hushed conversations. The main workstation, located under a flickering neon sign boasted the parlor's name. A leather-clad tattoo artist leaned over a client, deftly etching intricate designs onto his skin. The artist's arms were adorned with his own masterpieces, a walking advertisement.

The shelves lining the room displayed an array of vibrant ink bottles, each telling a story of its own. Flash sheets, showcasing tattoo designs ranging from traditional symbols to contemporary art, were neatly organized, inviting clients to choose their own personal expression.

In one corner, a cozy waiting area with plush leather sofas and magazines spanning from art to pop culture offered respite for those anticipating their turn. The faint hum of music, a blend of alternative tunes and classic rock, added to the ambiance without overpowering the intimate conversations between artists and clients.

The walls were a mosaic of tattooed canvases, a living gallery of stories etched in ink. From minimalist linework to intricate sleeves, the artistry on display reflected the paradoxes of individuality and self-expression.

All heads turned towards the door in response to the jingling of the bell attached to the frame.

Patrons and staff stiffened at the sight of Detective Williams standing in the doorway. Conversations stopped mid-sentence. Art who had just come from the back room in response to the door recognized who Brad was by his attire. He approached him.

"What can I do for you?" He asked, his tone more a challenge than a question.

"Are you Art?" Brad asked.

"That depends on who wants to know," he remarked.

Brad flashed his badge, "Detective Brad Williams, Pensacola PD," he responded, ignoring Art's demeanor, he continued. "I'm working on a cold case and I'm trying to identify a tattoo." He reached into the manilla folder he was carrying and pulled out a picture, not of Hammond's foot but of a drawing made by the PD artist. "Can you tell me what this is or what it signifies?"

Realizing that the detective was not there for anything involving him or his business Art's posture changed.

"Sorry, detective, didn't mean to be rude or anything..." Art went on to explain how "suits" are always coming by to harass him for one thing or another. "Let me see what you've got."

Art examined the drawing, recognition coming to his face immediately. "This is an Ouroboros. It's a mystical symbol from ancient time. It's a serpent devouring itself. It's supposed to represent the unity of all things, which never disappear but perpetually change form in the eternal cycle of death and recreation."

"Do you have any idea what it means today?"

"None, other than what I've told you."

"Thanks for your time," Brad offered.

"Anything else I can help you with? A tat perhaps," Art offered with a smirk.

As Brad turned to leave, activities within the shop resumed. As if someone had pressed the play button on the paused activities. He headed back to his car. His next stop would be the library. He needed to see what more information he could find out about the Ouroboros.

In the research department of the public library, he found numerous references to Ouroboros. He discovered there were several animals that bit their tales, giving the appearance of the Ouroboros: the armadillo girdled lizard, the European Hake, the Portuguese Pescada, but there seemed to be no connection there, at least none that he could relate. Digging further he found a Japanese wrestling organization used this symbol in its promotion. He noted that as, something to follow up on. The more he dug the more he found. It appeared that many noted scientists had used this symbol in their work, from cosmology to biology, to psychology, even chemistry. "Why had he never heard of this creature until now?" He thought.

When he read about the Swiss psychiatrist, Carl Jung, he thought he had hit on something. Jung defined the relationship of the Ouroboros to alchemy. Brad read the quotation, "The Ouroboros is a dramatic symbol for integration and assimilation. It symbolizes the One, the 'prima materia'."

"It's a cult, some kind of cult, religious or secular cult," Brad whispered to himself. This revelation led him to delve into Hammond's life, peeling back the layers of his public image and private persona. Interviews with friends and associates painted a picture of a man who was not only a benefactor but also a seeker of knowledge and truth. Hammond's charitable work, it seemed, was driven by a deeper quest for understanding the human condition.

Peter M. Browne

CHAPTER 13

Brad's perspective on Hammond began to shift as information gathered referred to a clandestine organization known as The Ouroboros Society that he appeared to be a member of. This group shrouded in secrecy, was rumored to explore the boundaries of moral and philosophical thought. Intrigued by this lead, Brad pursued it with fervor, aware that it might be the key to understanding the paradox at the heart of this case.

The investigation encountered numerous dead ends and misdirection, as if forces were at play to keep the society's secrets hidden. However, Brad's persistence paid off when he went digging back through the boxes of evidence.

"There's got to be something in here that I'm missing," he mumbled to himself, as he shuffled papers around, fanned through documents and dug down to the bottom of each box. Wedged in the corner of the last box was a small envelope, the kind you might get from a bank teller when you make a withdrawal. It appeared to be empty. It was caught in the bottom seam of the evidence box, almost out of sight. Brad had to tug at it to pry it loose. Inside was a solo key with numbers printed on the key's bow. Brad's eyes lit up when he saw it. It appeared to be a safety deposit box key. He could only hope.

Brad got on the phone with Richard. He was a bank VP and could tell him how to recognize a safety deposit key and how to gain access. As much as he disliked Richard he was not above using him to help solve this case. Richard was surprised by the call but kept his tone neutral, offering the level of civility expected when speaking to a police detective.

He explained that the number should represent the routing number of the bank containing the safety deposit box and with a name and a court order he could gain access. Brad politely thanked Richard for his help.

Richard had told him the routing number on the key belonged to Gulf Bank and Trust in nearby Ferry Pass.

Brad knew what he had to do. First he filled in his boss, Detective Sergeant Mike Brown in on what he had discovered, next he prepared the warrant application for the judge. He made sure he gave the judge sufficient information to approve the application. No sooner did he have the warrant in hand he was headed for Ferry Pass. The bank was on Main Street only seven miles from the Pensacola Police Station.

The bank manager was expecting Brad. He had called ahead. Brad, thought that armed with a warrant, this would be a simple transaction. However, the warrant indicated that it was for Ralph Hammond's safety deposit box. When the bank manager checked his files there was no safety box issued under that name and the bank could not reveal the owner without a separate court order.

"Nothing's ever simple," Brad groused, as he left the bank. It would take another elaborate warrant application before Brad would get access to the safety deposit box but it would turn out to be worth it.

The safety deposit box contained a passport, bank accounts, property deeds, and other documents in the name of Ralph Baker but the photographs were of Ralph Hammond. In addition, there was an address book containing some fifty names and addresses. Further investigation would reveal that a few of these names were prominent citizen from around and within the state of Florida, Alabama and Georgia. The other names were unknown with the exception of Roger Greer, the ex-chief of police. Greer was now in a nursing home after suffering from a massive stroke.

Brad thanked the bank manager for his assistance and left pondering his next move. He was definitely going to have to meet with Roger Greer, but he could see this was now becoming a delicate situation. It was time again to talk with his boss and garner some advice as to, exactly, how to proceed without embarrassing the police department. The "blue wall of silence" is an unwritten code among police officers not to report on a colleague's errors, misconduct, or crimes.

When Brad approached Sergeant Brown about his dilemma regarding what he had uncovered at the bank, Brown suggested that they talk with the chief.

"This is a touchy subject, with all the oversight happening around the country due to police misconduct," Brown pointed out.

Eric Dahl was the current chief, a no-nonsense kind of guy, who didn't suffer fools lightly. What that really meant was, if you did anything to cast the department in a poor light the fury of his position would come crashing down on you. As a result, people tiptoed around the chief not wanting to incur his ire.

"Come in guys. Have a seat. What can I do for you?" he said warmly.

"Chief, Williams has uncovered some evidence in the Hammond cold-case that we thought you should be aware of. I'll let him explain," said Brown.

Brad started out by giving the chief a "Reader's Digest" version of the case and where things stood.

"I think we can solve this one," Brad offered, "but we've uncovered what appears to be the involvement of ex-chief Greer." Brad stopped waiting for Chief Dahl's reaction before delving further.

The office got quiet. Brad and Sergeant Brown shifted uncomfortably in their seats, their eyes shifting from Dahl to each other and around the room. They knew that Dahl had worked under Greer in his early career and held him in high regard.

"Perhaps this hadn't been a good idea, to involve the chief before they had more information," thought Brown.

Chief Dahl who had been sitting back in his seat, leaned forward and rolled his chair up to his desk, placing both arms on the desk and leaning forward.

"I don't like it," he said, a stern expression on his face.

"Oh, shit, here it comes," thought Brown, pushing against the back of his chair, subconsciously, in an attempt to increase the distance between him and the chief, as if those few inches could protect him from the chief's anticipated fury.

But, the chief's following remarks were calm and measured, "I want to see what comes out of your further investigation before I decide how the department will respond," he said, his jaw tight but his voice soft. "There will be no cover ups on my watch." He stopped, "But Chief Greer is a good man." And he left it at that.

On their way back to Brad's desk, Brown cautioned him, "Just do your job. I've got your back." Brad nodded.

The Seaside Nursing Home was in East Bay Heights, a short drive down route 296. As promised by its name it was in fact seaside, its rooms having a view of East Bay on one side and the Gulf on the other.

Brad introduced himself at the front desk, flashing his badge and explaining his presence.

One of the nurses pointed out Greer sitting in a wheel chair in the main lounge.

"You know Mr. Greer has had a serious stroke. His right side is paralyzed and he has difficulty speaking."

Brad asked if someone could assist him. A nurse directed him to follow her.

Greer was just sitting there staring off into space as they approached.

"Mr. Greer, you have a visitor," the nurse spoke in a soft tone.

Turning to Brad, she said, "He cannot speak in long sentence and prefers to use his bell to answer yes and no questions, one for yes, two for no and three if he does not know or understand. So, if you could formulate your questions in that fashion it would be helpful"

Brad nodded, noticing the bell mounted on the wheel chair by Greer's left hand.

Brad started by telling Greer who he was and that he wanted to ask him a few questions, if that was okay. Greer acknowledged with a single ding of the bell.

Realizing that Greer could not ask him what the questions were in reference to, he decided to start with a brief narrative.

"I'm here to ask you some questions about the Hammond murder. It has been reopened as a cold case." Brad looked for a reaction from Greer but got none.

"Did you know Mr. Hammond?" Ding.

"Did you know him well?" Ding.

"Do you know anything about the Ouroboros Society?" Silence.

Brad decided to press. "We're you a member of the Ouroboros Society? Silence.

Do you know who killed Mr. Hammond? Greer became agitated, Ding, Ding, Ding, Ding. He pressed the joy stick on the wheel chair spinning it around and proceeded to drive away leaving Brad in his wake.

Brad returned to the precinct and headed straight for Detective Sergeant Brown's office. He filled Brown in on his attempted interview with Greer.

"Let's leave the guy alone. Doesn't look like you're going to get anything more out of him. Follow up on your other leads and we'll circle back to Greer if that's where the investigation leads."

Brad nodded in acknowledgement and headed to his desk. At his desk he pored over the documents from the safety deposit box. He decided to check out the deeds to see if anyone was claiming ownership following Hammond's death. That turned out to be a dead end. The deeds were out dated with the current owners having had possession prior to Hammond's death. That left just the address book. He did not dare to approach any of the prominent people listed but decided to try to track down one or more of the anonymous names on the list. This became an agonizing tedious endeavor. He was frustrated. He felt he was so close to solving this case but was missing a key piece of the puzzle.

Benjamin Wheeler was the last name on the list. Wheeler lived in the Tallahassee area. He was in the Pensacola PD database because he had gotten stopped for a DWI involving a traffic accident years ago. Brad looked up the records on that case and found that the charges had been mysteriously dropped.

Brad decided he would go to Tallahassee to meet with Wheeler but he felt unless he took a different approach to this meeting he was just going to encounter another brick wall. He had an idea but it raised both legal and ethical concerns or did it? Police are allowed to use deception during interrogations, pretending to have a witness who has implicated them is allowed. He decided he would go for it. But he was going to have Wheeler brought into the Tallahassee Police Station, put in an interrogation room and then he would drop the bomb on him.

"Mr. Wheeler, my name is Detective Williams and this is my associate Detective Grimes. Do you have any idea why we asked you here today?" Brad had arranged with the Tallahassee PD for Detective Grimes to back him in the interrogation. He had slightly misrepresented the facts pointing to Wheeler's guilt.

Wheeler was a heavy-set man now in his mid-sixties, balding, his attire suggesting he had seen better days.

"What is this all about?"

Brad came right at him. You're suspected of the murder of Ralph Hammond of Pensacola, Florida. We have an informant who has told us that you are the perpetrator. That you, under the direction of members of the Ouroboros Society killed Ralph Hammond in Willow's End Park, as a result of a dispute with the organization..."

Brad dropped this bomb on Wheeler full of suppositions and conclusions he had garnered from his investigation and just let it hang in the air."

Wheeler's face went pale, his jaw agape.

"Brad pounded him with another round of supposition. "We know you're a member of the Ouroboros Society. We know you were in Pensacola at the time of the murder and we know that you had help." Wheeler's mind was racing. This all happen over 10 years ago. He had put the Ouroboros Society behind him.

"At your age and your condition, you won't survive in prison. So, tell us what you know and we'll see what we can do for you."

Wheeler started out with, "I don't know what you're talking about."

For effect, Brad pulled out Hammond's address book and read a couple of names.

"I have a book full of people who say otherwise."

"I didn't do it."

"Didn't do what? Brad pressed.

"I didn't kill Hammond."

"I don't believe you," Brad replied dripping with sarcasm.

At that point Wheeler broke down. He began to sob, "I don't know anything, I don't know..."

"You are a member of the Ouroboros Society are you not?"

"I was. That was a long time ago."

Brad felt this was his opening. "Tell us about it. What caused you to quit?"

Grimes playing good cop offered Wheeler a tissue and some water. It took Wheeler a few minutes to gain his composure.

"I was young and idealistic at the time. I was an associate professor of psychology at Tallahassee Community College. This was about the time of the Vietnam war. Debates were taking place about the morals and ethics of the war, discussions about the killing of innocent people and about the greater good of preventing the spread of communism. You know the 'domino theory'. I got swept up in that and ended up finding and joining the Ouroboros Society." Wheeler paused to catch his breath and to recall memories from days long past.

"Perpetuo Progredi, Iustitia Omnium Pretium. Translated from Latin, it means 'Ever Forward, Justice at All Costs'. The motto reflects the society's relentless pursuit of the greater good. They were willing to pay any price for justice, as they define it. That is why I quit."

"What about Ralph Hammond?"

"He was the first to point out that the organization was going too far and that it had become a vehicle to benefit the greater good of its members and not society." Wheeler looked up at Brad. "I met with him that evening to warn him. I had heard that he needed to be silenced 'for the greater good'. When I left him, he was still alive. I have no idea who actually killed him. But when I found out about his death I was done with the organization."

"Who would have given the order?" Brad stared directly at Wheeler.

"The leader of the organization is called the Primus Circuli, First of the Circle. He and his council would make that decision. I'm sure their names are in your book. Any of a hundred followers could have actually committed the murder."

"Why do you think your name is in Hammond's address book?"

"Perhaps that is a list of like-minded people and not the leadership."

"Who then is the Primus Circuli?"

"Back then it was Albert Finnley. I have no idea who it is today."

Brad, satisfied he has gotten all he could from Wheeler nodded to Grimes. "I think we are done. Thank you Mr. Wheeler for your cooperation."

Relief washing over his face, "I'm not being charged with anything?" Wheeler asked.

"No, you are free to go. One last question. Why didn't you come forward when Mr. Hammond was killed?"

"I thought if I did I'd be next."

The meeting with Benjamin Wheeler was the piece of the missing puzzle. Brad now confirmed that Hammond's murder was not just a crime of passion or greed but a philosophical statement, an execution by someone who believed Hammond had betrayed the ideals of the Ouroboros society.

Brad had always been fascinated by the duality of human nature, the way light and shadow played within a person's soul. But this case, with its layers of deceit and revelation, fell beyond the pale.

Brad and Detective Sergeant Brown sat down once again with Chief Dahl.

"Chief, Williams has discovered that the Hammond case reaches deep into the political and social elite in and around Pensacola and Tallahassee. I'll let him tell you about it."

Brad told the chief what he'd uncovered about The Ouroboros Society and who some of its most prominent members were and that he believed that Chief Greer was a material witness. He named Albert Finnley as the head of this secret society. Finnley was also one of the seven justices on the Florida Supreme Court.

"I need to know how I should proceed with the investigation. We have a credible individual, a former member of this organization, who acknowledges that Hammond was murdered by someone under orders of the leadership of this organization." Brad paused to allow the Chief a moment to assimilate the information.

Brown interjected. "Is this something we want to continue to pursue? Or do we return the evidence boxes to storage and move on?"

The Chief swallowed hard. This was the last thing he needed, a highly charged political case. "We don't walk away from our duty to uphold the law. But right now, we don't know who we can trust, who isn't a part of this organization or affiliated with them. If word gets out that we are on to something two things are going to happen: powers that be will attempt to shut it down and your informant will be the next one in the morgue."

Looking at Sergeant Brown, "This investigation has become too big for us to handle on our own.

We need to carefully escalate this up to the federal level. We're going to have to avoid the state courts for any judicial warrants. All information shared from this point is on a 'need to know' basis only." He looked at both men seated before him. "I want you to do nothing and say nothing to anyone until I get back to you."

As the men got up to leave, the Chief called to Brad, "Williams, excellent police work."

CHAPTER 14

There was no shortage of cold cases. They were cold because the original investigators were unable to solve them in one, two, five years and they had been put on the shelf while new cases demanded their attention.

The Marston murder was the next case assigned to Brad while the Hammond case was escalated to a joint task force of combined federal and local authorities. It had been reassigned, renamed, and Brad no longer had a "need to know" what was happening, so he lost track of the case.

Fredrick Marston had been murdered while he slept. Marston was married and in his early thirty's when the crime occurred, more than ten years ago. Since there were no signs of forced entry his wife became the only suspect. She was in the house at the time. She said she never heard or saw anything. She was initially charged with capital murder and was about to go to trial when a similar crime in Texas made the front-page news. Oliver Thorn was murdered while he slept. His wife and three children were home at the time but only Oliver was killed, his throat slashed, from ear-to-ear. It was the same M.O. Mrs. Thorn claimed that things were out of place in the kitchen, but there were no signs of forced entry.

After poring over the file, Brad decided to head over to the location of the crime. The notes indicated that the murder had occurred in a house that was close to the interstate highway. He wanted to see the crime scene for himself. Brad drove to 141 Creek Road. He parked out front. Through the trees he could barely see I-10 no more than a few hundred yards down an embankment and he could hear the thunder of the traffic. "Who would want to live this close to the highway?' he thought. He didn't bother to go inside. He didn't want to disturb the residence and he certainly didn't want to tell them there had been a murder in their home, if they didn't know it.

Back at the office, he went over to the Florida State map that was on the wall and marked the location of the murder. He then, on a hunch, searched for the location of the other murder on a Texas map, he got from AAA.

Over a period of six years investigators in separate jurisdictions had now investigated seven murders stretching along I-10 from Jacksonville, Florida to El Paso, Texas. All these murders happened within a few hundred yards of the interstate but no one had thought to consider the interstate to be a factor in these crimes.

Brad went back to AAA and got maps for all the states involved. He pinpointed each location and then one-by-one, with a magic marker in hand, he back-traced the route from each house to the nearest exit/entrance to the interstate. None of the houses were anywhere within easy access. He concluded that anyone committing a crime of opportunity wasn't going to drive a bunch of back roads to reach any of these houses.

"They must be parking on the highway and approaching these houses on foot, but why?" he questioned.

Then he remembered the story that Buck Dyson had related to him about the truck driver committing murders along the interstate. He went back to the map to look at where the Marston murder happened. It was right on the Pearson's Point town line. He had remembered about that murder when Buck was telling him the tale. He now recalled the feeling he had that Buck wasn't telling a tale but relating a personal experience.

Brad sat down with his boss, Sergeant Brown, and went over his hunch.

"I don't know why no one has connected these dots before now. But just look at this." He had his map pinned to the wall of his cubicle. "All these crimes were committed in houses a few hundred yards from the interstate." Brown listened. "Who runs the interstate more than any other group of individuals? Truck drivers!"

Brown nodded, "It's a good observation. The only problem is…" He paused, "There are thousands of trucks and truck drivers on the interstate every day. Even if you're right, that's like looking for a needle in a hay stack."

"Yes but we can narrow that down. We have a time window for each of these crimes. Trucks don't just run up and down the interstate. There are Department of Transportation regulations governing hours behind the wheel, requiring drivers to maintain log books and even better there are weigh stations all along the road requiring trucks to stop and be inspected, creating a timestamp of their location."

Brown had listened intently to Brad's very thorough analysis before responding. "I hear you Brad. So now you've reduced the number of trucks from thousands to hundreds. How do you find that one driver, if your theory is even correct?"

"Who else could it be?" Brad challenged.

"How about a vagrant, a hobo, a hippy, traveling across the country? He could be hitchhiking, using truckers without their knowledge." Brown reached for his cup of coffee cooling on the corner of his desk. He had moved it to make way for Brad's map and had forgotten about it. "Just playing devil's advocate," as he sipped the tepid java.

"What if I told you I have a specific truck driver in mind. One, coincidently, I'd spoken to a while back, who seems to fit the description."

"O-kay, tell me more," Brown said, setting his cup back down.

Brad related the story of how he met Buck Dyson and the story he related to him and how it appeared he was retelling a personal experience. When he finished, he said, "So, let me work on this needle and see if he's just a good storyteller or if he's our guy."

Brad started by building a chart of the crime locations, the dates and times of each crime, the time in between each crime, the distance between locations, the average miles a truck travelled per day, and any other statistical data he could think of. He went out to the local Love's Truck Stop and spoke with a number of drivers about their log books, about their practices of pulling off the road to take rest stops overnight to sleep, why there always seemed to be a cluster of trucks pulled over in one location, how often would they pull off the road where there were no other trucks, how often trucks broke down, how quick was the repair services response times and then finally he asked if they were aware of the interstate murders. He was surprised to find out that his hypothesis was shared by many drivers. That brought Brad to his final question. "Have you ever met a driver that you might think capable of committing such crimes?"

The most frequent response was, "It takes all kinds."

Brad thought that weigh stations could provide some key evidence because truck drivers want to keep all their papers in order so that they can be in and out of a weigh station as fast as possible. His concern was retention. How long was the data retained before it was destroyed or discarded. Since weigh stations were controlled at the state level and not the federal, procedures varied from state to state, further complicating the matter.

The more Brad dug into the availability of weigh station data dating back over ten years the more it became apparent that this was not going to be a method he could use to track Buck Dyson's whereabouts. He needed Buck's log books. The truck drivers he interviewed had told him that it was not uncommon for drivers to keep them indefinitely as sort of a memoir of their time on the road. But how could he get those, if they still existed?

Brad reported back to Sergeant Brown that he had reached another dead-end. He spoke with investigators in other jurisdictions who found themselves in the same position.

"There's only one avenue left to pursue." Brad told Sergeant Brown. "We have to get ahold of Buck Dyson's log books."

"And how do you propose we do that?"

"We just ask him for them," Brad replied.

"Just like that. Just ask him, huh?"

"Worst he can say is no, right?"

"And why would he say yes?"

"Because he is an honest guy with nothing to hide."

Brown just shook his head. "How long have you been a police officer? Do you think there are really people like that? I thought by now you'd be more cynical."

"Well, this guy told me himself, 'nothing beats a try but a failure', so what have we got to lose?" After getting Dyson's information from the DMV, Brad called his house and spoke to his wife, Esther, who told him that Buck was retired.

Brad pulled up to Dyson's house, the big red rig still parked in the driveway. He had brought Detective Patterson from the Sarasota PD with him.

Buck answered the door. The detectives flashed their badges. Buck was curious what would bring police officers to his door. Esther had told him about the police's call but knew little else.

"How can I help you, detectives?"

"Just like to ask you a few questions about a case we're working on," Brad offered.

Buck, looking perplexed, "Sure come on in, guys. Can I offer you something to drink?"

"No thanks," came the reply in unison.

"What can I do for you then?

"I'm Detective Williams from the Pensacola PD and this is my associate, Detective Patterson, from Sarasota. We are working a cold case and we need your help." Brad watched Buck's face for any expression, any sign of concern or guilt, but saw nothing but curiosity.

"Come… have a seat. How can I help? You didn't tell Esther much on the phone."

"We are investigating what the media has been calling 'The Highway Murders'. We have spoken to a lot of truckers who have run I-10 over the past dozen years." His next statement was a lie. "We've been asking them to allow us to review their log books to find out if they were in the vicinity of the crime scenes at the times in question." He shifted the reference to make sure Buck would view this as the police looking for witnesses versus suspects. While he was talking he searched Buck's countenance looking for any "tells", indication of guilt. "Truckers tell me you guys keep your logs as mementos. What about you? Do you still have your log books?" Brad winced internally, waiting for Buck's reply.

"Sure, I have a garage full of log books stashed somewhere."

Brad was salivating internally while maintaining a cool exterior. "Would you mind if we borrowed them?"

"No not at all. They're just collecting dust. Esther has been trying to get me to clean out the garage for years. Help yourself."

"Thank you Mr. Dyson. We'll get them back to you." Buck waved them off. "I got no use for them. Esther will be pleased."

As the detectives were getting up to leave, Buck turned to Brad. "You look familiar. I've been thinking that we've met somewhere before. Have we?"

Brad lied again. "I don't think so. But I get that a lot. I have one of those faces, I guess."

Brad packed the boxes in the trunk and gave Buck a receipt detailing what was taken.

Brad would spend weeks, searching for relevant log books, going through log entries and cataloging them. He felt either Buck was the killer he was looking for or it was just a series of coincidences that put him in the area of more than one crime. He shared his findings with other jurisdictions who helped him build a case. When he thought he had probable cause, he met again with Sergeant Brown.

"This is our guy! I'll bet my badge on it," Brad asserted.

"How are you going to prove that? All your evidence is circumstantial, if it's even evidence," Brown pushed back.

"I want to get a warrant to search his house and truck. You know these guys love to keep mementos of their crimes."

"I think you're pushing it, detective," Brown admonished.

But Brad had come too far, dedicated too much time, his focus on Dyson laser sharp.

"People want these murders solved. We can't let this guy get away with it because he's been able to cover his tracks. I know it's him. I just know it."

Brad was able to convince a judge to issue a search warrant on Buck Dyson's home and vehicles.

After an extensive search, nothing was found in Buck's home but a hunting knife was retrieved from the glove box on Buck's truck along with blood stains that turned out to be human.

Peter M. Browne

CHAPTER 15

The sun was just peeking over the horizon as the convoy of police cars and armored vehicles rumbled across the short 10th Street bridge that separated Snead Island from the Bradenton mainland. The bridge, no longer than the narrow canal's width, provided a shortcut for boats traversing the Manatee River, headed for Terra Ceia Bay.

The air was thick with anticipation, each officer bracing themselves for the impending operation. The convoy's destination loomed ahead - the private enclave known as Amberwind Estates. To maintain the element of surprise, they approached cautiously, mindful of the eight-foot-tall locked gate guarding the entrance. Fortunately, an override existed for emergency personnel, granting them access without alerting their target.

As the gate slowly swung open, officers from the DEA, ATF, FBI, state and local police readied themselves for the assault. The task force leader gave the signal, and the convoy resumed its silent advance. The vehicles rolled slowly and quietly until they reached 1447 Amber Drive. To cover all escape routes, a State Police helicopter suddenly appeared, hovering over the water behind the property.

No sooner had the vehicles come to a halt than task force members surrounded the house with precision, like pieces on a chessboard moving into position. One group, armed with a battering ram, ascended the exterior stairs of the Key West-style home. This was a no-knock warrant, so they were not required to announce their presence until they had breached the entrance.

Vincent Moreno was startled awake by the thunderous crash of the front door below. Shards of glass from the leaded-glass door sprayed across the marble floor like a hailstorm, jolting him from his slumber. He reached for the 9-millimeter stored in his nightstand, his heart pounding in his chest.

Moreno was no ordinary man. His presence alone could command an entire room. Draped in the veneer of old-world refinement, he carried the quiet menace of someone who had seen — and caused — more violence than most could fathom. A man in his late sixties, with iron-gray hair slicked back to perfection, Moreno bore the sharp, angular features of an Italian marble sculpture. His tailored silk pajamas clung to his stocky, yet powerful frame, a testament to his disciplined workouts despite his age. But it was his eyes — cold, calculating, and the color of gunmetal — that left an impression. They hinted at the ruthlessness that had elevated him to the peak of organized crime and kept him there for decades.

The next sound he heard was the double bedroom doors being blown off their hinges, followed by the sight of a concussion grenade rolling across the floor.

Before he could react, the grenade exploded, sending shockwaves in all directions. Vincent was thrown against the headboard, disoriented and temporarily blinded by the blast.

As he struggled to regain his senses, Vincent found himself surrounded by a small army of law enforcement officers, their weapons trained on him.

"Vincent Moreno, you are under arrest for violation of the RICO statute, money laundering, and tax evasion," one agent declared, reading him his Miranda rights before leading him, handcuffed, out of the building and into one of the waiting armored vehicles.

The deafening blast of the grenade and the thumping sound of the helicopter blades had drawn the attention of the neighbors. Faces appeared on porches, in yards, and on the sidewalk, their expressions a mix of shock and disbelief.

The early-morning light revealed the decadence of the Moreno estate, a sprawling mansion more befitting a European nobleman than a Mafia kingpin. Despite his humiliation, Vincent held his head high, his mind already calculating his next move. For men like him, power was never just handed over—it was fought over.

Meanwhile, inside the house, agents descended like a swarm of locusts, tearing through drawers and cabinets in search of evidence. They left no stone unturned, their search methodical and thorough.

As a smaller convoy departed with Vincent Moreno in tow, bound for the Bradenton County Jail, the sun continued its ascent, casting a harsh light on the scene below.

The telephone rang at the reception desk of Wright and Wright, a prestigious law firm nestled in the heart of downtown Tampa, Florida, the receptionist lifted the receiver with practiced efficiency.

"Wright and Wright, may I help you?" she recited in her professional tone, her fingers poised above the switchboard.

"Chandler Wright," the voice requested.

"Mr. Wright is in the middle of a meeting. Can I take a message and have him call you?" she continued, her voice steady despite the urgency in the caller's tone.

"No! I need to speak to him now!" The voice on the other end crackled with tension, demanding immediate attention.

"Whom should I say is calling?" the receptionist inquired, her brow furrowing.

"Vincent Moreno," came the terse reply, sending a shiver down her spine. She knew the name all too well, and the implications it carried.

With a quick nod, the receptionist pressed a few buttons on her console, placing the call on hold then connecting to Chandler's office. "Mr. Wright, I have Vincent Moreno on line one. He says it's urgent," she announced, her voice carrying a hint of apprehension.

Chandler Wright, senior partner of Wright & Wright LLC, was a man who exuded an air of practiced authority, the kind of gravitas that came from years of navigating the treacherous waters of high-stakes litigation and corporate maneuvering. His custom-tailored navy suit clung to his lean frame with the precision of his legal arguments, and the platinum watch on his wrist subtly declared his success without shouting it. His silver-streaked hair, perfectly combed back, gave him the look of a polished statesman, while his piercing blue eyes carried the intensity of a man who left no clause unexamined and no weakness unexploited. Chandler had long mastered the art of looking unflappable, no matter the storm.

He felt a surge of anticipation as he halted the meeting already in progress. Rising from the head of the conference table, he adjusted his silk tie with a smooth flick of his wrist. "Gentlemen, I apologize for the interruption. I need the room," he declared, his voice crisp, measured, and utterly commanding. The room emptied without protest, his colleagues filing out with hurried nods. Chandler's word was law within these walls.

Once alone, he eased into his leather chair, leaning back slightly as his fingers steepled beneath his chin. The faint scent of cigar smoke from the office humidor mingled with the aroma of the espresso on his desk. But Chandler paid no mind to these luxuries now; his focus was entirely on the weight of Vincent Moreno's call. Even in his line of work, a call from Moreno carried an urgency that could not be ignored.

"Vincent, what can I do for you?" he inquired, his tone calm and smooth, though his mind churned with the possibilities. The faint crackle of static on the line punctuated the silence before Moreno's gravelly voice came through, agitated and rushed.

Chandler listened with his usual cool detachment, absorbing every detail as Vincent recounted the morning's chaos. His practiced ear picked up the panic beneath Moreno's barked commands, the raw anger barely concealed beneath the surface.

"I need you to get me out of here, now!" Vincent snapped, his fury tangible, even over the phone.

Chandler allowed a brief silence to stretch, not out of hesitation, but as a tactic — one he knew would calm even the most volatile clients. "I'll take care of it," he replied finally, his voice low but firm. "But Vincent, you'll need to follow my lead on this."

As he hung up, Chandler straightened his posture, already strategizing. Moreno was a complex client, a man whose empire relied on layers of legal ambiguity, and Chandler was the rare lawyer capable of navigating such intricacies. For Chandler, this wasn't just a job — it was a chess game, and he was already several moves ahead.

As Chandler hung up the phone, his mind examined the possibilities. He knew he needed to act fast if he was going to accommodate his client's wishes.

He summoned Jake Dyson, one of his most trusted senior associates. Jake entered the office with his usual quiet efficiency, a leather portfolio tucked under his arm and a look of unwavering focus etched on his face. Tall and broad-shouldered, Jake carried himself with the confidence of someone who knew his way around both the courtroom and the back channels of the legal system. His angular features bore a striking resemblance to his father, Buck Dyson, though Jake had worked tirelessly to distance himself from his father's rough, blue-collar reputation. Where Buck's hands had been calloused from years of manual labor and hard living, Jake's were smooth, his weapons a Montblanc pen and the cutting edge of the law.

"I need you to drop what you're doing and get over to the county jail," Chandler instructed, his voice clipped and authoritative. "Get Vincent Moreno out of there, no matter what it takes. We can't afford to waste any time."

Jake nodded solemnly, the weight of the task ahead settling heavily on his shoulders. He knew the risks involved in dealing with someone like Vincent Moreno, but he also understood the importance of loyalty to the firm. With a steely resolve, he rose from his seat and prepared to embark on the mission that lay ahead.

As he stepped out into the bustling corridors of the law firm, Jake couldn't shake the feeling that he was about to enter conflicting territory. He knew, dealing with this client blurred the lines between right and wrong, legal and illegal, moral and immoral. Each interaction with Vincent Moreno and Moreno Industries was a test of conscience. But for now, duty called, and he was determined to get Moreno out on bail, no matter what legal manipulations were required.

Moreno Industries sprawled like a malignant tumor across the economic landscape of the Gulf Coast, its influence seeping into every crevice of society. From the bustling docks where longshoremen toiled under the watchful eye of Moreno's enforcers, to the shadowy underworld of truckers smuggling illicit goods along the highways, the reach of Moreno Industries knew no bounds.

At the heart of the operation lay a tangled web of corruption and greed, with Moreno himself pulling the strings from behind the scenes. Banks and financial institutions, once bastions of integrity, had been infiltrated and manipulated to serve Moreno's insatiable appetite for wealth. Loan sharking became a lucrative sideline, with desperate souls falling prey to Moreno's predatory lending practices, their lives shackled to a never-ending cycle of debt and the threat of violence for nonpayment.

But it was in the illicit trade of contraband that Moreno Industries truly thrived. Drugs, both manufactured and smuggled, flowed like a toxic river through the veins of the Gulf Coast, poisoning communities and enriching Moreno's coffers in equal measure. Stolen goods, pilfered from unsuspecting victims or hijacked from freight shipments, found their way into Moreno's vast network of black-market distribution channels, disappearing into the ether with the ease of a magician's sleight of hand.

And then there was the darkest corner of Moreno's empire: human trafficking. Innocent lives, bought and sold like commodities on the open market, were subjected to unspeakable horrors at the hands of Moreno's henchmen. Women and children, torn from their homes and families, became little more than pawns in Moreno's twisted game of power and control.

But despite the pervasive darkness that shrouded Moreno Industries, there were whispers of resistance, of a brave soul willing to stand up to the tyranny of corruption and oppression. As Moreno's grip tightened, so too did the resolve of this single soul who dared to defy him, now a confidential informant working with the FBI. It was his information and months of investigation that lead to Vincent Moreno's arrest.

Jake had stopped by to visit his parents in Sarasota after leaving the Bradenton courthouse, where he had secured Vincent Moreno's release.

"We saw your TV press conference," Buck said, his tone heavy with disapproval, as he and Esther exchanged concerned glances. "Isn't Vincent Moreno a criminal?" Not waiting for a reply. "Why is your firm defending him?"

"Dad, it's complicated," Jake replied, his frustration bubbling beneath the surface. "Everyone deserves their day in court, guilty or not. It's our job to ensure that due process is served, regardless of our personal opinions."

"They've been trying to get this guy for years," Buck protested, his voice tinged with indignation. "Now apparently they have enough evidence to arrest him, and you're going to help get him off? That's not why we paid for you to go to law school."

"Dad," Jake sighed, running a hand through his hair. "Life is rarely as black and white as we'd like it to be. Our criminal justice system is founded on the principle of fairness and due process. Without proper representation, Moreno could be denied his fundamental rights."

"So, you put blinders on and try to find ways to get a known criminal off. Is that it?" Buck challenged; his eyes boring into Jake's with unwavering intensity.

Buck and Jake continued to debate the merits and shortcomings of the criminal justice system, their perspectives clashing like opposing forces in an unyielding battle. Buck saw the world in absolutes, while Jake understood the nuances and complexities that colored every legal case.

Finally, Buck asked, "What is RICO anyway? Is this some new law?"

Jake settled back on the sofa, gathering his thoughts before responding. "RICO, or the Racketeer Influenced and Corrupt Organizations Act, was enacted in 1970 to combat organized crime, particularly the Mafia. It targets 'patterns of racketeering activity,' which can encompass a wide range of illegal conduct." He paused. "In Moreno's case, they're alleging a number of associated crimes, which carry severe penalties, including forfeiture of assets gained from criminal activity."

"The wages of sin..." Buck remarked, shaking his head in dismay.

"Dad, it's not about passing judgment," Jake replied earnestly. "Our role, as his attorneys, is to provide a vigorous defense for our client, presenting the case to the best of our ability. Ultimately, it's up to the jury to weigh the evidence and determine guilt or innocence."

Realizing that they were unlikely to find common ground on this contentious issue, father and son agreed to table their discussion for the time being, each retreating into their own thoughts.

Moreno had requested a speedy trial. He and his council believed that this would be in his best interest. It would give the prosecution little time to prepare. The speedy trial act required the trial to begin within seventy days of the indictment. During that time, Wright and Wright did all they could to get the case dismissed, but the judge would have none of the legal shenanigans they disguised as just cause.

The courtroom buzzed with anticipation, as the trial commenced. Moreno sat stoically at the defense table, flanked by his legal team made up of several lawyers from Wright and Wright. Chandler Wright was not taking any chances with this case. He would be first chair. Jake Dyson was second chair.

Across the aisle sat the prosecution, spearheaded by Assistant U.S. Attorney Lisa Campbell, a woman whose reputation preceded her. Lisa had carved out a name for herself as a tenacious, razor-sharp prosecutor who didn't flinch in the face of high-stakes cases. Her tailored navy suit spoke to her meticulous nature, while the fiery determination in her eyes hinted at the fighter beneath her polished exterior.

Lisa's rise through the ranks of the U.S. Attorney's Office was nothing short of meteoric. A graduate of Georgetown Law, she had quickly distinguished herself with an uncanny ability to unravel even the most complex financial crimes. Her unrelenting focus on justice and her deep knowledge of the law had earned her the nickname "The Bulldog," a title she wore like armor in court.

As the trial began, Lisa radiated an almost intimidating calm, her every move calculated. She shuffled through her notes with the precision of a surgeon, her mind already dissecting Chandler Wright's strategy before he'd uttered a word. She glanced at Moreno, her steely gaze meeting his across the aisle. He didn't intimidate her — no one did.

This case was personal. Moreno's empire of corruption had destroyed countless lives, leaving a trail of broken families and ruined businesses in its wake. For Lisa, it wasn't just about securing a conviction; it was about sending a message to others like him that no one, no matter how untouchable they seemed, was above the law.

When the judge entered the courtroom and the trial officially began, Lisa leaned back in her chair, the faintest smirk tugging at her lips. She wasn't just ready for this fight — she was hungry for it.

"May it please the court, the United States calls its first witness," Campbell declared, her voice carrying across the hushed courtroom. Over the course of the trial, the prosecution meticulously laid out its case, presenting a litany of evidence and witnesses to support its allegations of racketeering activity within Moreno Industries. Documents detailing financial transactions, surveillance footage capturing illicit meetings, and testimony from cooperating witnesses painted a damning picture of Moreno's involvement in a wide range of criminal enterprises.

Lisa Campbell paced before the jury, her voice steady and commanding, as she called her next witness to the stand. "The prosecution calls Mary Johnson," she announced, her tone deliberate.

From the gallery, Mary Johnson rose and approached the stand with a quiet but confident presence. In her late forties, she carried herself with the precision of someone who had spent years uncovering hidden truths buried in financial records. Dressed sharply in a tailored navy blazer, her hair pulled back into a neat bun, she exuded professionalism. A Certified Forensic Accountant with an impressive track record, Mary was widely regarded as one of the best in her field. Her work had been instrumental in numerous high-profile cases, earning her recognition as an expert in financial crimes.

After taking her oath, she adjusted her glasses and sat upright in the witness chair, the model of composure. On the prosecutor's table lay thick binders of her reports and exhibits—evidence she had painstakingly compiled over months of investigation.

Lisa stepped closer to the stand, her voice steady and clear. "Ms. Johnson, could you please state your credentials for the court?"

Mary spoke with measured confidence, her voice carrying easily through the silent room. "Certainly. I hold a master's degree in forensic accounting from Georgetown University and am a Certified Public Accountant and Certified Fraud Examiner. For the past fifteen years, I've specialized in investigating financial crimes, including embezzlement, money laundering, and tax fraud. I've provided expert testimony in over two dozen federal cases, and my findings have been used to secure numerous convictions."

A ripple of approval passed through the jury as they nodded, impressed by her qualifications.

Lisa nodded, pleased, and continued, "And in your professional capacity, were you retained to analyze the financial records of Moreno Industries?"

"Yes, I was," Mary replied, her voice calm and professional. "Over the course of six months, I conducted a comprehensive forensic audit of Moreno Industries' financial records, transactions, and associated entities." She paused, her gaze steady as she addressed the jury. "My investigation uncovered a systematic and deliberate effort to launder funds, conceal taxable income, and channel money through offshore accounts and shell corporations."

Lisa moved to the prosecutor's table and picked up a chart. Unfolding it, she displayed a detailed flow of funds diagrams for the jury. "Ms. Johnson, could you walk us through this chart and explain how the funds were funneled into offshore accounts?"

As Mary began to explain, Chandler Wright rose from his chair with a flourish, his voice sharp. "Objection, Your Honor!"

The judge turned toward him with a raised brow. "On what grounds, Mr. Wright?"

"Speculation," Chandler declared, his tone clipped. "Ms. Johnson is presenting a narrative rather than facts. Unless she has specific evidence tying these accounts directly to my client, her testimony is conjecture at best."

Lisa stepped forward, unfazed. "Your Honor, the witness is providing expert analysis based on her forensic audit, which is admissible as evidence under Federal Rules of Evidence 702."

The judge deliberated for a moment before nodding. "Overruled. Proceed, Ms. Campbell."

Chandler smirked and leaned back in his chair, his eyes narrowing as Mary resumed her testimony. The interruption was classic defense strategy — throwing a wrench into the proceedings to rattle the prosecution and plant doubt in the jury's mind.

Mary, however, remained unshaken. She glanced at the jury; her expression unwavering. "To continue," she said, her voice steady, "the funds were transferred through a series of shell corporations — many registered in jurisdictions known for financial opacity. These corporations were used to disguise the true origin of the money, making it appear legitimate when, in fact, it was the proceeds of illegal activities."

The courtroom erupted into whispers as Mary detailed her findings, her testimony bolstering the prosecution's case against Vincent Moreno.

"And based on your analysis, what conclusion did you reach regarding Mr. Moreno's involvement in these activities?" Lisa pressed, her eyes narrowing in anticipation.

"It is my professional opinion that Mr. Moreno was intimately involved in the orchestration of these illegal transactions," Mary declared, her voice unwavering.

"The evidence leaves no doubt that he was the mastermind behind Moreno Industries' criminal operations."

With each witness testimony, the prosecution's case against Vincent Moreno grew stronger. However, Wright and Wright was prepared to mount a vigorous defense. At every turn, they challenged the prosecution's evidence, raising objections, filing motions, and cross-examining witnesses with precision and skill.

"Your Honor, the prosecution has failed to establish the existence of a criminal enterprise as defined under the RICO Act," argued Chandler Wright, his voice resonating with confidence. "They've presented a series of isolated incidents and attempted to string them together into a narrative of organized criminal activity. But where is the evidence of a structured hierarchy, ongoing operations, or concerted effort to commit crimes?"

The defense continued attacking the prosecution's case, posing challenges following every witness. "Objection, Your Honor! The prosecution is cherry-picking evidence and presenting a distorted view of my client's actions," interjected Jake Dyson, his brow furrowed in skepticism. "There is no pattern of racketeering activity here, only conjecture and speculation. Without concrete proof of a systematic course of criminal conduct, the charges against Mr. Moreno must be dismissed."

In dizzying repetition, the defense attacked every element of the prosecution's case. "Your Honor, we move to suppress the evidence obtained through illegal wiretaps and surveillance," declared Chandler Wright, his voice rising in indignation. "The prosecution's case is built on a foundation of unconstitutional searches and seizures, in clear violation of my client's Fourth Amendment rights. Without this tainted evidence, the prosecution's case crumbles."

As the trial progressed, tensions ran high in the courtroom, as each side raised compelling arguments and counterarguments in a battle of legal wits. Witnesses were cross-examined, evidence was scrutinized, and legal precedent was cited with precision.

The prosecution had saved their star witness for last. His name was Simon Weinstein. He had been the CFO of Moreno Industries, turned state's witness. The jury had seen images of him in surveillance photos and now they were about to meet the man, in person.

"The prosecution calls Simon Weinstein..." The anticipation in the courtroom was tangible as his name echoed through the hushed space. All eyes turned expectantly toward the rear of the courtroom, awaiting the appearance of the witness.

But as the seconds stretched into minutes, a sense of unease settled over the room. The doors at the rear of the courtroom remained closed, and there was no sign of Simon Weinstein.

Then, suddenly, the doors burst open, and a figure came rushing down the aisle. It wasn't Simon Weinstein. Instead, it was one of Lisa Campbell's associates, his face flushed with urgency as he whispered something into her ear.

Lisa's expression tightened, her jaw clenching in frustration as she turned to address the judge. "Your Honor, it appears Mr. Weinstein cannot be located," she announced, her voice tinged with irritation. "I would like to request a brief recess while we attempt to locate him."

A ripple of murmurs swept through the courtroom as the gravity of the situation sank in. Vincent Moreno sat calmly at the defense table, a knowing smile playing at the corners of his lips. He had anticipated this turn of events, knowing full well that Weinstein would never appear in court to testify against him.

The judge, sensing the seriousness of the situation, nodded in agreement. "Court will be in recess until 1 PM," he declared, pounding his gavel to signal the adjournment.

As the courtroom emptied, Chandler Wright and his team huddled together, their minds conflicted by the possibilities. They knew that Weinstein's testimony was critical to the prosecution and his absence could be a turning point in the trial, but they also understood the risks it posed to their defense should it be found that Moreno was the cause of his absence.

When court resumed after the recess, the tension in the air apparent. Lisa Campbell stood before the judge; her expression grim as she addressed the court.

"Your Honor, despite our best efforts, we have been unable to locate Mr. Weinstein," she admitted, her voice marked with frustration. "In light of his absence, the prosecution requests a continuance to allow for further attempts to secure his testimony."

Chandler Wright rose to his feet, his gaze steady as he addressed the judge. "Your Honor, we object to any further delays in this trial," he argued, his voice firm and resolute. "The prosecution has had ample time to prepare its case, and the absence of a single witness should not be grounds for postponement."

The judge considered their arguments carefully before delivering his ruling. "Given the peculiar circumstances surrounding Mr. Weinstein's absence, I am inclined to grant the prosecution's request for a continuance," he announced, his voice echoing through the silent courtroom. "Court will reconvene in one week's time to allow for further attempts to locate Mr. Weinstein."

As the proceedings concluded and the courtroom emptied once more, Chandler Wright and his team knew that the battle was far from over. With Weinstein's absence casting a shadow over the trial, they would need to redouble their efforts to secure Vincent Moreno's acquittal and ensure that the defense prevailed in the end.

The trial resumed a week later, the absence of Simon Weinstein loomed large over the proceedings. The courtroom buzzed with speculation and uncertainty, as both the prosecution and the defense prepared their arguments to the court.

In a sidebar, Lisa Campbell, stood before the judge, her expression determined as she addressed the court. "Your Honor, despite exhaustive efforts, we have been unable to locate Mr. Weinstein," she announced, her tone hinting her frustration. "However, we believe that the evidence we have presented thus far is sufficient to prove the defendant's guilt beyond a reasonable doubt."

Chandler Wright, also at the bench, his gaze steady as he countered, "Your Honor, the prosecution's case hinged on the testimony of Mr. Weinstein. Without his presence, their case crumbles like a house of cards. We move for a dismissal of all charges against my client."

The judge needed no deliberation before delivering his ruling. "While the absence of Mr. Weinstein is indeed concerning, it is not grounds for an automatic dismissal," he declared, his voice measured and authoritative. "The prosecution may proceed and the defense will have the opportunity to present its case."

With the judge's decision made, the trial resumed with renewed intensity. The prosecution recalled several witnesses, before resting its case.

Meanwhile, Chandler Wright and his team continued tirelessly to poke holes in the prosecution's argument, cross-examining witnesses, challenging the authenticity of evidence, and raising doubts about the credibility of the prosecution's case.

The defense had decided to call no witnesses. They were not required to mount a defense. The burden of proof was on the prosecution. They certainly didn't want to put Vincent Moreno on the stand and have him cross-examined by the prosecution.

And so, the trial reached its climax. Both sides delivered impassioned closing arguments, urging the jury to weigh the evidence carefully and reach a just verdict.

"Ladies and gentlemen of the jury, my client's involvement in certain activities may be regrettable, but it does not constitute racketeering under the RICO Act. Mr. Moreno was not privy to the inner workings of any alleged criminal enterprise. He was simply a businessman trying to navigate a complex and competitive market." Jake Dyson paused, turning toward his client and then back to the jurors. "My client is entitled to a fair trial, free from prejudice and bias," his eyes scanning the faces of the jurors. "The government's rush to judgment and overzealous prosecution have deprived Mr. Moreno of his fundamental rights. We urge you to uphold the principles of due process and deliver a verdict based on the facts, not on emotion or speculation."

As Jake's words hung in the air, his eyes instinctively scanned the courtroom. His gaze snagged on a familiar figure sitting near the back, a weathered man whose mere presence made Jake's throat tighten. Buck Dyson.

His father sat with his arms crossed, his piercing eyes locked on Jake, radiating an unmistakable aura of disapproval. It wasn't just the faint shake of his head that stung — it was the betrayal of the values that Buck had instilled in his children. In that moment, the courtroom walls seemed to close in.

Jake faltered ever so slightly, the next words catching in his throat before he forced himself to recover. He turned back toward the jury, refocusing with visible effort. But the damage was done. Buck's unspoken judgment lingered, clawing at the back of Jake's mind, a silent reminder of the line he had crossed in defending Moreno.

Even as the court reporter's keys clicked and the judge shifted in his seat, Jake could still feel his father's gaze boring into him like a scalding brand. Whatever came next, he knew this trial wasn't just about Moreno's innocence or guilt. It was about a battle of principles, legacy, and the choices that defined them both.

Finally, after weeks of testimony and deliberation, the case was turned over to the jury. As they filed out of the courtroom to begin their deliberations, the fate of Vincent Moreno and the future of Moreno Industries hung in the balance.

It would take days of deliberation, questions raised to the judge by the jurors, discussions about the reasons for the absence of Simon Weinstein and major arguments over testimony and the reliability of certain elements of evidence.

The tension in the courtroom crackled when the jury filed back in, their faces betraying little of their internal deliberations. Vincent Moreno sat at the defense table, his face a mask, as Chandler Wright and his team from Wright and Wright exchanged nervous glances.

"Will the defendant please rise," the judge instructed, his voice cutting through the silence like a knife. Vincent stood; his gaze fixed on the jury as the foreperson rose to deliver the verdict. The air seemed a hush of anticipation as the words hung in the air, each one carrying the weight of Moreno's future.

"We, the jury, find the defendant, Vincent Moreno, not guilty on all counts," the foreperson declared, the words echoing through the courtroom like a thunderclap.

A stunned silence descended over the courtroom as the magnitude of the verdict sank in. Gasps of disbelief filled the air, while Vincent's supporters erupted into cheers and applause, their jubilation spilling out in waves of relief and vindication. The prosecution shook their heads in disbelief.

Chandler Wright and his team struggled to contain their emotions, their faces a mixture of surprise and triumph. They had faced seemingly insurmountable odds, but their unwavering dedication to their client had prevailed in the end.

Outside the courthouse, reporters swarmed around Vincent Moreno, their cameras flashing as they clamored for his reaction to the verdict. But Vincent remained composed, his expression unreadable as he approached the press microphone.

"Justice has prevailed today," he remarked, a smile creasing his face. "God bless America!"

CHAPTER 16

Jake Dyson had been instrumental in getting Vincent Moreno off. This had been a high-profile case and he would be handsomely rewarded for his contribution.

But the victory had come at a cost. Jake had been avoiding his dad in recent weeks to sidestep the inevitable arguments about the case. Buck's disapproval of Jake defending Vincent Moreno and getting him off, continued to be a bone of contention, making every interaction feel like a sparring match Jake didn't want to participate in.

Jake was sitting in his office when the phone rang. It was his mother. "Hi Mom, what going on?" His mother never called him at work. "Is Dad okay? he quickly asked.

There was a long silence on the other end. His mother's voice was barely audible, a whisper, choked back by tears. "Your Dad's been arrested..." Her voice trailed off.

"Arrested for what"? Jake shouted back in disbelief. He knew his dad wouldn't even J-walk let alone commit a crime that would warrant his arrest.

"Where is he?"

Esther could not form a reply.

"I'll take care of it," he breathed into the phone. He hung up and immediately called the Sarasota PD and located his dad.

The trip from downtown Tampa to Sarasota took him an hour. By the time Jake arrived at police headquarters he was seething. He pulled up around the back of the police station parking in a spot reserved for patrol cars and sprinted inside. He spoke to the desk sergeant, who informed him that his dad had been booked on one charge of murder.

"There has been some kind of huge screw up and heads were going to roll," he thought.

Jake found his dad in a small room being interrogated by a couple of homicide detectives.

He interrupted the detectives, mid-sentence. "Dad, do not say another word." He turned to the officers, "I'm Mr. Dyson's attorney. My client is done talking."

Once Jake got his dad alone, he pressed him for details as to what was going on.

"They are trying to pin the 'Highway Murders' on me."

"What murder is this?"

"This all happened when you were a kid…," Buck went on to tell the story.

"How is that possible?"

"The police came down from Pensacola, where one of the murders took place, telling me that they needed my help?"

"For what? What did they want?"

"My log books. They said it would help them in their investigation."

"And you gave the logs to them? Without checking with me? What could you be thinking?"

"I was thinking I was helping the police solve a horrible string of murders. If I was one of the victims, I would want someone to do that for me."

"Didn't you think it was strange that your log books would point to someone else?"

"Never questioned their truthfulness. You know me."

"Yes I do. But Dad, everyone knows cops will say anything..." he didn't finish his thought. What was the point. His dad had been arrested and he had to deal with the here and now.

Under normal circumstances, a murder suspect would be denied bail but Jake was not about to let that stand. It could be months or longer before his case came to trial. He was not going to let his dad languish in jail for a crime he did not commit. He'd pull whatever strings he had to, call in whatever debts were owed. But before he could do that he had several things he had to do. Under Florida law he could not represent a relative without filing for an exemption. He would ask one of the partners at his firm, Wright and Wright to act as interim council. He was off to see Superior Judge Arthur Randall for a hearing to address the issue of representation.

Judge Randell was a no-nonsense man, his reputation built on equal parts legal brilliance and an unflinching dedication to order in his courtroom. A tall, silver-haired figure with sharp, piercing eyes that seemed to read a lawyer's intentions before they could speak, Randell commanded respect the moment he entered a room. His robes, always impeccably pressed, lent an air of formality that matched his precise manner of speech. Known for his sharp wit and occasional flashes of dry humor, he was a judge who valued efficiency but never at the expense of fairness or the law. As Jake sat in his office, Randell leaned forward, placing his arms on the mahogany desk as he spoke.

"I can allow you the role of 'second chair' in your father's defense, with the following understanding; You will not be required to testify as a character witness, you obtain an affidavit of 'advised consent' from the defendant and you make full disclosure to the prosecution."

"Thank you, Your Honor." It would be a week before Jake returned to see Judge Randall. This time it was to address the matter of bail. Jake felt he had done his homework and had a solid case for his petition.

"Your Honor, I am requesting bail in the case of Buck Dyson vs. The State of Florida on the following grounds." He went on to outline his petition.

"There is no true evidence in this case. There are no witnesses to the crime. The evidence is all circumstantial. In my opinion the charge should have never been made. This case is an overreach by an over-zealous district attorney." He went on. "Evidence was gathered through questionable means." After he completed the legal argument he explained that his father had lived in Sarasota for more than fifty years, his church affiliation, his community work, the fact that he has never had even a parking ticket.

"Your Honor, Buck Dyson is not a flight risk and he is certainly not a risk to public safety." When Jake had finished, Judge Randall looked down at the backup documents submitted and then back at Jake.

His response was slow and measured. "Mr. Dyson, I have reviewed your submission thoroughly and I am inclined to agree with the stature of this case." He paused. "But, nonetheless charges have been filed and we need to follow the law. The law says that the judge has discretion in these matters and as I see it your petition has merit. Therefore, bail is set in the amount of..." He stopped there and looked directly at Jake, as if waiting for him to finish with the amount Buck could afford. "I think $100,000 is reasonable under the circumstances."

Jake thanked the judge and with the court order in hand he secured his father's release with the stipulated conditions: he could not leave the area, he needed to surrender his passport, which he did not have, and wear an ankle monitor.

Jake would be 'second chair' in name only. He was clearly in charge of his father's defense. His first order of business was to make a motion for an expedited trial. He would claim the defendant's rights to a speedy trial, stating the age of the crime, the age and health of the defendant. The prosecution had no issue. In their view the case was cut and dry. In fact, they were in a hurry to close this age-old case. The motion was granted and a trial date was set for August 10th.

Buck's investment in Jake's education was about to payoff. Jake would go on the offensive, using every legal maneuver he could to win this case or get it thrown out. His next motion—to dismiss. This is usually a perfunctory move done by every defense attorney but Jake was going to turn this into a prosecution of the prosecution. In his motion he outlined the tactics used by the Pensacola PD to obtain, so called, evidence from Buck. Again, he pointed out the lack of any witnesses to the crime or anything linking Buck directly to the crime or the murder scene. He noted though the circumstantial evidence included Buck Dyson it also included hundreds of other truck drivers and thousands of people. The prosecution's response to Jake's motion came swiftly, a rejection to all of Jake's assertions.

With that, Jake began to prepare for trial. The prosecution's case would consist of mostly expert witnesses and log book entries that put Buck in the area at the time of the crime. The prosecution's star witness was Detective Brad William. He told the court how Buck unwittingly confessed the crime to him, years ago when he hitched a ride with him.

"He told me details that only the killer could know." Brad asserted.

On cross-examination Jake asked, "How do you know that these were facts that only the killer would know when there is no one who can tell what occurred in that house, that night?"

"He knew that the killer always had a meal after the murder and then cleaned up after," Brad shot back.

Jake was prepared for this. He had talked to his mom, the true crime aficionado, and she helped him locate a copy of the True Crime magazine containing the "Highway Murders" article that she had read to Buck on one of their trips together.

He walked over to his table and picked up the magazine and turned it to the marked page. He then walked over to Brad seated on the witness stand. He handed him the magazine.

"Please read the text that is highlighted in yellow."

Brad swallowed hard as he stared at the text, skimming it quickly before reading it.

"It's suspected that the killer took the time to prepare himself a meal and clean up before departing..."

"So, it appears this was public information not information only the killer would know. Is that correct, detective?"

Jake paused for affect and turned to look at the jurors, "No further questions, Your Honor!"

And this is how the prosecution proceeded, with each witness presented being summarily discredited by the defense. The forensic blood analysis fared no better. All they could say was that the blood found on the knife was the same blood type as the victim, AB positive.

"You point out that the blood found on the knife matched the victim's. What percentage of the population has AB positive blood; would you say?"

"About 4% roughly", replied the expert witness.

"So, 4% of the population of the United States are possible subjects." Before the witness could respond Jake provided the answer. "There are approximately 248 million citizens, which mean roughly 9.9 million have type AB blood who could have contributed the blood found on that knife, is that correct?"

"If you're math is accurate, that is correct."

Jake turned to the jury, would it surprise you to find out that I am one of the 9.9 million people and that I handled that knife and I rode in that cab."

"Objection, Your Honor," came a shriek from the prosecution. "May I approach the bench?"

Jake followed the prosecutor to the bench.

"Your Honor, the defense has just made himself a witness in this case. He cannot be council and a witness both. I want those comments stricken from the record and the jury instructed to disregard."

The judge turned to Jake awaiting his response.

"That was not testimony, Your Honor. I was just providing an example." The judge gave Jake a look that said — disingenuous.

"Sustained. The jury will disregard Attorney Dyson's last remarks and have them stricken from the record. Councilor, consider this a warning."

Jake felt okay with the Judge's admonishment. He had gotten his point made an he knew that once jurors heard something they wouldn't just unhear it during deliberations.

The prosecution rested its case and the judge called a recess for the day.

Jake wanted to meet with his client before the defense put on its case in the morning. "Dad, how are you feeling?" Jake asked.

"I feel like all those days on the road are paying off. I wanted to see you kids do better than I did career-wise and today you have made me proud."

"Thanks, Dad, but it's not over yet. We need to put on our case. We need to show the jury who you are so they can see that you could not have done this, no matter how the prosecution tries to portray you otherwise."

Buck sloughed back in his chair, exhausted by the pressure of this ordeal. "I'll be glad when this is over. I never realized how easy it is for the government to step into your life and change everything. Every truth becomes a lie. Every belief about the brotherhood of man comes into question." Buck took a long breath. "In the end who is the bad guy, the criminal who does the crime, the lawful who abuse their position? I guess both equally."

Peter M. Browne

CHAPTER 17

The ceiling fan spun lazily overhead, stirring the humid evening air as Brad Williams sat in his living room, a glass of bourbon untouched on the coffee table before him. His mother, Carla perched on the edge of the armchair across from him, her hands clasped tightly in her lap. She'd been in Pensacola all week, a constant presence in the courtroom, and now she was here, in his home, her expression as fierce and determined as ever.

"You're doing a great job in there, Brad," Carla said, her voice deceptively soft. "I can see the jury leaning toward conviction." Brad blinked, startled by the praise. Carla never handed out compliments unless there was an agenda lurking beneath them. Her words felt unnatural, like a stranger slipping into his mother's skin. What was she angling for? He studied her expression, but her smile gave nothing away.

Brad sighed, leaning back against the couch cushions. "Thanks, Mom. But it's not enough yet. The defense will come out swinging tomorrow, and I don't know if the jury's going to buy what we're selling without something stronger to tie Buck to the murder."

Carla tilted her head, her gaze sharp. "You've got everything you need already. The jury just needs a little nudge, that's all. Something to push them over the edge."

Brad frowned, sensing the direction this conversation was headed. "A nudge?" he repeated. "We're already presenting the facts, Mom. That's what we have to work with — the facts."

Carla leaned forward, her eyes narrowing. "And what if the facts don't tell the whole story? You know Buck's guilty, Brad. Everyone does. You've seen how he carries himself, so meek and mild. Do you really think he doesn't have it in him to commit murder? He's a chameleon, plain and simple."

"Knowing and proving are two different things," Brad said, his voice edged with frustration.

Carla's tone grew more urgent. "You're the arresting officer, Bradley. You're the one standing up for what's right in that courtroom. Sometimes, doing what's right means making sure the truth isn't buried under the technicalities and the lies Buck and his lawyer are spinning."

Brad ran a hand over his face, exhausted. "Mom, I know you want justice, but we have to follow the rules. If we cross the line, it all falls apart. The jury has already heard the evidence we've got. That has to be enough."

Carla stood, pacing the room, her heels clicking against the hardwood floor. "And if it's not? What happens if Buck walks free because the defense twists things just enough to create doubt? What happens to you then, Bradley? To your career? To your reputation? What happens to the victim's family?"

Brad clenched his fists, his thoughts churning. She was voicing the same fears that had been gnawing at him since the trial began. The prosecution's case wasn't solid, it lacked the kind of slam-dunk evidence that could wipe away any doubt.

Carla turned to him, her voice softening but her intensity unrelenting. "You've always done what's right, Bradley. I know that about you. But sometimes, doing what's right means making hard decisions. You have to think about what's at stake here — not only for you, but for everyone who's counting on you to bring Buck to justice."

Brad looked away, staring at the ceiling fan as it spun in endless circles.

"I can't talk about this anymore, Mom," he said finally, his voice barely audible.

Carla regarded him for a moment, then nodded. "Fine. I just wanted you to think about it, that's all."

She grabbed her purse and headed for the door, pausing with her hand on the knob. "You're a good man, Bradley. Don't forget that." There it was "Bradley". She always used his full name to make a point.

When the door clicked shut behind Carla, Brad let out a shaky breath. The silence in the room was thick, broken only by the faint hum of the air conditioner. He picked up the glass of bourbon she had poured for him, swirling the amber liquid before setting it back down, untouched.

Meredith's soft footsteps approached from the stairway. She leaned against the railing, her arms crossed, her expression one of careful concern. "What was that all about?"

Brad exhaled through his nose, running a hand through his hair. "Just mom being mom."

Meredith's eyes narrowed. "That's not an answer. What did she want?"

He hesitated, the weight of Carla's words still pressing on his chest. "She thinks I'm not doing enough to nail Buck," he admitted, his voice low.

Meredith's brow furrowed. She moved closer, crossing the room, taking a seat across from him. "And?"

"And she has this... uncanny way of getting under my skin," Brad said, rubbing his temples. "She keeps pushing, making it sound like I'm just one step away from wrapping this whole thing up if I would just... do more."

Meredith tilted her head. "Do more? What does that even mean?"

Brad avoided her gaze, staring instead at the untouched glass on the table. "It means she's Carla Peterson. She doesn't care how it gets done as long as it gets done."

Meredith's eyes widened slightly, realization dawning. "Brad, no," she said firmly.

"I didn't say anything," he shot back defensively.

"You don't have to." Her voice softened as she reached across to touch his hand. "I know how much this case means to you—how much proving yourself means to you. But not like this."

"Do you think I don't know that?" he snapped, pulling his hand away. He immediately regretted the harshness in his tone. He sighed, his shoulders slumping. "I'm just... stuck, Meredith. There are holes in this case big enough for a truck to drive through, and the defense is going to use every one of them. If Buck walks, everyone's going to look at me like I failed."

Meredith leaned closer; her tone steady but gentle. "It's not about what other people think, Brad. It's about you. If you cross a line now, you'll never come back from it. You know that."

He finally looked at her, his jaw tightening. "You think I don't know how much is riding on this? This isn't just a case, Meredith. It's my reputation, my career on trial. Do you know how that feels?"

She didn't flinch, holding his gaze. "I know how it'll feel if you win the wrong way. And I know how it'll change you."

Brad swallowed hard, the lump in his throat making it hard to respond. He stood, walking to the window. The night stretched out beyond the glass, quiet and indifferent to the storm raging inside him.

"I just... I need to think," he muttered.

Meredith stood too, but she didn't approach him. "Think all you want, Brad. But don't forget who you are." She lingered for a moment before heading down the hall, leaving him alone with his thoughts.

As the hours ticked by, Brad sat in the dimly lit room, the weight of Carla's words, Meredith's warnings, and his own gnawing doubts pressing down like a physical force. The crime scene photos flashed in his mind, the gaps in the evidence taunting him. He clenched his fists, staring at the glass of bourbon but never drinking it.

For a moment, the room seemed to close in on him, the silence broken only by the rain pelting the window. What if this guy is innocent? The thought cut through his resolve like a blade, unbidden and unwelcome. His pulse quickened as he tried to push it aside. Buck

Dyson was no saint, and the circumstantial evidence painted a damning picture. But doubts lingered, stubborn and persistent.

He shook his head, muttering under his breath. "Innocent men don't end up at the center of investigations like this." Still, the thought gnawed at him, refusing to let go. Was it really justice he was after, or was it simply the win? The career-defining moment that could cement his name in the legal world?

Brad leaned forward, burying his face in his hands. If Buck Dyson didn't do it, someone else did. But who? The question echoed in his mind, unanswered, as the clock ticked toward mid-night.

The next morning, Brad arrived at court, his expression unreadable, his movements calm and collected. As the trial resumed and the defense began their case, one nagging question hung in the air: What was Brad prepared to do?

Carla Peterson sat in the gallery, as she had throughout the trial. She was dressed in a sharp navy suit that exuded an air of understated authority. Her presence was impossible to ignore; she radiated a quiet intensity as her gaze remained fixed on the jury box. To the casual observer, she was merely there to support her son, Detective Brad Williams, but her real purpose was far more deliberate.

The defense's case would consist mostly of a long list of character witnesses except for one forensic expert to challenge the blood evidence found on the knife confiscated from Buck's truck. Buck himself would take the stand — a bold move, but one Jake Dyson believed was essential.

As the pastor from Buck's church, his lodge master, and several neighbors testified to Buck's good nature, Carla's irritation grew. Each glowing account chipped away at the prosecution's narrative. The jurors were shifting, their initial belief in his guilt, softening.

Then came Esther Dyson, Buck's wife, whose testimony was a calm yet devastating affirmation of her husband's innocence. Esther spoke of her interest in true crime and crime fiction, recalling how she and Buck had discussed the Highway Murders on long drives.

"Buck took a real interest in the Highway Murders because he spent so much time on the road. He mentioned the fact that he could have met the killer at one of the truck stops, even talked to him perhaps. 'How could you tell a killer from the rest of the truckers?' he asked. I told him I thought he would be able to tell. The person would have to have cold eyes, be mean-spirited, and have an ungodly appearance. He just smiled and said, 'Some people are like the one-eyed jack. You never see the other side of their face, and when you do, it may well be too late.'"

Jake asked gently, "How do you recall this incident so clearly after all these years?"

Esther straightened in her seat. "Life's made up of thousands, I guess millions, of events. Some stick with you while others don't. There was just something haunting about this murder." She paused, looking at the jurors, the judge, and then over at Buck at the defense table. "But I never thought it would bring us here."

The prosecutor seized the opportunity to undermine her credibility. "Mrs. Dyson, has your husband ever had a violent streak? Have you ever experienced any domestic violence?"

"No, never," Esther replied firmly, her disdain for the question evident in her tone.

"Before Buck went into the service, he liked to hunt and fish, correct?"

"Yes, but when he came back, he no longer had any interest in those sports. He said he'd seen enough killing to last a lifetime."

Esther was a rock. The prosecutor couldn't shake her testimony. She simply told the truth: Buck was a good and honest man.

Carla watched the jurors closely as the court broke for lunch. They seemed to lean toward the defense. She tightened her grip on the silver locket she wore, her focus sharpening.

When they returned, Buck took the stand.

He repeated Esther's story about how he came to be aware of the Highway Murders. "I often heard this phrase but never believed it to be true until now: 'No good deed goes unpunished.' I offered a stranger a ride out of Christian kindness, and he—turned out to be a liar and a scoundrel."

His eyes scanned the courtroom, landing on Brad. Buck's stare lingered, a cold, deliberate challenge.

"He lied to me that day," Buck continued, "told me he was heading to Pearson's Point, a place new to him. That reminded me of the true crime story where one of the murders took place on the outskirts of town. For reasons unknown, I started telling the story that Esther had read to me. I misspoke and called it crime fiction, but he corrected me, already knowing the tale I was telling but never letting on. Years later, he would appear again in my life, telling falsehoods, gaining my confidence, and when asked, denying we'd ever met."

Jake's calm questioning painted Buck as sincere and forthright, but Carla wasn't convinced.

She closed her eyes for a fleeting moment, her whispered thoughts cutting through the courtroom's tension like a blade.

Can't you see it? He's practiced this story a thousand times. He's manipulating you. Look at him. Feel the lie. You know he's guilty.

Juror number five, the young woman with glasses, shifted uncomfortably, glancing at the floor. Juror number three, the balding man, frowned slightly, as though doubting his own conclusions. Carla opened her eyes, satisfied.

When the prosecutor cross-examined Buck, the tension in the room thickened.

"I want to ask you about your time in the military. Isn't it true you were in Special Forces?"

"Yes."

"Did you have occasion to kill enemy combatants?"

"Yes."

"Can you tell us approximately how many?"

"I don't know."

"Take a guess."

Jake jumped up. "Objection, Your Honor. Asked and answered."

"Sustained. Councilor, move on," ordered the judge.

"Did you enjoy killing people?"

"Objection, Your Honor. Badgering the witness," Jake interjected.

"Sustained."

The prosecutor narrowed his eyes. "I want the jury to know that Mr. Dyson is a trained killer who has killed many people during his time in the service."

"Objection, Your Honor. Prejudicial and beyond the scope of direct."

"Sustained. The jury will disregard this question, and it will be stricken from the record," the judge admonished. "Councilor, move on."

The prosecutor glanced at Jake; his expression sharp. The unspoken message was clear: *Two can play at this game.*

"No further questions, Your Honor."

As the court adjourned for the day, Carla lingered in the gallery, her thoughts churning. She thought she had done what Brad couldn't, ensured Buck Dyson's conviction.

But as she walked to her car, a strange unease crept over her. Her whispered voice had been so sure, so resolute, yet now it faltered in the quiet of her mind.

What if you're wrong?

CHAPTER 18

Wilbur grabbed his backpack that was sitting on the floor next to the entrance. He stood by the door giving the place the once over. He didn't know how long he would be gone.

Wilbur was in his late sixties, his wiry frame and weathered face marking him as a man who had spent a lifetime on the road and under the sun. His skin was a leathery tan, etched with lines that hinted at hard work, hard living, and plenty of time to think about both. A thick salt-and-pepper beard covered most of his face, hiding a mouth that rarely smiled, and his steel-gray eyes held a quiet intensity. They were the eyes of a man who observed everything and trusted little. He wore a faded trucker cap that shaded his face, and his usual attire was a plaid shirt worn thin at the elbows, a pair of scuffed jeans, and boots that had walked more truck stop parking lots than he could remember.

Wilbur had the deliberate movements of someone who didn't waste energy on unnecessary gestures. Life had taught him to conserve his strength, whether it was for the long haul on the road or the unexpected curveballs that seemed to come his way. He wasn't a man who scared easily, but there was something restless about him lately, an unease that showed in the way his hands tightened around his coffee mug or in the way his steel-gray eyes would linger too long on nothing in particular.

"Junior," he called to his German Shepherd lounging on the couch. "Come. It's time to go."

Junior was Wilbur's one constant in his life. Wilbur had named all his previous dogs Wilbur Junior, as well, for reasons only he knew. His choice of name, always got a raised eyebrow or a chuckle from the few people he interacted with, but Wilbur didn't care. Junior was loyal, sharp, and always by his side, whether he was sitting on the couch, roaming the trailer park, or riding shotgun in Wilbur's rig.

His single-wide trailer at the Willow Grove RV Park was his sanctuary—a worn-down space that reflected his modest way of living. The siding was rust-streaked, and the roof leaked during heavy rains, but Wilbur didn't care much about appearances. Inside, the trailer was sparsely furnished, with mismatched chairs and an old couch that Junior, his German Shepherd, had claimed as his own. The place smelled of motor oil, dog hair, and something faintly burnt—Wilbur's attempt at cooking. He wasn't one for decorating; a couple of trucker plaques hung on the wall alongside a faded and out dated calendar from Moore's Auto Transport.

He knew many of his neighbors but he rarely spoke to anyone, except for Cindy, whose trailer was on the adjacent lot. Wilbur was pretty much a hermit, though he exchanged occasional nods or grunts, but rarely more, with neighbors in passing. The exception was Cindy, who had watched Junior for him a few times.

Cindy was a physical wreck, but she was dependable in her own way. Wilbur didn't judge her for her disheveled hair, missing teeth, or the stale smell of liquor that clung to her. He figured everyone had their baggage, and hers was just easier to spot.

He stepped down off the landing, with Junior following close behind. He walked around to Cindy's door and rapped on it gently.

"Cindy, are you in there?' When he got no response, he poked his head in and yelled, "Cindy, it's Wilbur. It's only me, you can come out." She poked her head around the curtain separating the bedroom from the rest of the trailer. Cindy was in her fifty's but the years had not been kind. She appeared twenty years older and worse for wear. Her hair was unkept, her smile toothless and she wore the smell of alcohol like it was perfume.

Wilbur yelled to her, "I need you to watch Junior for a few days. I gotta go outa town on business. His food is in the kitchen. The door's open."

Wilbur stepped inside and dropped some cash on the table. He looked down the short hallway. "Left you some money for your troubles and I'll have more for you when I get back."

Junior had stayed with Cindy before and had already made himself comfortable on the sofa.

As Wilbur closed the door to Cindy's trailer, she shuffled over to the table where he had left the cash. Picking it up, she counted the bills slowly, her fingers trembling slightly. It was several hundred dollars. Cindy's brow furrowed as she stared at the fist-full of bills. Wilbur had always been generous when it came to Junior, but this was beyond extravagant, especially for a few days of dog-sitting.

She glanced toward the door, as though expecting him to come back and explain, but the sound of his boots on the gravel outside was already fading. Cindy shrugged, slipping the money into her pocket with a crooked smile. She wasn't about to look a gift horse in the mouth — money was money, and she needed it.

But as she sat on the edge of the couch, idly scratching Junior behind the ears, a niggling thought crept into her mind. Why leave so much? Wilbur had only said he'd be gone a few days. A man like him couldn't afford to waste money. She dismissed the thought as quickly as it came, chalking it up to Wilbur being his usual odd self. After all, the guy named his dog after himself — who could figure him out?

Still, as she glanced around her dingy trailer, with Junior sprawled contentedly on the cushions, the faintest twinge of unease lingered in the back of her mind. She stepped to the window pulling aside the yellowed curtain and saw Wilbur removing his backpack from his shoulder as he reached his truck, a 1972 Ford pickup. He threw it on the passenger seat and climbed aboard.

Wilbur was headed to Pensacola. He had heard on the news about the capture of the Highway Murderer. He was following the case and he wanted to be there for the trial.

Wilbur had worked for Moore's Auto Transport. They were based in Jacksonville and had a fleet of twenty-five car carriers. Their business involved picking up foreign cars at their POE (port of entry) and delivering them to dealers across the country. His territory was Florida, south and west, as far as Texas, and states in between. Wilbur drove for them for 35 years before retiring on Social Security and a small pension. Wilbur was a loner. He had always been. He preferred his solitude, which made long-haul truck driving the perfect job for him. It kept people at a distance. He did much better with animals. Wilbur Junior was his third German Shepherd. They had all been named Wilbur Junior.

The first time he had asked Cindy to watch Junior, he had told her his name.

"That's a strange name for a dog, isn't it?" Wilbur told her that the dog's name was Wilbur but he called him Junior to avoid confusion. She had no idea what that meant, but she let it go. She had already figured out that Wilbur was an odd duck.

Wilbur met Buck Dyson, many years ago, the way most truckers meet, on the CB radio. The CB radio was a trucker's life line for communications, on the road. Truckers would alert each other when they passed a trooper hiding out trying to nab speeders.

"Breaker, breaker, Smoky at mile marker 185 westbound," would crease the silence, alerting truckers headed that way. The CB radio was also used as a means to kill time and alleviate the boredom and to obtain traffic information.

Drivers who frequented certain routes would look for each other en route, "Breaker-19, this is Junior-K," that was Wilbur's "handle". "Hey Buckeroo, are you out there good buddy?" That was Buck Dyson's handle. Once they connected they would switch to a clear channel and chat about the weather, food at the truck stop, the price of diesel, or whatever struck their fancy. The CB radio was the next best thing to picking up a hitchhiker, if you wanted company.

There were a couple of other truckers that ran I-10 regularly, George Alves, his handle was the "Ice Man". He drove a refrigerated truck delivering meat and produce to grocery chains along the way. Bobby Jones was known on the air as, "Postmaster-J". He worked for the USPS delivering mail between depots in Ocala and Galveston. On rare occasions they might encounter one or another, in person, at one of the many truck stops.

Wilbur was on I-10 headed west. As the mile markers passed his windshield, he thought about the last time he actually saw Buck. Traffic had been backed up on I-10 westbound. There had been an accident around mile marker 160. Some car veered from the passing lane into the travel lane sideswiping another vehicle sending one into the median, the other rolling over several times. Wilbur had been at least a few miles back when traffic came to a standstill. He turned up his CB radio to find out what was going on, when he heard Buckeroo talking to someone about the accident.

"Breaker-19, Buckeroo, this is Junior-K, go to 25 over." When Buck came on channel 25, he filled Wilbur in about the accident, letting him know they were going to be a while.

They agreed to meet up at the Love's truck stop at mile marker 7, just outside of Pearson's Point. That was just about five miles from the scene of the Marston murder.

Wilbur was jolted out of his reverie by an air horn from the 18-wheeler behind him. He found himself in the passing lane holding up traffic. "Old people shouldn't be allowed to drive," he thought. He used to be able to drive for hours without daydreaming.

He decided he should pull off at the next exit and get a cup of coffee. He only had another 50-60 miles to go but he was in no hurry, court wasn't until 9 AM tomorrow.

When Wilbur got to the court house the next morning, the prosecution had Brad Williams on the witness stand. He was walking him through exhibit 117. It was a map of interstate 10 showing pertinent mile markers and landmarks.

"This is the weigh station at mile marker 154, outside of Grand Ridge, Florida, correct?

"Yes."

"And what time does Buck's log show he arrived there?" the prosecutor asked.

"Six-forty-five PM."

"He next logged in at the Love's Truck Stop outside Pearson's Point at what time?"

"One hour and twenty minutes later, at eight-0-five, which means he was traveling the speed limit."

"And what is his next entry in his log?"

"He logged in at the Alabama weigh station, some 59 miles away, the next morning at 8:16 AM. Given he again was driving at the speed limit, he would have exited Florida around 7 AM."

"So according to his own records, Buck Dyson was in the area of the crime for at least eleven hours, is that correct?"

"Yes, that is correct."

When the prosecutor passed the witness, Jake jumped right on the obvious.

Jake approached the witness, his question loaded with sarcasm, "When do you normally sleep, Detective?"

"What does that have to do with anything?" Brad asked, looking at the judge for help.

"You're right. The question was rhetorical. Most of us sleep during the hours you noted that Mr. Dyson was immobile. It proves absolutely nothing, except that he like many other truckers slept in their cabs at Love's Truck Stop that evening."

"Objection, Your Honor. Is Mr. Dyson making a speech or asking a question, of the witness?"

"Mr. Dyson," the judge admonished.

"No further questions, Your Honor."

Wilbur was in the courtroom for the forensic testimony, when the defense paraded the army of character witnesses and for the summations to the jury. When the case was given to the jury for deliberation Wilbur was certain Buck would be found not guilty. Wilbur thought, "If it had weight, the reasonable doubt in the prosecution's case would have been measured in tons."

The jury deliberated over the weekend and for the next three days. On their initial vote, the split was stark: six guilty, six not guilty.

Carla Peterson was already feeling restless. From her perch in the gallery during the trial, she had done what she could to sway the jurors with her whispered influence. But now, sealed away in the deliberation room, they were beyond her direct reach. The waiting gnawed at her.

After five days, the foreman sent a note to the judge indicating they were deadlocked.

The judge instructed the jurors. "I am sending you back to deliberate. You have a moral obligation to try to reach a verdict."

Carla's nails dug into her palms as she listened. *A moral obligation? What about justice? Buck Dyson is guilty. He can't just walk away.*

She had tried influencing Brad, tried steering things in court with her whispers, but it wasn't enough. The jury had stalled. They need a push, she thought, a flicker of determination lighting in her chest.

Carla stayed behind, loitering in the lobby. She had no concrete plan—just a feeling, an intuition that she could do something to tilt the scales.

The building was quiet except for the occasional creak of floorboards and the echo of voices from distant offices. She searched the corridors looking for the jury room. As she turned the corner she saw the bailiff standing guard outside the room, his chair leaning back against the wall as he flipped through the pages of a paperback.

Carla took a deep breath and approached him, adopting a look of distress.

"Excuse me. I'm lost," she said, her voice almost a whisper, her steps unsteady. "I'm feeling a little faint."

The bailiff immediately stood up, concern flashing across his face. "Ma'am? Are you all right?"

"I—I don't know," Carla stammered, clutching the wall for support. "Everything's spinning."

"Hold on. Here, take my seat. Let me get you some water," he said, already moving toward the nearby office for help.

The moment he disappeared down the corridor, Carla sprang into action. She pressed her ear to the jury room door but could hear nothing through the thick wood. Her pulse quickened. There wasn't time to waste. She closed her eyes, focusing her energy, and pressed both hands against the door.

Her whispered words were inaudible, even to herself, but they carried an unmistakable force. As she pressed her hands against the wood, a faint warmth spread through her palms, growing into a prickling heat. Her pulse quickened, and for a brief moment, the world around her seemed to blur at the edges. *You're tired. You want to go home. He's guilty. You know it's true. You need to end this.* The thoughts projected outward, weaving their way through the wooden door filling the jury room.

She could feel the pull of her own energy, the way it ebbed and flowed as she focused her intent. *Come to the right decision. End this now.*

At the sound of footsteps, Carla snapped her eyes open and pulled back from the door, stumbling back into the chair to keep up the act as the bailiff returned with a bottle of water.

"Here you go, Ma'am," he said, handing it to her. "You should stay seated. Do you need me to call someone?"

"No, no," Carla said, shaking her head as she took the bottle. "I just need a moment. I'm partial to these dizzy spells" She smiled weakly, her face pale but convincing. "Thank you. You've been so kind."

The bailiff hesitated, clearly unsure whether to go for help, but Carla waved him off. "I'll be fine. Please, don't trouble yourself."

After a respectable period, Carla got up, thanked the bailiff and cast one last glance at the jury room door. A faint smile tugged at the corners of her mouth.

Inside, the deliberation room was a battlefield. Both sides were entrenched in their positions, and tension simmered with each passing hour.

A petite woman in her early fifties, who had taken copious notes during the trial, leaned forward, jabbing her finger at the table. "Look, he wouldn't have been charged if he wasn't guilty. They must have something on him. Did you see him? Sitting there like a statue during most of the testimony? He looked guilty."

The foreman groaned, rubbing his temples. "What kind of statement is that? We're supposed to be going on the evidence, not what the defendant looks like."

Another juror, a man with graying hair and a tired expression, chimed in. "What evidence? It's all circumstantial."

"That doesn't make him innocent."

"It doesn't make him guilty, either."

"What about reasonable doubt?" a younger juror added, her voice weary but resolute.

This back-and-forth had been going on for days. The jurors were worn out, their tempers fraying. They wanted to go home to their families, get back to their lives. Guilt or innocence seemed to matter less with every passing hour.

The tide began to shift. The petite woman who had been adamant about Buck's guilt sat a little taller. "I just keep coming back to this: why would the police arrest him if they didn't believe he was the guy? And what about the knife? The blood? That doesn't just appear out of nowhere."

The younger juror who had argued for reasonable doubt frowned. "But the defense poked holes in all that. The forensic expert said the blood evidence wasn't conclusive."

The petite woman shook her head. "Conclusive or not, it's enough for me. If he's innocent, why does everything keep pointing back to him? The knife. The truck. The timing. It all adds up. It's like the pieces of a puzzle—you can't ignore them."

The foreman, who had been leaning toward not guilty, hesitated. He glanced around the table, noting the weary expressions of his fellow jurors.

One by one, the others began to waver. The arguments that had seemed convincing just days before now felt hollow. Doubt gave way to exhaustion, and exhaustion gave way to consensus.

By day seven, they had reached a unanimous decision. The foreman sent a message to the bailiff, and the room emptied of tension.

While the jury had been deliberating, Wilbur had taken up residence at the Hotel Motel right off of I-10. One evening he decided to drive to the Love's Truck Stop. He had a yearning to see all the big rigs lined up and smell the diesel fuel. He drove up, parked around the side and entered through the rear door, went to the counter and ordered a ham and cheese sandwich and something to drink. He found a seat in the corner and watched truckers: as they came and went, as they sat in small groups talking and laughing, as they quickly ate their meals.

All these people were busy, living their lives. He felt a tinge of envy or more accurately a wave of jealousy. He thought about his childhood, reflected on the sea of events that had brought him to this place, this evening.

He had grown up in Jacksonville and had lived there most of his life. His parents, like so many poor families, struggled to make ends meet. His father, Wilbur Sr., had been a longshoreman, working at the same pier where he loaded vehicles destined for dealerships across the South. The hours were long, the work was grueling, and the pay was meager. Over time, his father became an angry man, directing his frustration at his wife and son—soft targets for his mounting rage. Alcohol became his escape, the salve to numb the pain of his daily grind. He blamed everyone for his lot in life—his employer, the government, neighbors, even family—and he unleashed the full force of that resentment on young Wilbur Jr.

He hated his father and hated his mother for not standing up for him. Hate became a way of life. He left home as soon as he could and joined the service. That is where he began driving trucks like the Chevrolet G-506 ½ ton 4x4. The social aspect of being around others in the barracks made him uncomfortable and he ended up almost going AWOL but he hung in long enough to get an honorable discharge. He had dropped out of high school, which kept him from getting many jobs. Moore's Auto Transport hired him on a trial basis. Being on the road away from other people seemed to agree with him. He did a good job and remained employed with Moore until he retired.

Wilbur was snapped out of his reverie when the busboy asked if he could clear his table.

"Yeah, oh, sorry, sure go ahead', he stammered.

He looked around. "What am I doing here? Why did I come to see this trial?" he thought. But he knew why. Buck had been the closest thing he had to a friend and he knew that Buck was getting a raw deal.

He arrived at the courthouse bright and early the next morning, the air thick with expectation. The word had already spread: the jury had reached a verdict. The halls buzzed with whispers, reporters hovered near the entrance, and the weight of the moment seemed to press down on everyone. When the courtroom doors opened, Wilbur slipped into a seat in the far corner at the back, his heart pounding in his chest.

The murmur of the crowd ceased as the clerk called the court to order.

"All rise," the bailiff commanded, his voice cutting through the stillness.

Judge Arthur Randall entered, his expression grave, and took his seat at the bench. "You may be seated," he said, his voice steady but devoid of warmth. "Has the jury reached a verdict?"

The foreman, an older man with a balding head and nervous hands, stood. He cleared his throat and spoke. "We have, Your Honor."

Wilbur watched every movement with hawk-like intensity as the foreman handed the folded verdict form to the bailiff. The silence in the room was oppressive, broken only by the soft shuffle of footsteps as the bailiff carried the paper to the judge. Wilbur shifted in his seat, his breath shallow, his hands gripping the edge of the bench.

The judge unfolded the paper, adjusting his glasses. His face betrayed no emotion as his eyes scanned the words. He handed the verdict form back to the bailiff, who now turned toward the jury box.

"Will the defendant please rise," the bailiff intoned, his voice steady, formal.

Buck Dyson stood slowly, his face pale but composed, his lawyer Jake Dyson rising beside him.

Wilbur could see the tension in Buck's shoulders, the way his hands clenched into fists at his sides.

The bailiff addressed the jury. "Ladies and gentlemen of the jury, in this entitled action, how do you find the defendant? Guilty or not guilty?"

In that moment the silence was deafening. For a moment, no one moved. The courtroom held its breath, the foreman clutching the verdict slip with trembling fingers.

Buck felt the air grow thick around him, the sound of his heartbeat drowning out the present. He stared at the bench, unseeing, his mind pulling him elsewhere.

The highway stretched out ahead of him, bathed in the soft golden light of late morning. It was a familiar rhythm—engine humming, wheels gliding over asphalt, radio crackling with static. Picking up hitchhikers had always been Buck's way of breaking up the solitude, adding some variety to the long hours on the road. Most didn't talk much beyond a polite "thanks" or "where're you headed?" And when they didn't talk, he would make an effort to draw them out.

Brad Williams, he'd said his name was—was sitting in the passenger seat with his backpack wedged between his knees, the sign reading "Pearson's Point" now folded in his lap. Brad had been wiry, quiet at first, his low-slung baseball cap shielding his eyes. Brad wasn't saying much so Buck decided to take the lead.

For no good reason, he could remember, Buck found himself telling Brad a story. He hadn't planned to, hadn't even thought about it in years, but it spilled out all the same—a tale Esther had read aloud from one of her true crime novels.

"The Highway Killer," Buck had said, letting the name settle between them. "Ever hear about him?"

Brad had stiffened slightly. Buck caught the movement from the corner of his eye but brushed it off, launching into the story with too much eagerness. He'd described how the killer prowled quiet, isolated homes near highways, pretending to pull off the road for a break and making things look like a normal rest stop. How he used the cover of night to slip into homes undetected, leaving carnage in his wake.

He and Esther had discussed the story, calling it "unreal." Buck had been fascinated by the killer's cunning—enough that he told the story now, as if it were his own memory. He even added details, offering how it might have played out.

When he finally trailed off, the cab had gone silent except for the soft hum of the engine. Then Brad had turned to him, his expression unreadable. "You sure know a lot about this guy," he'd said, his voice flat.

Buck had laughed, an uneasy sound in the close quarters. "Ah, it's just a story, kid. My wife's into crime stories."

But Brad hadn't looked convinced. And now, sitting in this courtroom years later, Buck realized his mistakes. If he hadn't picked Brad up that day... If he hadn't shared that stupid story, trying to pass the time... If he'd noticed how Brad seemed to know more than a hitchhiker should about the Highway Killer.

If not for any of those errors in judgment, he wouldn't be here right now. What had he been thinking... A harmless story to pass the time... No good deed goes unpunished!

The weight of it pressed against his chest like a heavy stone.

The foreman hesitated, visibly uncomfortable. His hands trembled as he adjusted his posture, as Buck snapped back to the present, his body rigid with tension.

The foreman averted looking at Buck and then he spoke, in a weak unconvincing voice. "We find the defendant, guilty of murder in the first degree."

Buck slumped down in his seat an expression of incredulity on his face. Jake placed a comforting arm on Buck's shoulder and lowered himself into the adjacent chair, speaking softly into Buck's ear.

In the rear of the courtroom Wilbur was no less shocked, but not surprised. From his years of experience in his encounters with authorities he felt they rarely got things right.

Buck was immediately remanded into custody, the bailiff stepping forward to handcuff him and lead him away.

Esther and Lily were seated behind the defense table. They burst into tears. Esther reached for Buck as he was led out of the courtroom.

Esther, turned to Jake, the question of what just happened on her face.

"Mom, don't worry. This verdict will not stand. I will make sure of it. I'll get dad home. It may take some time but I will do it. I promise!"

Esther and Lily joined together in a sorrowful embrace slowly walking up the long aisle to the exit.

When the verdict was read aloud — "Guilty" — Carla felt a rush of triumph, tinged with a faint sense of unease. Her work here was done.

But as she watched Buck Dyson's shoulders slump and his wife Esther collapse into sobs, something in her chest tightened. *Was this justice? Or something else?*

For a fleeting moment, she wondered what might have happened if she'd let the jury decide on their own. But the thought passed quickly, replaced by her certainty that she had done what was necessary.

Wilbur sat quietly, watching the spectators stroll out. Then he saw the two weeping women walking arm-in-arm and assumed it was Buck's wife and daughter. He wanted to say something to them but thought better of it.

Jake was at the defense table putting the last of his papers into his briefcase when Wilbur approached.

"Excuse me," he said to Jake, who looked up in surprise.

Reflexively, Jake asked, "Can I help you?"

"Yes, I need an attorney."

"You need to call our office," He reached into his pocket and pull out a business card.

"Please, let me explain," Wilbur persisted.

"Look," Jake responded abruptly, "I'm busy right now. My client was just wrongly convicted of murder."

"I can help you with that."

Jake looked at the person standing in front of him, elderly, somewhat disheveled and obviously not capable of helping him. Jake gave Wilbur a look that said, "I don't have time for this."

Jake made a move to push past Wilbur, when Wilbur grabbed him by the arm with a powerful grip. Before Jake could respond to his restraint Wilbur blurted out, "I'm the killer. I'm the man they want not your father."

Jake stopped dead in his tracks. He had experienced these kooks before, who confess to crimes they didn't commit looking for attention.

"Hear me out," Wilbur said forcefully, at the same time releasing his grip of Jake's arm.

"Look pal, I've got no time for this!"

"Buck and I go way back. You tell him Junior-K spoke to you. I'll be at the Hotel Motel on I-10 until 4 PM, and then I'm headed home." Wilbur turned and walked out of the courtroom.

Jake picked up his briefcase and ran back to the holding area to see if he could catch Buck before he was transported to the county jail. He was too late. Jake sprinted to his car. It was less than five miles to the Escambia County Jail on Pace Boulevard. As he approached he saw the sheriff's van entering the gate. He knew that he would not be able to see his father until he had been processed, so he parked his car and walked to the visitor's entrance.

Nothing the government does happens quickly. It was two hours later before he was able to sit down with his dad.

He didn't know how to broach the subject so he just jumped right in. "Dad, do you know a guy that goes by the name of Junior-K?"

Buck, was lost. The shock of being incarcerated had overwhelmed his senses. "What are you talking about, Son?"

"Some guy came up to me after the trial, said his name was Junior-K and that you went back a long way. Does that ring any bells?"

Buck was not thinking about CB handles and couldn't come up with anybody. Buck shrugged his shoulders.

"He told me he was the killer." Jake just let that hang out there.

"What did he look like?" Buck asked.

Jake went on to describe him, his appearance and manner.

"Oh, my God! Wilbur Knapp Jr. You have got to be kidding me. He was there that night! At Love's Truck Stop. He was in a real funk that night. His dog, Junior had died a couple days earlier." Buck looked up at Jake. "He actually said he was the killer? What do we do?"

Jake jumped up from the table. "Dad, gotta go! I'll be back soon."

Jake rushed down the hallway toward the exit, careful not to move too quickly, raising the concern of the guards always on alert for any unusual activity. Running in the corridors of the jailhouse, not a good thing.

When he exited the facility, he picked up his pace, making a mad dash for his car. Wilbur told him that he would be at the motel until 4 PM. It was now 3:43. He had seventeen minutes to get across town, in rush hour traffic.

Jake exited the county jail onto Pace Boulevard headed east. The lights were not in his favor. He arrived at I-10 at 4:01. He took the causeway paralleling the highway to the entrance of the motel. It was 4:08. At the front desk he asked for Wilbur Knapp's room.

"Sorry sir, he checked out this morning."

"Do you have a lounge or restaurant in here?

"No sir, but there's a couple of fast-food joints across the way."

Jake scoured the area but there was no sign of Wilbur. He could have called his buddies at the Pensacola PD and had them put out a BOLO (Be On the Look Out), but he didn't know what Wilbur was driving.

He needed to go back to visit his dad and find out where Wilbur lived, if he knew.

He hated leaving his dad in jail overnight, but there were going to be many more days in jail if he didn't get this conviction overturned.

Wilbur had parked outside the Hotel Motel until 4 PM at which point he decided to head for home. It was a good five-hour drive. As he was pulling out of the motel parking lot he scanned the area for any cars pulling in. He saw none. Frustrated he took the causeway to the entrance of I-10 East. He was headed home. He didn't know what else to do. He thought about going to the police and telling them his story but he had been around long enough to know that just getting a conviction, they were going to blow off anyone coming in with a confession as just a crackpot looking for publicity. He considered the newspaper but even if they believed him and printed his story, the police, again, weren't likely to reopen their investigation.

He was approaching the Love's Truck Stop exit when he made a snap decision. He had to turn sharply to make the exit ramp nearly causing an accident.

"Sorry!," he muttered under his breath, as he swerved back to stay on the ramp. He pulled up to the building near the payphone booths and got out.

He decided to see if he could find Buck Dyson's phone number in Sarasota and talk to his wife.

Information was able to locate a Buck and Esther Dyson. As the phone was ringing Wilbur was nervously tapping the glass.

The phone rang multiple times with no answer. Wilbur looked at his watch and realized that they had been at the trial this morning and could not have made it back to Sarasota and probably might even still be in Pensacola.

He decided to try several of the hotels close to the courthouse. He went inside the Love's store and got a bunch of change and started calling hotels in the downtown area. The Hilton had a couple of Dysons registered. The first room he called; he got no answer. When he got back to the hotel operator he requested the second room.

"Hello," came a voice on the other end of the line.

Wilbur stammered, "Er, Hello ma'am, my name is Wilbur Knapp." He paused, not sure how to broach the subject. "I am a friend of Buck Dyson and I have information about his case. Are you his wife, Esther?"

"Yes, this is Esther. How do you know Buck?" she enquired doubtful of the veracity of the caller.

"We go way back we were truckers together. He brought me a new German Shepherd puppy when my dog died."

"Esther knew about the time that Buck drove all the way to Jacksonville, to bring a puppy to a guy he knew. "That was Buck," she thought. "You're William, no Wilbur, am I right?"

"Yes, ma'am. I can help Buck. If you can get his attorney to call me. Tell him that I am going back to the Hotel Motel." He stopped to allow Esther to process the information.

"How can you help?" Esther asked.

Wilbur did not want to disclose to Esther that he was the killer and the cause for all of Buck's troubles.

"I know who killed all of those people and I have proof. Please have him call me."

Wilbur returned to the Hotel Motel and was assigned room number 110. He went across the way and picked up something to eat, a burger, fries and a root beer and headed back to his room. As he approached the door he could hear the phone ringing. He fumbled with his key, juggling his drink and food bag trying to get the door open. By the time he got to the phone the last ring was fading.

"Hello, hello," he shouted into the receiver but was only greeted with a dial-tone.

Wilbur decided not to panic. They would call back. He sat down at the little table and tore open the bag containing his sandwich and fries. He grabbed the remote and turned on the TV. The news was on every channel and they were all covering the trial, blow by blow. He turned off the TV and focused on his dinner.

About a half hour later, as Wilbur was about to doze off, slumped in the arm chair he was brought back by a knock on the door. Shaking off the veil of sleep he rose and walked to the door. Before he could open it, the knocking was repeated.

He opened the door cautiously and recognized Jake.

"Come in," Wilbur offered. "I thought you'd call but meeting in person is much better." He looked around.

"There's not much space in here but have a seat," he said pointing to the chair he'd just been sleeping in.

Jake nodded, and as he approached the seat, he introduced himself. "I'm Jake Dyson. Buck is my father and I am also his attorney."

"I assume you have spoken to Buck about me."

"Yes I have and I want to apologize for not hearing you out earlier today, but I hope you can understand my suspicion by your unexpected confession."

"Understood," Wilbur replied.

CHAPTER 19

Jake assured Wilbur that he had come to listen, without judgement.

"Before I begin, there is one thing I would like to ask of you. Whether you answer yes or no, I will still give you my full confession." Jake waited in silence.

"I'd like for you to represent me. I have no money and no means to retain a lawyer. I know I could get a public defender but I'd like to have someone I can trust."

Jake looked at Wilbur, "Give me a dollar." Wilbur did not ask any questions. He reached into his wallet and handed Jake a dollar bill.

"There, you have retained me. I am your lawyer," he said smiling.

"I have known Buck for many years. We initially met on the CB radio. Over time we would share many hours over a cup of coffee or a baloney sandwich. We'd come as close as truckers on the road can be.

"I'm sure you know he's the kind of guy that would give you the shirt off his back.

"The only one I felt closer to was Junior. Junior was my first German Shepherd. I had him for fourteen years. He died from old age. Buck knew about him because he used to ride with me. When I told him, Junior had passed, he saw the look in my eyes, but he only said he was sorry. That next week he called me, and told me he had something for me. He wouldn't say what it was. He drove 250 miles from Sarasota to Jacksonville to bring me a puppy. Can you believe that? I will never forget that as long as I live. Well, Junior-two passed a while back and now I'm on to Junior-three." Wilbur paused to take a breath.

"Junior is an unusual name for a dog," Jake remarked, begging the question.

"That's what everyone says to me. I name all my dogs Wilbur Jr., 'cause they are like my children, but I call them Junior to avoid the confusion."

Wilbur continued. "Buck Dyson is a saint. He could never hurt anyone, anyone who knows him knows that." At this point Wilbur was stalling. He knew he needed to tell Jake about the murders but he really didn't want to talk about it.

Jake picked up on Wilbur's reticence, so he tried to nudge him into it.

"When you approached me in the court room you told me you were the killer the government was looking for. Can you tell me about the murders?"

Wilbur swallowed hard, shifted uncomfortably on the bed, where he was seated.

His eyes were down cast as he began. "Let me start with the one that Buck is being tried for and we can go on from there if you wish.

"Junior had died a few days before and I was feeling very low. There had been some kind of accident on I-10 westbound that had brought traffic to a standstill. I jumped on the CB radio to see what I could learn. I heard Buck's voice. I called to him and we switched channels and chatted for a while. We agreed to stop at the Love's Truck Stop outside of Pensacola. We ate and talked for a bit and said good night.

"I ran this route regularly, transporting vehicles to dealerships along the I-10 corridor. As I drove I would scout for houses that were visible from the highway. These were my targets. When I felt the urge, I would pick one, park my truck like I was taking a break or sleeping. I would change into my ninja gear and proceed through the woods. In my backpack was the equipment I needed to unlock doors, neutralize individuals and my tanto knife that I used for the killings.

"That night I had parked a few miles past Love's Truck Stop, changed and proceeded up the embankment. It was about 12 AM everything was dark. There was no moonlight and the sky was overcast, a perfect cover. When I reached the house, a blue ranch with a one car garage, I circled around the property, as I always did, to make sure there were no watchdogs and then I headed for the back door. They were always easiest to open and always lead to the kitchen where I would set up."

"What does that mean when you say 'set up'" Jake asked?

"In circling the house, I had determined where the bedrooms were. I preferred single story houses; they were easier to navigate." Wilbur paused, looking up, making eye contact with Jake.

"I never killed women and children, only men. But in order to make sure I would not be interrupted; I first would visit the spare bedroom and tranquilize anyone I found. Then I would enter the master and tranquilize the husband and wife. I used Propozine, a product used by vets to operate on animals. They use it because it was quick acting and short lasting, allowing them to do their surgery and have the patient wake up within thirty minutes or so based on dosage.

"I would then cut the husband's throat with one blow of my knife.

"For some reason this ritual made me hungry. I would always make my breakfast, clean up and leave things as I found them."

Wilbur had been recounting his crimes with an unnerving calm, as though he were reliving a mundane memory. Jake sat frozen, his hands gripping the arms of the chair so tightly his knuckles turned white. The words "cut the husband's throat" echoed in his mind, and a wave of nausea rolled through him.

"You... you made breakfast?" Jake finally stammered, his voice low and uneven, unable to hide the mix of horror and disbelief.

Wilbur raised an eyebrow, his expression neutral. "Always did. It kept me grounded, gave me a sense of normalcy after the... act. Eggs, toast, sometimes bacon if they had it."

Jake shot up from his seat. He turned his back to Wilbur and pressed his palms against the wall, as if trying to steady himself. His breaths came short and quick. He felt trapped, cornered by the calmness in Wilbur's voice, the absolute lack of remorse.

"Jesus Christ, Wilbur," Jake muttered under his breath, shaking his head. "You're talking about this like it's... like it's nothing." He turned back to face Wilbur, his eyes wide, his voice rising. "Do you even hear yourself? You killed people—human beings—

and then what? Sat down for a snack like it was just another day at work?"

Wilbur didn't flinch at Jake's outburst. Instead, he regarded him with a steady gaze, as if waiting for the storm to pass. Finally, he spoke, his tone flat but deliberate. "Getting angry doesn't change what's already done, Jake. I'm not asking for your forgiveness or your understanding. I'm just telling you what happened."

Jake blinked at him, incredulous. "Why? Why now? Why the hell are you telling me this?"

"You asked," Wilbur said simply, as if that explained everything.

Jake fell back into the chair, his hands trembling slightly. He rubbed his temples, trying to piece together the enormity of what he was hearing. The words *tranquilize, tanto knife, ritual* swirled in his mind, refusing to settle. He took a shaky breath and gestured for Wilbur to continue, though he wasn't sure he wanted to hear more.

Wilbur nodded and picked up where he left off, his voice still eerily calm. "I neglected to mention that before I left the master bedroom, I would take a 3x5 card and press the wife's thumb onto it. A memento, you could say. That way, I'd taken something from the house without disturbing anything else."

Jake's expression hardened. "A memento?" he repeated, his voice thick with disdain. "You're sick, you know that? Absolutely sick."

Wilbur shrugged. "Perhaps. But that's what I did, whether you like it or not."

Jake leaned forward; his eyes locked on Wilbur's. "What was your motive? What possessed you to want to kill someone in the first place?"

Wilbur stared down at his hands, his fingers tracing invisible patterns on the bedspread. "I have no answer to that question," he admitted. "All I can tell you is that something would come over me. A compulsion. Like a pressure on my brain, building and building until I satisfied the tanto knife with a life."

Jake shook his head, "Go on."

"Then I slipped out, locking the door behind me and returned to my truck. The entire execution taking less than one hour.

"After, I drove my truck at least fifty miles before stopping for the rest of the night."

Jake recoiled slightly, the cold detachment in Wilbur's words sending a shiver down his spine. He rubbed his jaw, his mind racing. "Who is going to believe this story?" he murmured, almost to himself, as the weight of it all began to crush him.

"As far as the officials are concerned they have their killer. Case closed."

"Perhaps you weren't listening when I told you I took fingerprints of the victim's spouses." Wilbur reached for his backpack on the floor, unzipped a pocket and handed Jake, a baggie with seven 3x5 cards, each with a single thumbprint.

"One of these cards is the fingerprint of Marston's wife and the others are of the other spouses. How would I have these? What more proof do you need?"

Jake took the cards that were housed in a baggie, the expression on his face was unreadable.

"May I keep these?

"You may, I have copies."

Jake's mind was swirling from information overload. "Are you willing to come with me now and turn yourself in?"

Wilbur nodded in the affirmative.

They had talked for a long time. When they arrived at police headquarters it was around 11 PM. The front door was locked after 10 PM so they had to press a buzzer to alert the officers that someone wished to enter. Once inside, Wilbur sat nervously in the dimly lit lobby. Jake sat beside him. Jake had spoken to the Desk Sargent making him aware of the situation. Due to the serious nature of the claims being made an on-call detective had been summoned. They were awaiting his arrival.

Wilbur's confession weighed heavily on him as he contemplated the gravity of his decision to come forward. Jake watched over his client with a mix of emotions — part disbelief, part anger, and part a flicker of hope that this might finally clear his father's name.

Earlier that day, Jake had sat in the courtroom, stunned, as the jury pronounced Buck Dyson guilty. He knew in his heart that his father was innocent, and the evidence — or lack thereof — only reinforced that belief. The case had been a web of circumstantial threads, but nothing concrete tied Buck to the murders. Jake's instincts as a lawyer told him that the jury hadn't been convinced by the evidence; they'd been worn down. After days of deliberation, they had deadlocked. Exhausted and desperate to go home, they'd done what good people sometimes do under pressure — they made the wrong choice. Jake had seen it in their faces when the verdict was read: a flicker of guilt and unease, but also relief that it was finally over.

Now, as Wilbur sat beside him, ready to confess to the very crimes Buck had been convicted of, Jake couldn't help but feel a surge of vindication. The truth was finally within reach, though the law and those invested in the verdict would not be easily swayed.

Detective Brown arrived, appearing a bit disheveled, displeasure in his eyes, his lips tight. He ushered Wilbur and Jake into a small interrogation room. As soon as they were seated he jumped right in without introduction.

"What is this about? I was told about a murder confession."

With a deep breath, Wilbur leaned forward in his chair, "I'm the person you want for the 'Highway Murders'. I killed those people not Buck Dyson." The detective, listened attentively but remained skeptical. Confessions are not uncommon in law enforcement, but they're often met with caution, especially when they come after a conviction has already been secured. There were always kooks out there looking for attention.

Jake leaned forward, his presence commanding respect. He introduced himself as Wilbur's attorney and stressed the seriousness of the situation. Despite his professional demeanor, Jake's concern for his client was evident. He knew what was at stake here. His father's freedom hinged on the credibility of his client.

The detective hesitated, unsure how to proceed. On one hand, Wilbur's confession could potentially overturn Buck's conviction and bring about justice. On the other hand, the timing and circumstances of the confession raise doubts about its credibility. The detective decided to err on the side of caution.

"We appreciate your cooperation, Mr. Knapp," the detective began, "but given the late hour and the complexity of the situation, we'll need to do the following. We'll take your statement, remand you into custody, and notify the detective in charge of Buck Dyson's case as well as the district attorney. They'll need to review the evidence and assess the validity of your confession."

Jake nodded in understanding but pressed the detective to expedite the process.

"We have indisputable evidence that places my client at the scene of the crimes, that we will make available to law enforcement."

Jake knows time is of the essence, and every moment that passes could mean the difference between incarceration or freedom for his father.

Detective Brown read Wilbur his Miranda Rights, asked if he understood his rights and when Wilbur acknowledged in the affirmative, he pressed record and nodded to Wilbur to begin his confession. Wilbur repeated the story he told Jake earlier, at the motel, providing in depth details of his actions on the day of the Marston murder. When he finished Wilbur was booked: finger printed, his mug shot taken, his personal possessions bagged, and he was placed in a holding cell for the evening.

Jake arrived at police headquarters promptly at 9 AM. Detective Bradley Williams and Assistant District Attorney Marlow Atkins were already assembled in Police Chief Dahl's office discussing the recent turn of events in the Buck Dyson case.

"Who is this guy, Wilbur Knapp? Was he on anyone's radar? Or is he just some kook?" The Chief went on firing questions at Detective Williams without getting any responses.

Jake tapped on the office door, that was ajar.

"Ah, Mr. Dyson come on in. We've been expecting you." Jake exchanged nods with the group, who responded in kind.

"What can you tell us about Wilbur Knapp?" The Chief inquired.

"Gentlemen," Jake acknowledged... "I am here representing Wilbur Knapp, who has confessed to the 'Highway Murders' and I am in possession of irrefutable evidence of his presence at the crime scenes. I am prepared to turn that evidence over to you here and now."

"Where did this evidence come from?" Brad shot back, his question a clear challenge to Jake's veracity.

"This evidence was given to me by Mr. Knapp and has been in my possession since yesterday evening."

"What could you have that is so irrefutable?" Brad remarked, the distain in his voice unmasked.

"For one, I have the murder weapon and more importantly, I have evidence that puts my client in the home, with no other explanation as to how he could have obtained this evidence."

With that, Jake reached into Wilbur's backpack he had been holding and pulled out the tanto knife.

"And who says that's the murder weapon?" Brad's determination to discredit the evidence not lost on anyone.

Jake then reached into the backpack and pulled out the baggie holding the 3x5 cards.

"These seven cards contain the thumb print of each of the seven victims' significant other, taken by the killer while in the residence."

At that point Bradley William's jaw dropped open, but was quickly concealed by his next challenge.

"How do you know that?"

At this point Jake has become exasperated by Brad's constant chides, "I am going to leave that to this office to obtain the fingerprints of the parties in question and make that confirmation."

"I say this guy is a kook and made this all up. Anybody can put fingerprints on cards and claim they are the victims."

"Let the evidence speak for itself, Mr. Williams. And just so this confession and evidence does not get swept under the rug I will be holding a press conference and giving copies of the fingerprints to the press. I'm certain that the spouses of the victims want the right person in jail and not one who is most convenient for the police."

Brad made an attempt to respond but Chief Dahl cut him off.

"Let me assure you, Mr. Dyson, we will get to the bottom of this and if Mr. Knapp's confession and evidence prove to be valid we will act accordingly."

Marlow Atkins, who had remained silent, offered his assurance, reinforcing the Police Chief's sentiment.

"We, in the DA's office, will do the right thing. Be assured."

As promised, Jake called a press conference, on the steps of the police station.

"A person has stepped forward identifying himself as the 'Highway Murderer'. He has provided evidence that is being corroborated by the authorities. To ensure transparency, in this case, a key element of the evidence is being provided to the public."

The wheels of justice turn slowly and so it was with Wilbur's confession. The parties involved in Buck Dyson's conviction were in no hurry to be proven wrong. As Wilbur stated, the seven finger prints on the 3x5 cards were a match. His information about the use of Propozine was confirmed by multiple forensic labs. It could render a person unconscious immediately upon injection. The design of the Tanto knife was such that it could slice a man's throat with a single blow. Blood found on the knife was inconclusive, however.

At the end of the investigation, it was clear, from the evidence Wilbur Knapp was their killer. But Jake Dyson would have to push hard to overturn his father's conviction.

Jake followed the investigation closely and knew when it concluded. However, no one was making any effort to address his father's innocence.

Jake filed a petition with the court to vacate the conviction based upon the confession of Wilbur Knapp and the corroboration of his guilt by the supporting investigation.

A hearing was held but it was brief, the prosecution indicated to the judge that they had no objection with the petition to vacate.

Assistant DA Marlow Atkins told the court, "Your Honor, we are convinced that the truth has been revealed and have no objection to this petition."

Atkins took his seat and the judge immediately responded.

"Based on the arguments by the defense and the remarks of the prosecution, and considering the newly discovered evidence of innocence brought forward by the defense, this court finds that there exists clear and convincing evidence of the defendant's innocence.

Accordingly, the conviction entered against the defendant Buck Dyson for the offense of capital murder is hereby vacated and set aside.

"The court acknowledges the prosecution's support of vacating the conviction and concurs with their assessment of the credibility and significance of the newly discovered evidence. Justice demands that we correct any miscarriage of justice, and in light of the compelling evidence presented, it is the duty of this court to ensure that the defendant is exonerated and his innocence affirmed.

"Furthermore, any associated penalties, fines, or sentences imposed upon the defendant as a result of the wrongful conviction are hereby nullified. The defendant is to be released from custody immediately, and any remaining legal obligations or restrictions imposed as a consequence of the conviction are hereby lifted.

"The court extends its sincere apologies to the defendant for any wrongful deprivation of liberty endured as a result of the erroneous conviction. We trust that this decision brings some measure of solace and closure to the defendant and his loved ones.

"This court orders that all records related to the conviction in question be expunged or amended accordingly to reflect the vacatur of the conviction and the exoneration of the defendant. The clerk of court is directed to notify all relevant parties of this decision and to take all necessary steps to effectuate this order.

"This court stands committed to upholding justice and ensuring the integrity of our legal system. May this decision serve as a reminder of the importance of vigilance in safeguarding the rights and liberties of all citizens.

"Court is adjourned."

Bradley Williams who was seated in the back of the courtroom could only wince, hearing the judge's remarks. He had really screwed up this case, sending the wrong person to prison based primarily on a story told to him while hitchhiking a ride many years ago. What caused him to pursue this case with such vigor? He would ask himself this question over and over again. But he knew the answer—his mother. He wanted to make her proud. She had always seen him as a failure, but he had turned out to be a good detective. When he spoke with her about the case and his concerns about getting a conviction she had convinced him to manipulate the situation to his advantage. She never told him to falsify Buck Dyson's log entries or to tamper with the blood evidence but he knew that's what she was hinting at—what she would do if it were her.

But right now, he had bigger problems. The Chief had told him he wanted to see him in his office following the hearing.

Carla was at home. She had just returned from grocery shopping and was in the pantry when the breaking news alert flashed across her TV screen. She barely registered the anchor's words at first, her mind focused on her task.

"…The Highway Murders case has taken a stunning turn. Just moments ago, Judge Randall overturned the conviction of Buck Dyson.

The can of tuna she was placing on the shelf slipped from Carla's hands, the edge crashing down on her instep sending a shooting pain to her brain. She winced in pain brought by the tuna can and the news.

The screen cut to footage of Buck Dyson and Jake walking down the court house steps into a crowd of reporters.

Carla limped into the living room staring at the screen, a heavy silence settling over the room. Her mind raced as she tried to make sense of it. "No," she whispered, shaking her head as though that would undo the reality playing out in front of her.

The anchor continued, her polished voice at odds with the raw chaos Carla felt inside.

Carla lurched forward and turned off the TV with a sharp click. The room seemed too quiet now, her own heartbeat pounding in her ears. She felt nauseous, as though the ground had tilted beneath her feet.

She sank into the couch, her head in her hands. How could this have happened? Buck was guilty. He had to be. She'd been so sure. She had watched him in court, felt his guilt in her gut, in her bones.

Or had that been a manifestation of her own desire?

Her mind replayed the night she had convinced herself to act. The bailiff. The jury room door. The thoughts she'd projected into the air like an invisible whisper. She had believed it then—in the righteousness of what she'd done.

But now?

Her stomach churned. Her foot ached. *I tipped the scales. I made them see what I wanted them to see. And I was wrong.*

She tried to shove the thought away, but it clawed its way back, sharper this time.

The house felt suffocating, the air too thick. She pushed herself up from the couch but the throbbing of her instep made her sit back down. Her own voice mocked her, sharp and unrelenting. *What have you done?*

The phone rang, slicing through the suffocating silence of the room. She stared at it for a moment, dreading whoever might be on the other end. Finally, she lifted the receiver, pressing it to her ear.

"Hello?"

"Carla, it's Richard," his voice came through loud and sharp, already charged with emotion. "Looks like Brad really screwed up—again!"

Carla closed her eyes, gripping the phone tighter. She didn't respond. She was in no mood for conversation.

Ignoring her silence, Richard continued, "The media's tearing him apart. How does this even happen? First, they nail Dyson, and then the real killer comes forward. It makes them all look like a bunch of fools."

She felt her stomach churn. The weight of his words bore down on her, sharp and unforgiving.

"And you know how this works," Richard said, his voice dipping lower. "They'll be looking for a scapegoat, and you know who that'll be. Brad."

Her mouth went dry. She tried to swallow, but the lump in her throat wouldn't budge. "I... I don't know," she stammered.

"I'm just saying, he better get ready. They're gonna throw him under the bus to save their own hides. Watch and see." He exhaled sharply, clearly agitated. "Anyway, I thought you'd want to know."

Carla couldn't respond. Her throat felt tight, her pulse racing. She mumbled something about needing to go and hung up, ignoring Richard's puzzled goodbye.

The line clicked, leaving her alone with the dead silence of the receiver. Slowly, she replaced it on the cradle, her hands trembling.

Richard's words echoed in her mind. *They'll be looking for a scapegoat... Brad.*

Carla's chest tightened. She sank back into the couch, the weight of everything pressing down on her.

Her whispered words from the jury room came back to haunt her. *You know it's true. He's guilty.*

But it wasn't true.

For the first time in her life, Carla felt the crushing weight of her actions — the consequences she had never imagined.

Tears welled in her eyes, but she refused to let them fall. She couldn't take it back. She was going to have to live with it. No one knew what she had done and it would remain that way — if in reality she'd done anything.

Peter M. Browne

CHAPTER 20

Chief Dahl's office was standing room only when Brad Williams arrived. He poked his head in and the Chief waved him in.

"Have a seat, detective," the Chief offered, as Brad looked around the room. His boss, Detective Sargent Brown, was already seated. Assistant DA Atkins was seated on the couch along with Lieutenant Nathan Strong from Internal Affairs.

The Chief began, " Lieutenant Strong has been looking into the Dyson case to see where we went wrong in the investigation. It appears that there have been some irregularities. Would you care to comment before the Lieutenant begins?"

Brad looked around the room. He knew where this was headed but didn't know how to respond.

"I've tried to be diligent and thorough in my investigations. I guess I got a little over zealous with the Dyson case. But..." Brad stopped himself there. He wasn't about to self-incriminate.

Strong picked up the conversation. "Detective, it appears that you were moving fast and loose with the evidence. Wouldn't you say?"

"No sir. I thought Dyson was guilty based on the evidence I uncovered."

"The DA's office is here because they are concerned that you may have lied on the witness stand when presenting Buck Dyson's whereabouts, the day of the murder."

"No sir, even Knapp's confession states that they were together prior to the murder."

At this point Atkins jumped in. "We are not going to pursue any of this, there has already been enough bad press surrounding this case, but your credibility as a witness of fact is in jeopardy, to put it politely."

It was Chief Dahl's turn to weigh in. "A single incident of poor judgement would be grounds for a reprimand but it appears we are dealing with a pattern of bad choices."

Brad looked startled by the Chief's remarks. *What pattern?* he thought, but wasn't about to challenge the Chief.

It was as if the Chief had read his mind. "The FBI task force recently wrapped up their investigation into the Hammond murder and the infamous Ouroboros Society. Their findings indicated that Hammond's death was from natural causes. The coroner had noted it as undetermined, somehow it got changed to homicide.

"The Feds had his body exhumed and a second autopsy performed. The report states that Hammond had a stroke, fell and busted his head open. He died of exsanguination. As for the conspiratorial nature of the Ouroboros Society, the fact of the matter is they are nothing more than a bunch of radical thinkers not killers."

As the Chief spoke Brad could feel himself becoming smaller and smaller in the eyes of those present. He was about to disappear when the Chief address him by name.

"Detective Bradley Williams, you are hereby discharged from the Pensacola Police Department."

The Chief's words reverberated in the room, but for Brad, they might as well have been muffled echoes. His vision blurred as the weight of the moment pressed heavily on his chest. A lump formed in his throat, but he forced it down.

His mind raced backward, dragging him through the debris of his life—a vivid, painful slideshow of failure he couldn't seem to escape.

He thought of his first marriage, how bright and promising it had seemed. But he had married too young, too naïve. In no time, they grew apart. The divorce felt like a failure, though he didn't know what else he could have done to save the marriage.

Then there was the lawn business. It had started with so much potential, a chance to be his own boss and carve out a little stability. But when his equipment was stolen and he had no insurance or savings to replace it, the business collapsed. Poor planning.

After that, he'd moved back to Pearson's Point, tail between his legs, hoping for a fresh start. It had been humiliating, packing up his few belongings and leaving the city behind, knowing full well the whispers waiting for him back home. "Bradley Williams couldn't hack it."

And then there was "Your Move". God, what a disaster. The moving company had been his chance, his ticket out of mediocrity. He had sunk his savings into it, only to watch it crumble when his very first customer's trailer unhitched and caused a massive accident.

And now, here he was again. Another venture, another failure. He had thought this time would be different. That being a detective—a real cop, in a real department—would prove that he could finally be something other than what his past had made him. But it seemed he was programmed for failure.

Brad clenched his fists under the table. He didn't want to admit it, not even to himself, but he was tired. Tired of trying, tired of failing, tired of the endless cycle of disappointment. Maybe his mother had been right all along. Maybe he wasn't cut out for anything.

The Chief's voice snapped him back to the room.

"Detective Williams, do you have anything to say for yourself?"

He looked up, his lips parting as if to speak, but no words came. What was there to say? That he'd tried his best? That he wasn't as bad as they thought? That somehow, despite his intentions, everything always fell apart in his hands?

The silence stretched out awkwardly, and he realized the Chief was still waiting. Brad stood slowly. He straightened his jacket, met the Chief's gaze for a fleeting moment, and gave a small nod.

"No, sir," he finally said.

"I'm going to need your badge and your gun," the Chief replied, his voice devoid of sympathy.

Robotically, Brad placed his badge and gun on the Chief's desk. Then, without another word, he turned and walked out of the office, out of the police station, and into his most familiar role—failure.

He got into his car and headed out of the parking lot with no idea where he was going. Home wasn't an option. He couldn't face Meredith right now. The thought of explaining what had just happened — how he had let it happen, how he had made it happen — was unbearable.

Brad drove aimlessly, his thoughts a chaotic storm, until a strip mall appeared ahead. He pulled into the parking lot, his movements mechanical, like a man on autopilot. Fletcher's Liquor Store caught his eye. Without really thinking, he parked, got out, and wandered inside. The smell of stale alcohol and the buzz of fluorescent lights greeted Brad as he stepped inside the store. He grabbed a fifth of Smirnoff's Vodka from the nearest shelf, the cold glass heavy in his hand.

The clerk was hunched behind the counter, a man well past his prime, with wiry gray hair that stuck out in uneven tufts around a balding scalp. He wore a faded blue polo that hung loosely over his thin frame, the name "Gary" embroidered in red above the pocket. Gary's glasses were smudged, and his eyes looked tired, like he hadn't had a decent night's sleep, in weeks.

Brad watched as the man bagged the bottle with hands that trembled faintly, the veins on the backs of them like rivers on a map. His movements were slow, deliberate, as if even this simple task required effort.

"Ten twenty-five," Gary mumbled, his voice hoarse and gravelly, like he'd been chain-smoking for decades.

He didn't make eye contact, didn't bother with small talk, and Brad was grateful for that. The anonymity was a comfort. No judgment, no questions — just a quick transaction, like any other faceless customer. Brad handed over a crumpled twenty and watched as the clerk shuffled to make change, his fingers fumbling slightly with the bills.

For a moment, Brad wondered about the man's story. Did Gary have a life outside this dim little store? A family? Dreams he'd never managed to chase? Or had he been stuck behind this counter for years, slowly fading into the fluorescent haze?

The thought was fleeting, quickly drowned by the oppressive ache of his own despair.

Back in his car, he unscrewed the cap and took a long, stinging pull. Across the lot, the neon glow of a CVS Pharmacy flickered, catching his eye. A thought crept into his mind — subtle at first, then louder, more certain. A path formed, as if it had been waiting for him all along.

The vodka burned in his throat as he walked across the parking lot, bottle in hand. He pushed through the automatic doors of the CVS, not caring how he looked to anyone else. The harsh fluorescent light was jarring, making his head pound. He found the aisle with sleep aids and stared blankly at the rows of bottles and boxes until his hand landed on the largest package of SleepEase sleeping pills — 100 capsules. It felt heavy in his hand. He took it to the counter, handed over cash, and left without saying a word.

The drive to the BudgetTel motel on the outskirts of Pensacola was a blur. He didn't even remember pulling into the parking lot, but here he was. The cheap plastic sign flickered above him, and the building itself seemed to slump under the weight of its own insignificance. Brad sat in his car, the bottle of vodka resting between his knees, the box of pills on the passenger seat. The night was quiet, except for the hum of the nearby highway and the occasional burst of music from a passing car's radio.

He sat there for what felt like an eternity, unscrewing and tightening the cap of the vodka, sipping occasionally, waiting for it to do what it would do—numb the pain. But, the dull warmth wasn't enough. The ache in his chest remained, a steady, unrelenting weight.

He tightened his grip on the steering wheel, the cool leather grounding him for a moment. He asked himself the question he'd been avoiding since the Chief's words had shattered his world: *What have I done?*

The thought reverberated in his mind, cold and merciless. *What-have-I-done?*

Brad looked down at the box of sleeping pills on the seat beside him, then at the vodka bottle in his hand. His fingers trembled as he took another swig, the alcohol burning all the way down. The edges of his vision fuzzy as despair settled over him like a heavy, suffocating blanket. He couldn't see a way out.

He had no recollection of how he got into the hotel room. It was as though he had floated there on the fumes of his despair, carried by an autopilot he didn't remember engaging. The flickering neon light from the BudgetTel sign outside seeped through the gap in the curtains, casting the room in a cold, pale glow. The half-empty vodka bottle sat on the table beside him, its label peeling at the corners from where his sweaty hand had gripped it too long. Next to it lay the package of SleepEase pills, their cheerful branding a stark contrast to his dark thoughts.

Brad stared at the pill bottle, his vision swimming as he swirled the vodka in his hand. His lips curled into a bitter smile. "If I had my service pistol, this would all be over by now," he muttered to no one. "Bang. Done. No fuss, no dragging it out. Just a clean escape." He tilted the vodka to his mouth, its fiery trail offering no relief, only a momentary distraction.

He picked up the bottle of sleeping pills, held it up to the light as though it might reveal some hidden truth. His fingers fumbled with the cap, but he set it down again, unsure. A part of him hesitated. A part of him still clung to... what? He couldn't name it.

"Are you going to do this or not?" His own voice startled him, louder and sharper than he intended. He laughed bitterly, his words slurring now. "Coward. Weakling. You can't even make up your mind. Just do it! End this miserable excuse of a life."

The laughter turned to sobs, but he silenced them quickly, embarrassed even in his solitude. With shaking hands, he tore off the safety seal, the crack of plastic loud in the oppressive silence of the room. He poured a handful of pills into his palm, staring at them as though they were tiny soldiers lined up for battle. Then, without giving himself time to second-guess, he tipped his head back and threw them into his mouth, swallowing hard. The chalky bitterness of the pills clung to his tongue. He chased it with vodka, the burn searing down his throat.

It wasn't enough. He felt committed now, a grim determination overtaking him. He poured another handful, then another, washing them down until the bottle was empty. He dropped it onto the carpet, where it rolled lazily under the table. The vodka followed soon after, its weight making a soft thud as it landed beside the empty pill bottle.

He slumped back in the chair, his head rolling to one side as his limbs went limp. His breaths came shallow and uneven, a dull haze closing in around him. "Finally," he thought. Relief washed over him—not from the pills or vodka, but from the idea that this would all soon be over. No more shame. No more pain. No more failure.

But peace did not come. Sometime after midnight, his stomach began to churn, a deep, ominous rumble that stirred him from his stupor. His chest tightened, his throat burning as bile clawed its way up. Before he could react, his body convulsed violently, a torrent of vomit spewing forth in a grotesque, unstoppable wave. It splattered across the room, soaking the chair, the carpet, even the curtains. Brad doubled over; his body racked by spasms as his system purged the toxic cocktail with a vengeance.

Again and again, the waves came, each one more brutal than the last. His back arched, his stomach clenched, his throat raw from the acidic burn. He gripped the sides of the chair, his knuckles white, as though holding on for dear life. When the vomit finally stopped, the dry heaves began, his body refusing to believe the ordeal was over. He gasped for air, his chest heaving, his entire body trembling with exhaustion.

By the time it was done, the room was a war zone, and Brad was its sole, broken soldier. He collapsed onto the bed, the sour stench of vomit clinging to him, his clothes, the air. He didn't care. He closed his eyes, hoping for unconsciousness to take him, but sleep was elusive.

When he awoke, it was nearly noon. Sunlight filtered through the stained curtains, illuminating the wreckage of the room. Brad sat up slowly, every muscle aching, his head pounding like a jackhammer.

He rubbed his eyes, his throat dry and raw, and looked around. He was alive!

Somehow, against all odds, his body had rejected his attempt to end it all. The irony was not lost on him. His first thought was bitter: "You can't even kill yourself right." But then, inexplicably, he smiled. A weak, crooked smile, but a smile nonetheless.

As he sat there, the fog began to lift. "I have plenty to live for," he thought, almost surprised by the realization. "A beautiful wife. A home. Friends who care. I can get through this. I can rebuild." He wiped his face with the corner of the blanket and stood, shaky but resolute. This wasn't the end. Not yet.

Brad went out to his car and retrieved a set of clothes he kept in the trunk for emergencies, returned to his room and got dressed.

At the checkout desk, Brad apologized to the clerk for the mess he left behind, dropping a couple of twenties on the counter. "For your troubles," he said with a faint, weary smile.

Walking to his car, he felt unsteady, a dull fog settling over him. The effects of the pills and vodka, no doubt. His vision wavered—objects up close were sharp, but everything at a distance blurred into indistinct smudges. He blinked hard, gripping the car door for balance, before settling into the driver's seat.

Brad was eager to get home, to fix things with Meredith. In his mind, he rehearsed the apology he owed her: the tears, the promises, the fresh start. The hope of reconciliation burned faintly within him, though it was nearly snuffed out by the dread of facing his mother and Richard. He'd just have to endure their judgment.

Opting for the quieter backroads, Brad drove past warehouses, empty parking lots, and rows of truck depots. The industrial district stretched in muted shades of gray, the streets deserted, the faint rumble of a passing freight train the only sound in the distance.

His thoughts churned, growing heavier with each mile. Meredith's face, the emptiness in her eyes during their last argument, haunted him. He should've done better—been better—for her. For himself.

As he neared the railroad crossing, the low rumble of the oncoming train grew louder, a mechanical growl that seemed to vibrate the air. But Brad wasn't paying attention. He was lost in the script playing in his head, preparing for the conversation he prayed would fix everything.

The train's horn blared, jolting him back to reality.

His head snapped up. The train was nearly on him, its enormous engine bearing down with terrifying speed. Brad thought of slamming on the brakes—but stopping wasn't an option. The realization hit him like a punch to the gut: got to go for it!

His breath quickened. "I can make it," he muttered, his voice shaking.

The Grand Am lurched forward as he floored the accelerator, tires screeching against the pavement. For a moment, hope surged through him. He could beat this monster. He had to. But he'd miscalculated.

The train struck the rear quarter-panel of the car with a deafening crash, the impact spinning the Pontiac like a toy. Metal shrieked and crumpled as the vehicle was dragged along the tracks, sparks flying in violent bursts. Glass shattered, scattering like crystal rain, and the grinding of steel-on-steel echoed into the afternoon air.

Inside the car, Brad was thrown violently, his body jerking against the seatbelt. The world became a chaos of sound and motion, then...nothing.

When the train finally screeched to a halt, the Pontiac was a mangled husk of twisted metal lodged beneath the engine. Smoke rose from the wreckage, mingling with the acrid stench of burning rubber and gasoline. The silence that followed was heavy, broken only by the distant wail of approaching sirens.

Brad sat slumped in the driver's seat; his head tilted at an unnatural angle. Blood trickled from a gash on his forehead, pooling on the crumpled dashboard. His eyes stared blankly forward, unseeing.

Meredith had called the police department the previous evening when Brad didn't come home. The officer on the other end had been curt, informing her only that Brad was no longer with the department. No further details. She had hung up the phone, confused and worried, her heart pounding as the hours stretched into morning.

When she saw the patrol car pull into the driveway around noon, her stomach dropped. Her first thought was that Brad had gotten into trouble—maybe he'd been arrested, or he'd done something reckless after losing his job. But when Detective Brown stepped out of the car and walked to her door, her fear took on a sharper edge. His face was grim, his movements deliberate. She opened the door before he knocked.

"Detective Brown," she said, her voice tight.

"Mrs. Williams," he began, his voice low. "May I come in?"

She hesitated. "What is going on? Brad never came home last night," she said, her eyes darting to his face, searching for answers.

Detective Brown removed his hat, holding it against his chest. It was a gesture she'd seen in movies; the kind of thing people did when delivering bad news. Her throat went dry.

"I'm sorry to have to tell you this," he began, his voice strained. "There was an accident earlier today."

Her breath caught in her chest. "An accident?"

He nodded, his eyes softening. "Brad's car was hit by a train over on Ridge Road. He… he didn't survive."

For a moment, Meredith just stared at him, the words hanging in the air like thick smoke. She blinked, once, twice, as if trying to process what he'd said.

"What?" she whispered; her voice barely audible.

"He's deceased," Brown said, his voice quieter now, his expression etched with regret. "I'm so sorry, Mrs. Williams."

Meredith staggered back a step, gripping the edge of the doorframe for support. The world around her seemed to tilt, her vision narrowing as the weight of his words settled over her.

"This can't… this can't be real," she murmured. Her voice cracked as tears welled in her eyes. "There must be a mistake. Brad wouldn't…" She stopped, shaking her head.

"If there's anything I can do…" Detective Brown trailed off awkwardly, unsure how to console her. "Is there someone you can call? Family, a friend?"

Meredith didn't respond right away. Her mind was racing, memories of Brad flashing before her: his laugh, his stubbornness, the way he always insisted on doing things his way. She thought of their last conversation, the tension between them, the things left unsaid.

Finally, she shook her head. "I... I need to be alone," she said, her voice hollow.

Detective Brown hesitated. He wanted to say something — anything — to ease her pain, but no words seemed adequate. With a reluctant nod, he turned and walked back to the patrol car, leaving Meredith standing in the doorway, her arms wrapped tightly around herself.

As the car pulled away, she closed the door and sank to the floor. She pressed her palms to her face, sobbing into the quiet of the empty house. Somewhere in the back of her mind, a question lingered, nagging at her like a splinter: Was it really an accident?

CHAPTER 21

Dr. Mercer was surprised to see Carla. She had terminated her visits with the therapist years ago, with a clear understanding of her path to personal improvement, if she chose to follow it.

"I was surprised when I saw your name on my calendar. What brings you here today?"

Carla crossed the room with the composed elegance of someone attending a social function, not a therapy session. Her cream-colored blouse was pressed, her tailored slacks sharp and crease-free, and her gold earrings perfectly matched the chain around her neck. But there were cracks beneath the polished exterior. Her eyes were puffy, betraying sleepless nights or a flood of tears that she had wiped away long before walking through the door.

She headed for the couch and collapsed onto it unceremoniously. She smoothed her slacks as she settled into the cushions, folding her hands carefully in her lap.

"My son, Bradley, is dead." Her voice was flat, devoid of any tremor or emotion. "The police killed him. And I..." She hesitated for a beat, her lips tightening. "I haven't cried. Not once."

Dr. Mercer tilted her head slightly, her sharp eyes studying Carla. "What is wrong with me?" Dr. Mercer just allowed that question to linger in the air. She was not in the habit of answering questions. She did the asking.

Minutes passed in silence until Carla realized what was happening and began talking. She felt it important to bring Dr. Mercer up to date.

"I stopped pretending to be something I'm not," Carla said suddenly, her tone sharp and defensive. "All that phony compassion, the endless amends. None of it made me happy, so I stopped. It was pointless." She smoothed her blouse, a nervous habit that seemed at odds with her cold detachment. "But now... I feel nothing. Not for Brad. Not for anyone."

Carla continued to ramble on about her displeasure with life, with Richard, with everything that wasn't about her. When she had finished and a respectable period of silence had passed, Dr. Mercer asked, "So, why have you come here today?"

Carla sat with her legs crossed on the couch, her hands laced in her lap, rolling her thumbs back and forth slowly. She looked up to meet Dr. Mercer's eyes.

"I needed to talk to someone, someone who knows the real me. Where I can be real and that's you Doc."

"So then let's get down to what you really want to say to me."

Carla's head descended once again, her eyes down cast. "I'm the one responsible for Bradley's death. There I've said it. I'm the one who killed him, not the police."

Dr. Mercer was aware of the facts reported in the newspaper regarding Bradley Williams' death being a potential suicide.

"Tell me more," was the doctor's reply.

He was working on the murder case, a multiple murder case and he thought he had found the guy who did it, but the evidence wasn't coming together for him and the guy was most likely going to get off." Carla paused and shifted uncomfortably on the couch.

"I convinced him to get the evidence he needed, if he had to make it up himself. I told him it was his duty not to let this guy go free." At this point Carla was shaking her head from side to side.

"Well, I don't know if he took my advice. But, he got the guy convicted. Bad news, the guy turned out to be innocent." Carla got up from the couch and walked over to the window and stared out into the parking lot. It was as if she couldn't face the doctor with this truth.

Staring out the window, as she spoke, "He had come to see me the night before the hearing to determine if the convicted guy was going to be freed. Richard couldn't resist getting his digs in, telling him how he screwed up big time. I wanted to defend him, but I silently agreed with Richard and Bradley could see it in my face." Carla stopped, turned around placing her hands on the back of the couch and leaning in toward the doctor. "I killed him, just as if I drove his car into that train."

"Do you feel guilt, remorse?

"None of those things."

What are you feeling?"

I feel angry." She came around and sat back down.

"I'm angry at Bradley for not being more of a man, for not being able to stand up to me or for himself, for disappointing me."

"Don't you see how those emotions don't fit the circumstances?" the doctor said, telling not asking.

"I know that, that's why I asked you when I first arrived what is wrong with me? But you won't answer me," Carla's body language adopting a childish demeanor. "Am I a sociopath?"

Dr. Mercer felt compelled to answer, without actually answering.

"Sociopath is a label. I don't deal in labels. I deal with individuals." She stopped, set her notepad on her side table.

"Feeling uncertain about your own behaviors or tendencies can be unsettling. It's important to remember that labels like 'sociopath' are complex and not something we can diagnose with a simple yes or no answer. What's more important right now is to explore what's prompting you to ask this question. Let's talk about your thoughts, feelings, and experiences so we can gain a deeper understanding together. Our goal is to work through any challenges you're facing," Dr. Mercer said calmly, "and support you in finding clarity and peace of mind."

Carla rolled her eyes ever so slightly, a flicker of impatience crossing her otherwise composed face. "Doctor, we've done all that before. I've tried to change—tried to be empathetic, an active listener, a team player. I've even let others take the lead." She scoffed, a dry laugh escaping her lips. "But those things? They're not me. It's not my nature."

She paused, lifting her chin to meet Dr. Mercer's gaze directly, her expression equal parts defiance and challenge. "I am who I am, and I make no apologies for it."

Dr. Mercer studied her for a moment, her pen resting idly against the notepad in her lap. "If that were true," she said evenly, "you wouldn't be here."

Carla's head tilted slightly, intrigued but unconvinced. "Think about it," Dr. Mercer continued. "Something is missing in your life, and you're searching for it—whether you want to admit that or not."

Carla's polished exterior faltered, just for a second, as if a hairline crack had formed in the armor she wore so effortlessly. "How will I know when I've found it?" she asked, her voice quieter but tinged with skepticism. Dr. Mercer waited, sensing that Carla wasn't finished.

"I'm a contradiction," Carla admitted, her tone gaining momentum, more like the Carla Dr. Mercer remembered. "When I'm with a man who wants to take charge, I rebel. Push back. Fight him every step of the way." She exhaled sharply, brushing an invisible speck from her slacks. "But when I find a man who lets me have my way, who bends over backward to please me..." She shook her head, her lips curving into a wry, self-deprecating smile. "I don't respect him. I grow bored. And then I'm off looking for someone who will challenge me."

She leaned back against the couch, crossing her legs with deliberate precision, the smile on her face widening slightly as a thought struck her. "I'm like Goldilocks," she said, a hint of amusement creeping into her voice. "The porridge is always too hot or too cold."

Dr. Mercer leaned forward; her expression still composed but thoughtful. "And do you think there's a 'just right' out there for you?" she asked gently.

Carla's smile faded, her gaze turning inward as if the question had landed somewhere deep. She was reluctant to answer. She looked away, folding her hands in her lap. "No, I've settled on Richard.," she said with a sigh.

The room went silent once again. Carla fidgeted on the couch. Dr. Mercer watched her. She noticed that Carla could not remain still for more the a few seconds. She would shift in her seat, adjust her hair, look around the room, stare at her hands and finally she had to get up and move around again.

"It appears to me that you are uncomfortable, in your own skin…" The doctor remarked and she just let that message float in the air.

"I don't like being alone, but I don't like people bothering me. I need to be doing something all the time or my mind starts racing, thinking about all the 'what-ifs' of my life. That is why I'm here."

"Carla, our time is up for today, but it appears we have made some progress. You know why you came. Of all the other things you could be doing today you chose to be here.

After Carla left, Dr. Mercer sat at her desk, the late afternoon light slanting through the blinds, casting striped shadows across her notes. She thumbed through the pages, revisiting years of sessions and observations. It was clear to her that Carla did not fit the classic definition of a sociopath. A sociopath operates without conscience, but Carla... Carla seemed to dance on the edge of that void, flirting with its darkness but never fully stepping inside. There was something else at work — something she couldn't quite put her finger on.

Dr. Mercer jotted a note in the margins of the file: "Borderline sociopathy with undefined variables." She paused, tapping her pen against the desk, and continued writing:

"Carla exhibits an exaggerated sense of self-importance and entitlement. She expects special treatment, believes herself superior to others, and demonstrates a striking lack of empathy. However, she does not entirely disregard others — there is a subtle struggle beneath her surface, as though she knows what she should feel but chooses not to. This is not indifference; it's a deliberate decision, almost an act of rebellion against vulnerability."

Typically, a narcissist exaggerates their achievements or talents, Dr. Mercer thought, but Carla had no significant accomplishments to bolster her grandiose self-image. Her superiority seemed to stem from sheer will — a relentless, almost magnetic energy that defied reason or merit. It was as though Carla operated on a frequency that bent others to her will, despite the absence of substance behind her facade.

Continuing on, she wrote, "She craves admiration, employs charm and manipulation without hesitation, and disregards the emotions of others when they conflict with her goals. Yet, she does not derive satisfaction from the chaos she creates. Instead, she seems to view it as an unfortunate but necessary byproduct of getting what she believes she deserves."

Dr. Mercer leaned back in her chair; her pen stilled. The diagnosis was straightforward enough, but the "undefined variable" lingered like an itch she couldn't scratch. There was something about Carla—an unnameable force—that set her apart. It was as though she had been born with an unshakable sense of her own centrality in the universe, an instinctual conviction that the world owed her something, though she couldn't articulate what or why.

In her prognosis, Dr. Mercer wrote:

"Carla seeks results without committing to the process. She has consciously chosen to embrace her condition rather than confront it. Psychotherapy has run its course. Recommend group therapy as a means of engagement with others, for greater self-awareness, though prognosis remains uncertain."

Even as she wrote the words, Dr. Mercer felt a pang of doubt. Could a support group, with its collective vulnerability and shared humanity, truly reach someone like Carla? Likely not. But it was the only path left to recommend.

At their next session, Dr. Mercer handed Carla a note torn from her script pad, containing information about a local support group that met twice a month at the Y. "Carla, I believe we've reached a crossroads. We've done all we can do together. You have the knowledge and tools to make meaningful changes—if you choose to act on them."

Carla accepted the paper with an unreadable expression, her manicured nails plucking it from Dr. Mercer's hand as if it were an invitation to an event she had little interest in attending. "We'll see," she said with a faint smile, neither dismissive nor committed.

When the session ended, Carla rose, smoothed her tailored skirt, and walked out without a goodbye or a glance back. No thank you. No acknowledgment of their years of work.

Dr. Mercer watched the door click shut and felt no surprise. If anything, the lack of closure was the most fitting conclusion to their time together.

Sitting at her desk, she glanced at the file once more, the phrase "undefined variables" standing out like a taunt. She closed the folder, resisting the urge to write anything further. Some questions, she knew, were not meant to be answered.

Peter M. Browne

CHAPTER 22

It had been over a week since Jake had secured Buck's release. Life had settled back into a familiar rhythm—or at least it seemed to, on the surface. Buck spent his days helping neighbors, working at the church, and tending to his garden. But Esther knew better. She had seen the way he lingered, sitting in his rig daydreaming.

That truck had been his companion on the road for decades, a steel testament to years of hard work and freedom. Buck hadn't driven it since retirement, yet he couldn't bring himself to sell it. Esther had tried, gently at first, then firmly, to nudge him into letting it go. "It's just gathering rust," she'd say. He always promised to "look into it," but the promises never amounted to action. And lately, Buck had been spending even more time inside the cab, sitting in the driver's seat like he was trying to recapture something that had slipped away.

She watched him now, as he sat across the dinner table. His fork hovered above the plate, piled with meatloaf and mashed potatoes, but he wasn't eating. Instead, he stared at his plate, lost in thought.

"You think you know someone," he said finally, breaking the silence. His voice was low, more to himself than to her. "If you'd asked me, I'd have sworn Wilbur couldn't hurt a fly. Murder?" He shook his head. "No way. Sure, he was a loner, and yeah, he had his quirks, but..." Buck trailed off, stabbing at his potatoes with his fork. "We spent a lot of time talking over the years. I thought I knew him."

Esther watched him carefully, her heart aching at the confusion and betrayal etched into his face. Buck shoveled a forkful of potatoes into his mouth, chewed, and swallowed before continuing.

"I've been turning it over in my mind," he went on. "If he did kill all those people and got away with it, why confess? What's the sense in that?"

Esther reached across the table, placing her hand gently on his. His rough, work-worn hand was still, but she could feel the tension in him, coiled and ready to spring. "Jake asked him that very question," she said softly. "Wilbur told him he wanted to repay your kindness. He said giving him that German Shepherd puppy all those years ago... it meant something to him. He never forgot it."

Buck looked up then, his eyes meeting hers. There was doubt in his gaze, like he was trying to reconcile the Wilbur he thought he knew with the man who had confessed to being a killer.

"All the same," Buck said, after a long pause, "I've got to see him."

Esther frowned, concern flickering across her face. "Buck..."

He cut her off gently. "I keep having this dream. Same one, night after night. Me and Wilbur, talking on the CB radio, like old times. Then, out of nowhere, the cops come screaming in with their lights flashing. They arrest us both."

He sat back in his chair, rubbing a hand over his face. "I don't know what it means, but I can't shake it."

Esther held her tongue. She could see the storm brewing inside him — the restless need for answers. But Wilbur was a dangerous man, and part of her wanted Buck to let sleeping dogs lie. Still, she knew better than to try to stop him. Once Buck had made up his mind, there was no changing it.

Buck sat at the kitchen table; the phone pressed to his ear. "Still in Escambia County Jail?" he repeated, frowning as he listened to Jake on the other end. "Alright. Thanks, Son." He hung up; the decision already made.

Buck had called his son Jake and found out that Wilbur Knapp was still in the Escambia County Jail awaiting extradition for the other murders that occurred outside of Florida.

"I'm headed up to Pensacola, to visit Wilbur Knapp. He's still in the Escambia County Jail, awaiting extradition for the other murders," he told Esther.

"Do you want me to go with you, for the company?"

"No, you stay here. I'll only be gone overnight. I'm going to take my rig, this one last time. I'm going to put it up for sale when I get back. Promise! It's time to move on," he told Esther, with a tentative look.

She tilted her head, searching his face. "Do not pick up any hitchhikers, Buck. Promise me."

He gave her a weary smile. "I promise." But he couldn't deny the tug in his gut, remembering Brad Williams — the man who set this whole mess in motion.

The next morning, Buck rose before dawn. Esther watched him from the front window as the old big rig roared to life, a sound that once carried promises of freedom and adventure. It didn't feel like that now.

Hours later, Buck pulled into the Flying J outside Ocala. He climbed down from the cab, stretching his legs as he scanned the lot. No familiar faces, but the place still felt like home — the smell of diesel fuel, the rhythmic hum of idling engines. For a moment, he let himself savor it. There's nothing else like it, he thought. A bittersweet pang hit him.

By the time he hit the entrance ramp to I-10, Buck's thoughts began to drift. The turnoff brought back memories — clear as the road stretching before him. This is where the nightmare started, he thought.

Had he not stopped to pick Brad Williams up none of this would have happened. But his thoughts were conflicted. "If it wasn't for Brad this case would have never been solved. Wilbur would not have confessed," he suspected.

The miles rolled by, and Buck's grip on the wheel tightened as the Escambia County Jail came into view. The complex loomed on the horizon, its walls stark and lifeless against the afternoon sky. Just seeing it again sent an icy ripple down his spine. The last time that he had been here he was the prisoner.

"I'd still be in there if it wasn't for Wilbur," Buck whispered as he pulled into the lot. He parked the rig and sat for a long moment, staring at the gate. The irony wasn't lost on him. Wilbur had put him in jail, and Wilbur had gotten him out.

Buck took a breath, squared his shoulders, and climbed down from the cab. The gravel crunched under his boots as he approached the entrance, each step carrying the weight of unfinished business.

Jake had called ahead to make arrangements for Buck's visit, so everything was in order—at least on paper. Still, Buck couldn't shake the sense of unease as he stepped out of his rig and into the shadow of the Escambia County Jail.

The building loomed ahead, an ugly gray slab of concrete and steel that seemed to absorb the sunlight, refusing to give any back. High fences topped with coils of razor wire cut jagged lines against the blue sky. The distant clang of metal doors echoed faintly in the air, like a warning that this was a place where freedom went to die.

Buck walked toward the entrance, his footsteps loud and deliberate on the cracked pavement. A small, square glass enclosure greeted him—more like a guard post at a military compound than a place for visitors. Inside, a uniformed guard stared through the thick glass with the blank, expressionless face of someone who'd seen it all. His eyes—hard, gray, unwelcoming—locked onto Buck's the moment he approached, as though daring him to step out of line.

Buck cleared his throat. "I'm here to see Wilbur Knapp. My name's Buck Dyson. My attorney called ahead to schedule the visit."

The guard said nothing, didn't even nod, just flicked his gaze downward to a clipboard on the desk. He ran a calloused finger down the list, moving slowly, deliberately, as if he enjoyed making visitors wait. Finally, he stopped.

"ID," came the clipped response, sharp as a bark.

Buck fished his wallet from his pocket and slid his driver's license through the narrow slot beneath the glass. The guard snatched it up, inspected it with exaggerated care, and then passed it back without another word. A buzzer sounded, and a metal gate unlocked with a harsh click. "Follow the arrows," the guard said flatly, jerking his head toward the painted yellow lines on the floor. Buck stepped through; the door groaning shut behind him like the gate of a tomb.

The interior of the prison wasn't much better. Fluorescent lights buzzed overhead, casting a pale, sickly glow that made everything look washed out and grim. The air was stale, smelling faintly of bleach and sweat, with a chill that crept under Buck's skin.

He followed the arrows down a narrow corridor, his boots echoing in the silence. The walls were bare except for chipped paint and a few signs warning against contraband, unauthorized communication, and breaches of conduct. Buck wasn't sure whether it was the building or the people inside that made the place feel like the walls were closing in.

At the end of the corridor, a second guard waited by a heavy steel door. This one was larger, barrel-chested, with a shaved head that gleamed under the lights. Unlike the first guard, he didn't seem to have the patience for theatrics.

"Pass," the man grunted, holding out his hand.

Buck handed it over. The guard inspected it with a quick, practiced glance, then pulled open the door with a loud, metallic creak. The sound made Buck flinch.

"Through here. Take a seat. The prisoner'll be brought in shortly."

The visiting area wasn't crowded, but it was far from quiet. A handful of prisoners sat across from their visitors at scuffed, bolted-down tables, their conversations low and murmured, punctuated by occasional bursts of laughter or tense silence. Everything felt observed — the guards stationed along the walls, the security cameras mounted high in the corners, the way people avoided eye contact as if the simple act might betray them.

Buck chose a table near the back, where the shadows softened the harsh glare of the lights. He sat down, folding his hands on the cold metal surface, his eyes wandering to the doorway across the room. He didn't have to wait long.

The door on the far side opened, and Wilbur Knapp stepped through, led by yet another guard. Even from a distance, Buck could see that Wilbur had changed. His shoulders sagged, his clothes hung loose on his wiry frame, and his face was paler than Buck remembered — haunted, almost hollow.

But when their eyes met, something sparked. Wilbur's step quickened, as though he'd found the only familiar face in a sea of strangers.

Buck started to stand instinctively, but the guards' warning rang in his ears. No body contact of any kind. He sank back into his seat, his movements stiff.

Wilbur reached the table and sat down across from him. For a moment, neither man spoke. Buck could hear the hum of the lights, the low murmur of other voices, the clank of doors being opened and closed somewhere distant.

Wilbur offered a faint smile — tired, almost apologetic.

"Buck," he said softly.

Buck nodded, leaning forward slightly, trying to find the words. "Wilbur."

The guards hovered nearby, close enough to be seen but far enough to avoid intruding. But Buck still felt their eyes, their presence pressing in on him like the walls of the prison itself.

"What are you doing here?" were the first words out of Wilbur's mouth as he pulled his chair closer. His voice was hoarse but carried a hint of surprise. "Not that I'm unhappy to see a familiar face."

Buck had watched him approach, and his gut clenched. Wilbur didn't look good. His once wiry frame now seemed frail, his skin pallid, his movements slow and deliberate as if every step cost him something. There was something hollow in his eyes, too—like a man already halfway gone.

"Are you okay?" Buck blurted, his concern tumbling out before he could stop it. "Are they treating you all right in here?"

Wilbur gave a tired half-smile as he lowered himself into the seat across from Buck. "As well as can be expected, given the circumstances. How are you holding up?"

Buck studied him for a beat, noting the shadows under his eyes, the unnatural stillness of his hands. "You don't look well," Buck said gently.

"I'm not," Wilbur admitted, his voice matter-of-fact. "But I'm glad you came. I wanted to reach out to you, but..." He trailed off, looking down at the table as if the words were too heavy to finish. "I didn't know if you'd want to speak to a convicted murderer. Especially one who almost got you put away for life."

"I'm here," Buck replied softly. He leaned forward, resting his elbows on the cold metal table. "I wanted to thank you—for coming forward when you didn't have to. But I have to say, Wilbur, I was shocked. I still can't wrap my head around it. You, a killer? I spent years talking with you. I thought I knew you."

Wilbur looked up then, his gaze steady, something unreadable flickering across his face. "Fear not, my friend," he said softly. "If I may still call you that?"

Buck nodded without hesitation. "I don't judge you, Wilbur. I just don't understand it. What would compel you to do something like that?"

Wilbur smiled — a strange, quiet smile — and leaned in slightly, lowering his voice to a whisper. "I didn't do it."

Buck blinked. "What?"

"I'm not the murderer," Wilbur said, watching as Buck's expression shifted from disbelief to confusion.

"But..." Buck stammered.

"Do you remember Kelvin Hart?" Wilbur asked, his voice steady. "The driver I worked with at Moore's Auto Transport? He lived in the same trailer park as me."

Buck frowned, the name tugging at the edges of his memory. "Yeah, I remember him. He was a strange one, mostly kept to himself."

Wilbur nodded. "That's him. Kelvin took to the sauce pretty bad. One night, he came to my trailer with a backpack. Said he'd been diagnosed with cirrhosis of the liver and was dying. He looked it, too — skin yellow, eyes sunken. He told me he didn't want to take his sins to the grave."

Buck felt a chill creep over him. "What sins?"

Wilbur paused, as if searching for the right words. "He confessed to killing those people, Buck. All of them. He told me how he did it, why he did it. Even showed me the knife he used, the ninja outfit, and..." Wilbur swallowed hard, "...the fingerprints he took as trophies."

Buck stared, stunned into silence.

Peter M. Browne

"I didn't know what to say to him," Wilbur continued. "He was a dead man walking, and I think he just wanted someone to know the truth before he went. He died a few days later."

Buck sat back in his chair, his mind spinning. "But...why didn't you go to the police? Why confess to something you didn't do?"

Wilbur sighed, his shoulders sagging further. He continued in a conspiratorial tone, "Do you think the police care about the truth, Buck? Look at what they did to you. They twist evidence, manufacture it, do whatever it takes to make their case stick. I knew if I walked in with that backpack, they'd pin it on me anyway. But when they convicted you—" Wilbur broke off, his voice thickening. "I couldn't let you rot in here for something you didn't do. I attended every day of your trial, hoping they'd come to their senses. When that guilty verdict came in, I knew what I had to do."

"But confessing to murders you didn't commit?" Buck's voice cracked. "That's madness."

"Maybe," Wilbur said softly. "But you came to my rescue once in my time of need. I couldn't do any less for you."

Buck shook his head, trying to make sense of it all. "I gave you a puppy, Wilbur. A puppy. That's not the same as giving up your freedom."

Wilbur smiled again, a faint glimmer of satisfaction in his eyes. "Freedom is relative, Buck. You've noticed I don't look well."

Buck nodded; his throat tight.

"I'm dying," Wilbur said simply. "Terminal cancer. Doctor gave me a year, months ago. I figure I've got weeks left, maybe days. My freedom's already gone, Buck. So, what does it matter?"

Buck's face fell. He opened his mouth to argue, to protest, but nothing came out.

"There's one thing you can do for me, though," Wilbur continued, pausing to catch his breath. "I left Wilbur Junior — my dog — with my neighbor. Told her I'd be back in a few days. Could you check on him for me?"

Buck swallowed hard, nodding. "Consider it done."

"Good." Wilbur exhaled as though a weight had been lifted. "As for my reputation? Don't worry about that. I've got no family, no one to care what they say about me. What's done is done. But at least you know the truth now."

"Your time's up!" barked the guard from behind Buck.

Buck turned, startled. He'd forgotten they weren't alone, that their conversation had ticked away on the clock.

Wilbur smiled faintly, his eyes holding Buck's for a long moment. "Take care, my friend."

Buck stood slowly, his legs feeling unsteady. He wanted to say something — anything — to make sense of what he'd just heard, but the words wouldn't come. He looked at Wilbur one last time, as the guard moved in to escort him away.

"Wilbur..." Buck started.

But Wilbur just shook his head, offering a small, peaceful smile. "Goodbye, Buck."

Buck nodded and turned toward the exit, his thoughts swirling. He had come looking for answers, and now he had them. But somehow, the truth weighed heavier than the questions ever had.

After leaving the prison, Buck searched for a pay phone. He dialed home, and when Esther picked up, he kept it brief.

"I need to make a stop in Jacksonville," he said. "I'll explain everything when I get back. You won't believe it." He hung up before she could ask questions.

Buck climbed into his rig and pointed it eastbound on I-10, the five-hour drive ahead of him. He decided to push on until dark and then finish the last stretch at sunrise.

By 8 a.m., Buck pulled into Willow Grove RV Park. Wilbur's trailer wasn't hard to find—faded, sagging, and quiet as a tomb. Tied next to the neighboring trailer, Buck spotted Junior. The German Shepherd was a miserable sight: ribs jutting out like piano keys, fur dull and matted.

"Junior," Buck called softly. The dog's ears perked, and in an instant, he was up, tail whipping back and forth, a glimmer of life sparking in his eyes.

Buck's face tightened with anger, but he kept his stride steady as he approached the neighbor's door. He rapped on it sharply three times.

A bleary-eyed woman who appeared to be in her 50s opened the door, a cigarette dangling from her lips. She squinted at Buck through the smoke. "Yeah?"

Buck took off his cap, holding it in his hand as a show of civility, though his tone was firm. "Morning, ma'am. I'm here about Wilbur Knapp's dog—Junior. Name's Buck Dyson."

The woman glanced lazily at the Shepherd. "Yeah, what about him?"

Buck's eyes narrowed. "He's starving, that's what. Wilbur asked me to check in on him, and it's clear you haven't been taking care of him."

Buck stiffened, but he bit back his anger. "Wilbur trusted you to look after him, and from where I'm standing, you haven't done a lick of that."

The woman shrugged, her voice carrying a weary defensiveness. "He gave me a few bucks and told me he'd be gone a few days. What am I supposed to do? I'm not made of money, ya know. I fed him when I could. It's not my fault." She brushed him off with a wave of her hand and took a long drag of her cigarette.

Buck slipped his cap back on, pulling it low over his brow as he leaned in slightly, his voice low but firm. "Listen, lady. I'm taking the dog. He deserves better than this, so I'm taking him with me."

The woman let out a sigh—not frustration, but something closer to relief. She wasn't uncaring; she was just poor, stretched too thin. "Fine. I didn't know what else to do for him, anyway."

She hesitated as Buck stepped toward Junior, then asked softly, "What about Wilbur? Is he... okay?"

Buck froze for half a beat. He didn't want to linger, didn't want to explain, but he also couldn't ignore the question. Keeping his gaze steady, he replied tersely, "Wilbur won't be coming back."

The woman's face fell, and she looked down, fiddling with the cigarette between her fingers. She nodded quietly, as if the answer had confirmed something she already suspected. "I'm sorry to hear that," she murmured.

Buck didn't give her another look. He untied Junior from the post, scooping the rope into his hand. "Come on, fella," he said, his voice softening as he led the Shepherd toward the truck.

Junior wagged his tail, limping slightly but eager to follow. Buck hoisted him carefully into the passenger seat of the rig, patting the dog's side. "You're safe now, buddy," he murmured. "We'll get you fed and back on your feet."

Before hitting the road, Buck stopped at a mall parking lot. He grabbed dog food, a couple of bowls, and fed Junior right there, watching the Shepherd inhale the meal like it was his last. Once satisfied that the dog had eaten his fill, Buck hit the road again, headed for home.

When Buck pulled into the driveway, Esther was already outside waiting.

"How was your trip?" she called, shading her eyes from the sun.

Buck jumped down from the rig, a hint of a smile playing on his face. "Meet my new friend," he said, gesturing toward the passenger side.

Junior bolted from the cab, bounding toward Esther like a runaway freight train. Before she could react, the dog leapt up, nearly knocking her backward.

"Whoa, big fella!" she exclaimed, steadying herself.

While Esther rustled up lunch, Buck sat at the kitchen table and relayed everything Wilbur had told him—leaving out none of the shocking details. He talked about Kelvin Hart, the confession, and Wilbur's sacrifice. Esther sat in stunned silence, shaking her head from time to time, disbelief etched across her face.

Buck wasn't done. He grabbed the phone, called Jake, and asked him to come by. "You'll want to hear this," he promised.

When Jake arrived, Buck grabbed a couple beers from the refrigerator and they headed out back. After repeating the story one more time Buck wanted to know what they could do to help Wilbur.

"What can we do, Son?" he asked.

"There's nothing we can do, Dad. He is going to die before any attempt to exonerate him could run its course. Plus, we don't want to jeopardize your situation. Your charges were dismissed 'without prejudice' which means they can revisit the case. Let's just let sleeping dogs lie. The authorities have no desire to resurrect this case and chase after a dead Kelvin Hart. Trust me on this!"

It wasn't Buck's nature to just let it go. But before he could do anything he received word that Wilbur had passed away. He knew that Wilbur had no one so with Jake's help he petitioned the courts to take responsibility for Wilbur's funeral arrangements. Wilbur had been a military veteran, eligible to be buried with military honors, but it would take Buck jumping through hoops and Jake threating legal action to make it happen.

Wilbur was buried in the Sarasota National Cemetery with full military honors, with all its rights and privileges.

The Florida sun shone bright on the manicured grounds that day. The military honor guard stood in crisp formation, folding the flag with practiced precision. It was a quiet ceremony — no speeches, no mournful crowd. Just Buck, Esther, Jake, and Junior, who sat obediently at Buck's side, looking healthy and well-fed.

As the final notes of Taps echoed across the cemetery, Buck whispered under his breath, "Rest easy, Wilbur. You were a better man than they'll ever know."

Junior let out a low, soft whine, as if in agreement.

CHAPTER 23

Years ago, before anyone knew his name or the horrors he'd committed, Kelvin Hart sat at a truck stop diner, blending into the crowd. He always did.

Kelvin Hart slumped at his table, his wiry frame half-disappearing into the shadows cast by the buzzing fluorescent lights. He had the kind of build that suggested malnourishment rather than lean fitness—his shoulders were bony and slightly hunched, giving him a vulture-like posture. His jeans hung loose on his hips, stained with oil and dust, as though they hadn't seen a washing machine in weeks. The stiff denim crunched faintly when he shifted his legs beneath the table.

His face was narrow and angular, as if his skin had been stretched too tightly over his skull. A patchy beard clung stubbornly to his jaw, tufts of graying brown coarse against his pale complexion. Deep-set eyes peered out from beneath a low brow, the irises a murky hazel that appeared almost yellowish in certain lights—feral, like a predator's. They didn't dart or fidget but moved with slow deliberation, scanning the truck stop patrons one by one, settling on a subject just long enough to make them feel observed without knowing why.

His mouth was small and tightly drawn, but the corners of his lips twitched occasionally, as if he found some private joke in the chaos around him. It wasn't quite a smile—just an involuntary quirk that appeared and vanished in seconds, leaving nothing behind but an unsettling hollowness. His hands, large and calloused, rested lightly on the table, but there was something deceptive about the way they lay so still— like coiled traps, waiting.

Everything about him seemed deliberately inconspicuous. The clothes—work-worn jeans, steel-toe boots, a dingy flannel shirt over a grease-stained undershirt—blended into the scenery of trucker life. But it was his stillness that gave him away. While the rest of the crowd bustled, shouted, and clattered silverware against plates, Kelvin sat like a rock in a stream—unmoving, observant, apart.

He had chosen his table because it was away from everybody and he could observe all the comings and goings, parents with their kids yelling and screaming, demanding candy or ice cream, couples seated together acting all cozy with one another, the single guy, like himself, devouring his food like someone was about to claim it, as their own and then there were the other truckers, in all shapes and sizes, male and female. Occasionally he would see a hooker, working the truck stop, pop in for a bottle of water and dash back out. They never sat down.

He marveled at the way all these truck stops were set up. The first thing you encountered when you entered was the gift shop with it tons of knick-knacks, bric-a-brac, souvenirs, and other worthless junk. Next came all the fast foods: candy, chips, soft drinks, crackers, premade sandwiches, and frozen treats. Following that was the lunch counter, where you could order meals of various kinds. Past the lunch counter were the tables and chairs for dining and all the way in the back were the restrooms.

If you came in to use the bathroom you were first going to be tempted by all the ways they could take your money. And you had to run the gauntlet on your way back out, two chances to entice an impulse buy.

As he scanned the crowd he noticed a fellow trucker he knew, Wilbur, one of his co-workers and neighbor, jaw boning with another guy. He thought of joining them but he preferred being alone.

He had ordered the Salisbury steak and mashed potatoes from the lunch counter, but it sat on the table untouched. For some reason he had lost his appetite between the counter and his table. He was hungering for something else but that would have to wait.

The calendar said it would be a moonless night and the day promised a heavy cloud cover for this evening. "It will be perfect weather conditions," he thought as a sardonic smile passed over his lips, disappearing as quickly as it came.

He moved the mashed potatoes around on his plate, then set the fork back down; took a sip of his coffee and wiped his mouth on his shirt sleeve.

Normally truckers were on the move. They'd stop for food; a quick meal and they were back on the road. Time was money. But he was in no particular hurry this evening. He'd make up for lost time later.

He finished his coffee and decided to head out to his rig. The rear exit led to the back of the building where truckers parked if they planned be there awhile; taking a required rest break.

He stepped outside, looked around then threaded his way through the parked 18-wheelers to his rig. He climbed onboard and crawled into the sleeper. It was 8 PM. He planned to be back on the road by midnight.

Kelvin Hart had been a sniper in Vietnam, and he'd enjoyed every second of it. Vietnam had given him the opportunity to perfect his craft, far from the rules and prying eyes of the real world. Officially, he'd been a sniper, patient and precise. He liked the way one clean shot could end everything—how a man could go from smoking a cigarette or chatting with a buddy to crumpling lifeless on the ground in the blink of an eye. One moment alive, the next gone. It never got old.

It wasn't like hunting deer or rabbits. With animals, there was no fear in their eyes, no last moment of knowing. People were different. That flicker of awareness, the brief recognition that this is it—that was the part Kelvin liked best.

War suited him. He thrived in it, really. His commanders thought he was reliable, just another soldier who followed orders without complaint. But they didn't see the deeper satisfaction behind his still, calculating eyes. They didn't notice how much he enjoyed waiting, sometimes for hours, for his prey to step into his sights. Killing wasn't duty for Kelvin. It was pleasure.

But Vietnam wasn't all perfect. Officers could be a problem—especially the ones who got too big for their britches or tried throwing their weight around.

Fragging wasn't unusual back then. Everybody knew what it was, even if nobody talked about it out loud. "Fragging" was what they called it when soldiers turned on their own. Maybe it was a grenade rolled into an officer's tent while he slept. Maybe it was a bullet from the jungle that nobody questioned too hard. It happened enough that some officers stayed awake at night, too scared of their own men to close their eyes.

Kelvin had fragged a man once. An Army captain who'd threatened to bring him up on charges of insubordination. The captain had shouted at him in front of the whole unit, calling him a loose cannon, promising Kelvin he'd see his ass in a court martial. The man didn't live to make good on that promise.

Kelvin didn't use a grenade—that was messy, too loud, too obvious. Instead, he waited. He watched the man head out on patrol, walking ahead of the others like some goddamn hero. Kelvin set up, slow and steady, his finger relaxed on the trigger. He didn't even have to use his issued rifle. He preferred the Mosin-Nagant, an old bolt-action weapon he'd taken off a dead Viet Cong weeks earlier. It felt fitting—poetic, almost. The captain never saw it coming. One shot, right between the eyes.

When they found the body, the enemy rifle lying next to him, everyone assumed it had been an ambush. Kelvin kept his mouth shut, like he always did, and no one asked too many questions. It wasn't uncommon, after all, for officers to end up dead.

When the war ended, Kelvin came home to a country that didn't want him. People spat at veterans like him, called them murderers and baby killers. He didn't understand it—how he'd been the one risking his life out there, doing what he did best, and now the world acted like he was the villain.

That's when it all started to unravel. PTSD—back then, nobody had a name for it. They just called you "shell-shocked" or "damaged goods." Men like Kelvin didn't talk about the nightmares, the sweating, the racing heart. He'd wake up at night with his hand curled around an imaginary trigger, his body tense and ready, but there was nothing there. No jungle. No war. Just the ceiling above him and the endless noise in his head.

Others turned to booze or drugs, but Kelvin didn't need that. He found his own relief—his remedy. Killing brought calm, like a wave washing over him. And not just killing—it was the hunt. The plotting, the waiting, the precise moment when the target realized it was too late. It was the only thing that silenced the noise.

When he came back, he found work driving trucks for Moore's Auto Transport. It was the perfect job. Hours on the open road, no one to bother him, nothing but the hum of the engine to keep him company. People left truckers alone, never looking twice at them. Invisible. That's how Kelvin liked it.

He couldn't say exactly when he decided to start killing again. It wasn't some grand plan, just... instinct. A need that grew stronger the longer he ignored it. He spent months preparing, perfecting his tools. He bought himself ninja gear—tight black clothing and a hood that swallowed his face. He read books on ninja weapons and ordered a fukiya—a blowgun—and a tanto blade, short and deadly. It wasn't hard to practice. He'd sneak into the woods at night, testing his tranquilizer-laced darts on wild animals until he got the dosage right.

Once he felt ready, he started scouting. A blue ranch house off the highway caught his eye. It sat back from the road, barely visible through the trees. Perfect. He'd stopped there before under the pretense of a breakdown, checking the area out. There was even a widened shoulder nearby, enough space for his rig. The stars had aligned.

And tonight? Tonight, was a moonless night, cloud cover rolling in thick as smoke. The kind of dark where shadows disappeared completely.

The buzzing of the alarm jolted Kelvin awake, a sharp crack through the stillness. He blinked, rubbed his eyes, and adjusted to the low light filtering through the sleeper cab. For a moment, he just sat there, staring into the darkness. Then he smiled faintly. It was time to hunt.

Sliding out of the sleeper, he climbed into the driver's seat. The diesel engine grumbled awake under his touch, its steady idle filling the silence like a purring beast. He reached for his backpack, fingers brushing over the contents — each piece of equipment laid out with precision. He took quick inventory, checking his tanto blade, the fukiya blowgun, and the darts laced with tranquilizer. Satisfied, he pulled the bag shut, adjusted the seat, and eased the rig into gear.

The truck rumbled quietly out of the parking spot. Most everyone was asleep — rows of darkened cabs and trailers standing silent as tombstones. Through the diner's windows, he spotted the night crew mopping floors, heads down, preparing for the day ahead. No one looked up. No one ever did.

He slipped onto the empty highway, the vast dark stretching out before him. There wasn't another vehicle in sight. The rig hummed beneath him, steady and reassuring, as mile markers ticked by. Kelvin didn't need a map; he had the spot memorized.

A few miles later, he saw it. He flipped on his emergency blinkers and guided the massive truck onto the shoulder with the precision of a surgeon, ensuring the entire trailer sat well off the road. The hazards clicked rhythmically in the cab as he jumped down to deploy the triangular reflectors, placing them in a careful line several feet behind him. The rig had to look like a mechanical failure—ordinary, unremarkable.

Once satisfied, Kelvin climbed back into the cab. He turned off the blinkers, killed the engine, and doused the exterior lights. Silence fell around him again, dense and absolute.

Now cloaked in darkness, he changed. The ninja outfit hugged his wiry frame, swallowing him in black. He pulled on the NVGs—night vision goggles that cast the world in ghostly shades of green—and slid over to the passenger side. Cracking the door, he slipped down to the ground, landing silently in a crouch.

He moved like a shadow, crouching low as he ducked into the woods. Up the embankment he climbed, stepping carefully over twigs and branches, pausing at every sound. When he reached the road, he stopped.

The world here was perfect—pitch black, utterly still. Across the street, a single lighted door buzzer burned against the darkness like a beacon. Kelvin's pulse quickened.

In a burst of movement, he dashed across the road and circled the house, his head swiveling as he scanned for dogs or movement. If there'd been a dog, he'd have handled it—one dart was all it took—but the yard was quiet. Too quiet. He allowed himself a satisfied breath.

Returning to the rear door, he crouched and pulled his lockpicking tools from his bag. The deadbolt gave way with barely a whisper. Kelvin opened the door a crack, holding his breath and listening.

Nothing.

He stepped inside. The house smelled faintly of lavender and laundry soap—homey, domestic. Kelvin felt his lips twitch. It was strange, how lives could seem so neat right up until the moment you ended them.

Moving stealthily down the hall, he checked the first guest bedroom. Empty. The second—empty as well. The master, he thought, already knowing they'd be there.

He eased open the master bedroom door. Inside, bathed in the faint green glow of his NVGs, a man and a woman lay asleep, tangled in blankets. The man faced away, his back to the door. Kelvin crept closer, silently raising the fukiya to his lips. The blowgun's dart flew true, embedding just below the man's left ear. A second dart followed an instant later, sinking into the woman's throat.

Kelvin waited, counting slowly in his head. One... two... Ten seconds. That was all it took.

He moved into the room, removing the darts with surgical care and tucking them into his bag. Quiet as a ghost, he stepped around to the man's side of the bed. The man lay there, his body limp, breathing shallow. Kelvin reached for the tanto blade strapped to his back.

In one fluid motion, he brought the blade around and drove it downward. The knife sank deep — straight into the man's neck. Kelvin felt the jolt as steel met bone, and then the warmth that spread around the blade as it slid free.

For a moment, everything fell silent. Kelvin closed his eyes, as the rush hit him. It rose like a wave, a flood of elation so pure it almost took his breath away. It spread through his limbs, curling in his stomach, buzzing in his fingertips. And then, as quickly as it had come, it ebbed, leaving him hollow but satisfied.

Kelvin backed away, leaving the man sprawled lifeless on the bed. He turned his attention to the woman. Her chest rose and fell faintly, her body heavy from the tranquilizer. For a moment, he stared at her face — her mouth slightly open, the lines of her brow relaxed in forced sleep. It was her turn... But, he had other plans.

He told himself it was a code — his code — and it set him apart from the stories they used to whisper about Vietnam vets. The accusations, the atrocities... No. He wasn't like the others. The thought filled him with a peculiar satisfaction, as though it lent purpose to the chaos. Kelvin didn't kill women or children.

Instead, he crossed to her side of the bed and crouched low. Reaching into his backpack, he pulled out an ink pad and a neat stack of blank index cards. With deliberate care, he lifted her limp hand, pressing her thumb to the ink and then onto the card. A perfect, dark print appeared — a little piece of her he could keep.

Kelvin held it up to the faint light, examining the impression for flaws. Satisfied, he wiped her thumb clean with a rag, tucked the card and ink pad back into his bag, and stood.

He paused, giving the room one last look — the man lifeless in the bed, the woman drugged and unaware.

The adrenaline drained from him suddenly, replaced by something simple and primal. Hunger. He turned and headed for the kitchen, already imagining what might be in the fridge.

He stepped to the refrigerator and pulled out a carton of eggs, a jug of orange juice, and a foil-wrapped slab of what looked like leftover meatloaf. The cold air hit his face as he paused, staring into the depths of the fridge as if waiting for something to emerge.

The kitchen was silent, save for the ticking of a clock on the wall. He cracked the eggs into a bowl, whisked them with deliberate strokes, and poured them into a skillet. The meatloaf sizzled as he reheated it. He sat at the table, his posture straight, his movements mechanical. Fork to mouth, chew, swallow.

When he finished, he washed the dishes, wiped the counters, and returned everything to its rightful place. The house looked as untouched as it had when he arrived.

Outside, the night was thick with humidity. Kelvin locked the door behind him, testing the knob twice before heading down the embankment. At the passenger side of his truck, he paused, scanning the area. The road was almost empty, except for a single passing car. The light washing over him and passing quickly returning the road to darkness.

Satisfied, he climbed into the cab, peeled off his gear, and stowed it in his backpack. The fabric of his shirt clung to his back, damp with sweat. He started the engine and eased onto the road, the hum of the tires on asphalt a steady companion as he merged westbound onto I-10.

This routine worked. It kept the noise at bay. But routines had limits. The relief they offered was limited thinning, fraying at the edges, with its repetition.

When it wasn't enough, he turned to whiskey. When whiskey wasn't enough, there were pills. Each swallowed dose dulled the roar in his head, but it didn't silence it. Nothing ever did.

Months would dissolve into years and years into decades. He was terminated from Moore's Auto Transport, Inc. for a DWI and drinking became his fulltime job. He collapsed one evening in front of his doorway. Junior found him, barking wildly, as he and Wilbur were passing by. EMT's were called. During his treatment, blood drawn indicated the need for more testing, the results, he was diagnosed with cirrhosis of the liver, kidney failure and fluid in his lungs. Having no medical insurance, he was never admitted.

The following evening just as the sun was setting he was at Wilbur's trailer pounding on the door.

"Let me in. I know you're in there," he yelled in a drunken stupor. When Wilbur opened the door, he stumbled in and staggered to the sofa.

"I'm gonna die!" he wept with a mournful tone.

Wilbur just stared, not knowing what to make of this display. Anytime he had seen him he was stoic and removed.

Junior did not want to go anywhere near Kelvin, it was as if he could smell the evil. He went and sat in a far corner and covered his muzzle.

When Wilbur was finally able to calm him down he began to speak softly and deliberately.

"I don't want to die," his eyes pleaded, as if Wilbur could alter the facts.

"I'm going to hell. I've done terrible things. I don't know why I did them. Forgive me, Lord, I enjoyed them." He continued to ramble.

Wilbur made him some coffee and after a while Kelvin's thoughts became more organized than the earlier bursts of verbal excrement.

When he was done he had told Wilbur his life story, the terrible treatment he had received as a child, the terrible things he visited on others and the fact that he was the "Highway Murderer". He showed Wilbur his backpack with all its evil contents.

Wilbur had let him talk, because once he got started Wilbur was struck by his story. Their lives had not been that dissimilar, unhappy childhood, loner, Vietnam veteran, even worked for the same trucking company. But there their lives had diverged.

Wilbur thought for a moment. Could this have been me? What was that critical instant, that fork in the road marked good and evil?

Now calm, Kelvin staggered out of the mobile home. The next time Wilbur would see him he was being taken out of his mobile home on a gurney, a sheet covering his face.

Wilbur thought of going to the police and then thought better of it. The murders had stopped. He was dead. It served no purpose, until his friend Buck was wrongfully convicted.

During all the retelling of the story Wilbur only referenced Kelvin by name once. After that Wilbur would only refer to him as "he". In Wilbur's mind, the man was "pure evil". A name not to be spoke for fear that by mentioning his name it was like conjuring up the devil.

EPILOGUE

Carla was in her 100th year having recently celebrated her 99th birthday, a few days before. Celebrate was probably not the best word to describe the occasion. That day, as she sat alone in her room at the Blackwater Nursing Home, a female orderly arrived with a cupcake with a single lighted candle. She was joined by another member of the staff, who wished Carla happy birthday without the accompaniment of the song. They left as swiftly as they came restoring the solitude that had become her life.

Carla's room, at the nursing home, was a 9 x 12 space containing: a bed, a dresser, a single chair, a nightstand and a single window, that had a sliver of a view of the Blackwater River shoreline, if you got close to the glass and craned your neck to the right.

The room was otherwise unadorned, but for a single photograph of a male dressed in clothes that spoke of the early 1900s.

This had become her life. She was the sole survivor among her family, friends, neighbors, associates, as well as husband and ex-husbands. She had outlived them all. Something that gave her a sense of pride, a sense of accomplishment, a sense of revenge, and a sense of victory.

Her parents had long ago passed. Her father, Ramon, the only man she ever really cared for, had lived to a ripe old age, passing quietly in the night. There had been a large funeral, for him, as was the Muscogee custom. She remembered sitting graveside and the tears she shed, a unique moment in her life that would rarely be repeated.

Gregory, her eldest, was the next male to leave her, a casualty of war. When the military came to notify her of his death all she felt was empty. She never really knew her son. He reminded her too much of her first husband. The revenge she could not obtain against Tom was visited upon Gregory.

She had not been there for him, in his formative years, she was too busy, working and taking care of her needs. Her brother and sister-in-law had been more parents to him than she had been. She never had the chance to make amends.

Bradley, her youngest, was another story. She had driven him away, pushed him out of the house, told him he was never going to amount to anything, like his father, but was given a second chance when he returned to Pearson's Point. She had tried her best to muster that missing maternal instinct. But in the end her misguided advice had caused him to make a tragic mistake, one that would cost him his life. With Brad's passing came the return of the icy cool exterior, her trademark, a skin she had tried unsuccessfully to shed. Her efforts and concerns with amends — frozen.

Since the day her first husband, Tom, left she had wished him ill. But much to her dismay, he had gone on to become a successful entrepreneur, acquiring wealth, owning multiple properties and having many exotic toys; a yacht, several Mercedes, and a 6-place twin engine aircraft, that he piloted himself.

Tom had box seats and season tickets to the Tampa Bay Buccaneers. His wife Suzanne had been a 5th runner-up for Miss America and was a clothing model for a major Florida department store chain.

Tom had received awards from the Pensacola Chamber of Commerce and was a member of the Board of Directors at Habitat for Humanities

Each accomplishment he achieved was a dagger in Carla's heart. She had turned Gregory against him, telling him that his father had deserted him and refused to pay child support, neither of which was true. Tom tried his best to be involved in his son's life which Carla did her best to sabotage.

When Carla received the news that Tom's plane had crashed, she secretly wished, his wife Suzanne was onboard too, but she was not.

Tom was on a flight back from Tampa, after a Buc's game. He usually didn't fly at night and would stay over and fly back in the morning. It was never determined why he chose that night to fly. It was a clear night and a short flight for the twin engine Beechcraft, about two hours, straight across the Gulf of Mexico. Tom would have flown on instruments as there were no visual landmarks at night. He had filed a flight plan and was on course when he disappeared from Radar.

Search and Rescue were able to locate the downed aircraft the next morning. The NTSB investigation determined that Tom's aircraft must have had some kind of mechanical problem otherwise, if he had had a medical event autopilot would have continued to fly the plane.

Carla learned about the crash on the news. As she watched the watery sight of the crash and the news report that the pilot was dead, a sardonic smile pierced her lips. She thought, "I finally beat him at something!", as if outliving him was some kind of personal achievement.

Carla's second husband had been easy to beat. He had died many years earlier from a drug overdose. Her dislike of Reggie was mild in comparison to her hatred of Tom, for reasons only she knew.

Richard's death had been very different. He had been diagnosed with stage four prostate cancer. He never bothered to have his PSA tested until it was too late.

There are no happy endings when it comes to life's final chapter, but cancer is an ugly and painful way to go. It is slow, agonizing and degrading, robbing a person of all human dignities.

Carla was unable to summon the compassion one would expect of a grieving spouse. She would go to the hospice center but she would sit just far enough away from Richard so as to be unable to touch or physically comfort him. He had asked her to bring him home so he could die in familiar surroundings. She promised him she would but always had an excuse as to why it would be in a day or two. The worse Richard became, the shorter and less frequent Carla's visits became. He would die alone one silent sunny summer afternoon, as Carla sat at home reflecting on the past and pondering her future, without a man in her life.

She had waited long for this moment, not that she was wishing Richard's death but she accepted it.

The irony, the paradox, was that Carla always wanted to be independent but as much as she hated to admit it she needed a man, for what he could provide. There were the creature comforts of course but more so, she needed to be the object of someone's affection, to be loved emotionally as well as physically.

She was always curious of female friends, who as they got older lost interest in sex. She could not understand that, for Carla sex was rejuvenating, a feeling that only came from being with a man. She needed the intoxication it provided. It was a salve coating all the meaningless moments in between.

When Richard passed, at seventy-six, she was financially independent but still not free.

With no one left to care for her, at the age of eighty-one, she moved into the Blackwater Nursing home. There was the occasional conjugal visit from one of the residents still able to perform but it was empty and unsatisfying. And so, the days wrapped around themselves, protracted and seemingly never ending.

On a gray Florida day, Carla awakened early to the sound of birds just beyond her window. She thought she heard someone at her door. She sat up on her elbows and turned her ear toward the door to listen. When she looked back a shadowy figure stood before her, veiled in black. Fog rolled in around the figure, curling and shifting like the smoke of forgotten sins.

Carla's breath caught. "Who are you? What do you want?" The figure stepped forward, the air growing colder with each measured step. A voice emerged, one that seemed to echo from every corner of the room and none at all.

"It is *He Whose Name Is Never Spoken*. I've come to you many times, Carla," the voice said, the words heavy with a knowing weight. "Sometimes as your Aunt Millie, cautioning you in the only ways I could. But you never heeded my warnings.

Carla's pulse quickened. "What...what do you want from me?" she stammered.

The figure's voice darkened, carrying a cold, undeniable truth. "It is not about what I want. It is about what you owe." The fog thickened, the air pressing against Carla's chest. "You thought your gift made you untouchable, that it was your ticket to outwit the source of the power. But every action carries a cost. What you took, Carla, must eventually be repaid. You have paid a portion, but the debt is not yet settled."

Carla's chest tightened. "Debt?" she whispered, barely able to form the word.

"You blamed Brad for his misfortune, but you were the cause," the figure intoned. "You twisted the power to serve yourself, to gain love, wealth, admiration. And each time, the scales shifted. But the universe requires balance."

"No," Carla whispered. "That's not true."

"It is," the figure said, softer now, its voice carrying an almost mournful edge. "When Brad suffered, when his life crumbled under the weight of failure, the universe was extracting its due. You saw his misfortune as weakness, as punishment for his inadequacy. But it was your punishment, Carla. The universe demanded payment for your selfishness, and Brad was the currency."

Carla shook her head, her face contorting with denial. But deep down, the words struck a chord she couldn't silence.

The figure loomed closer, the veil parting just enough for Carla to glimpse a void where a face should have been. The voice grew sharper, laden with dark triumph. "You believed that outliving your children, your husbands, your friends made you superior to them. But you are wrong."

The air around Carla thickened, her breath shallow as the figure continued. "Old age is no prize, Carla. It is part of the price you pay. Your punishment. Your mind clouds, memory fades, eyes grow dim, limbs ache, and teeth fall away. Your body, mind and spirit — all wither. And for all your misdeeds, you will die with nothing gained."

Tears welled in Carla's eyes as the weight of the words settled over her. "I didn't mean..." she began, her voice breaking, but the figure cut her off.

"You always believed the gift made you untouchable," it said, "but it was never about the power. It was about the choices you made. The knife in your hand could have healed, but instead, you chose to cut. And now, the wound festers."

The figure's silhouette loomed larger, the fog swirling around Carla like a suffocating embrace. "You think you can avoid the consequences, Carla. But you cannot. As I told the farmer who begged for his wife's life long ago: There is always a price to be paid."

Carla's voice cracked as she screamed, "Get out! Get out!"

A passing orderly, hearing her screams, hurried into Carla's room. He reached for Carla, shaking her gently as she writhed on the bed.

"It's okay, Ms. Peterson, you were dreaming," the orderly said, his voice soft, but distant, as if coming from another world.

Carla lay still, staring at the ceiling. Her chest rose and fell in shallow gasps, her hands clutching the sheets as though she might slip away if she let go.

Was it a nightmare? Or was the nightmare waking up in this empty room, old and alone?

As the orderly left, Carla's gaze drifted to the window. Outside, the gray sky churned like an unsettled ocean, and somewhere in its depths, she imagined the shadow watching her still.

She thought of Brad. For the first time in years, the image of his face summoned an aching sorrow. She had blamed him for years, but the truth clawed its way to the surface now. Brad's pain was never his alone; it had always been hers, born of her choices. His suffering had been her reckoning, though she had refused to see it.

The fog lingered in the edges of her mind, and with it, the voice's final words: *There is always a price to be paid.*

Carla would die alone as Aunt Millie had predicted. And in her final moments, she would find herself surrounded by only silence and regret.

* 9 7 8 1 7 3 6 0 2 1 7 6 7 *